Slowly, she raised her eyes to his.

Harriet could not read his expression in the dim light that filtered through the window, but she did see the muscle leap in his jaw. The air between them crackled with intensity, and her pulse responded with a lurch and a gallop. She licked at her dry lips as he moved closer. His gaze fastened on her mouth, sending desire sizzling through her. Pure instinct tilted her head, lifted her lips to his.

The most delicate of touches. Lip to lip… sweet, gentle…almost worshipping. Memories of love and laughter and pure joy. They had been so young. A shared future planned. They had followed the instinctive desires of their youthful bodies. She had felt so secure in his love for her. *Before…*

Author Note

Saved by Scandal's Heir is the second of two linked books—the first of which, *Return of Scandal's Son*, was published in October 2015. This is, however, a stand-alone title, and it's not necessary to have read the first book in order to enjoy the second.

Benedict Poole, hero of *Saved by Scandal's Heir*, is the friend and business partner of Matthew Damerel, hero of *Return of Scandal's Son*, and both Matthew and his new wife, Eleanor, appear in this book. You might be interested to note that, as a peeress in her own right, Eleanor has not become Mrs Damerel but retains her title of Lady Ashby.

The heroine of *Saved by Scandal's Heir* is Harriet, Lady Brierley, who first appeared in *From Wallflower to Countess* (April 2015) as the hero's former mistress. The hero and heroine of *Wallflower* (Richard, Lord Stanton, and his wife, Felicity) also appear in this book.

I do hope you enjoy reading about the dire predicament Harriet finds herself in following Benedict's reappearance in her life, and that you, like me, have fun revisiting old friends from my previous books.

SAVED BY
SCANDAL'S HEIR

Janice Preston

First published in Great Britain 2016
By Mills & Boon, an imprint of HarperCollins*Publishers*
1 London Bridge Street, London, SE1 9GF

Large Print edition 2016

© 2016 Janice Preston

ISBN: 978-0-263-26309-1

Our policy is to use papers that are natural, renewable and recyclable
products and made from wood grown in sustainable forests.
The logging and manufacturing processes conform to the legal
environmental regulations of the country of origin.

Printed and bound in Great Britain
by CPI Antony Rowe, Chippenham, Wiltshire

Janice Preston grew up in Wembley, North London, with a love of reading, writing stories and animals. In the past she has worked as a farmer, a police call-handler and a university administrator. She now lives in the West Midlands with her husband and two cats and has a part-time job with a weight management counsellor (vainly trying to control her own weight despite her love of chocolate!).

Books by Janice Preston

Mills & Boon Historical Romance

Men About Town

Return of Scandal's Son
Saved by Scandal's Heir

**Linked by Character
to *Men About Town* duet**

Mary and the Marquis
From Wallflower to Countess

Visit the Author Profile page
at millsandboon.co.uk.

To my wonderful editor, Julia,
who first sparked the idea of rewarding
Harriet with her own Happy-Ever-After.

Chapter One

Mid-February 1812

Harriet, Lady Brierley, paced the lavishly furnished drawing room at Tenterfield Court, mentally rehearsing the words she would say to Sir Malcolm Poole. If she had known the baronet was hovering so close to death, she would never have made the journey from London at this time of year. She had not known, however, and, now she had come all this way into Kent, she might as well ask the questions to which she sought answers. She had come to Tenterfield to find the truth of the past, in order to help her friend Felicity Stanton come to terms with her sister's death…and Harriet was certain that Sir Malcolm held the key to that particular puzzle.

Felicity's older sister, Emma, had been just eighteen—an innocent girl seduced and impregnated, who had seen no way out of her predicament other than to take her own life when the man she'd believed loved her had cruelly abandoned her.

Harriet suppressed her shiver. She could so easily have suffered the same fate. Was that why she had been so quick to come to Tenterfield? The empathy she felt for Felicity's poor sister? *There but for the Grace of God...*

She crossed the room to stand again before the portrait of the baronet, painted in his younger days, although he was still far from being an old man even now. He gazed down at her, devastatingly handsome, with his lean aristocratic features, dark auburn hair and deep green hooded gaze. Harriet shuddered, partly at the knowledge of what this man was—or what he had been, in the past—partly at his resemblance to... Resolutely, she steered her thoughts in a different direction. This trip was bound to resurrect painful memories... She must rise above them...concentrate on—

'Lady Brierley. To what do we owe this pleasure?'

Harriet froze. It could not be. Had she conjured him up in the flesh, just by allowing her thoughts one tiny peek at those memories? Moisture prickled her palms even as her mouth dried. She drew a calming breath, gathered her years of experience in hiding her feelings and turned.

He was framed in the open doorway.

Benedict.

After all this time.

He had the same long, lean legs and wide shoulders, but this was a man, not the youth she'd once known. His chin was just as determined but the high forehead under the familiar fox-red hair now sported faint creases. His lips were set in an uncompromising line and his leaf-green eyes pierced Harriet as he stared into her face, his gaze unwavering. A cat stalking its prey could not be more focused.

Harriet swallowed past the jagged glass that appeared to have lodged in her throat.

'Good afternoon, Mr Poole.' Had those composed words really come from her lips? She took courage. She had faced worse than this. 'I apologise for calling uninvited. I did not realise your...' What was his relationship to Sir Malcolm again? All she could recall was that he had been Benedict's guardian. 'Sir Malcolm was so very ill. I had hoped for a few words with him.'

'He is my second cousin. I'm the only other Poole left now.'

'I'm sorry.'

The platitude slid readily from her tongue. She wasn't sorry. The world would be well rid of the Pooles. But she would remain polite. Let nothing of her bitterness show. Sir Malcolm had spent his life in pursuit of his own pleasures, a dissolute rake with not a care for the ruined lives he left in his wake. Felicity's poor sister had been just one of his victims. And Benedict had proved himself equally as contemptible, equally as careless of the heart-break he had left behind. Hardly surprising with Sir Malcolm as his only role model since childhood.

Benedict prowled into the centre of the room, nearing Harriet. The very air seemed to vibrate between them. She stood her ground, although she could not prevent a swift glance at her maid, Janet, who had accompanied her, sitting quietly on a chair near the beautifully carved stone fireplace. Benedict followed her gaze.

At least I am not alone.

'Why are you here?' The words were softly spoken. Benedict's green eyes bored into Harriet's. 'Did you think to wed another wealthy man on his deathbed?'

'Brierley was not on his deathbed! And I had no ch—' Harriet shut her mouth with a snap. She'd endured over seven years with that lecher. Seven years of misery and disgust, empty arms and a broken heart, all because of Benedict Poole.

She had not in a million years thought to meet him here. He had gone overseas—right to the other side of the world. And even that was not far enough away for Harriet. Hatred for this man rose as the long-suppressed memories cascaded through her thoughts.

His lying words. His false promises. All of it.

She concealed any hint of her feelings. He must never know how her heart still ached for what might have been. She braced her shoulders and raised her chin.

'If Sir Malcolm will see me, I should be grateful for a few words with him.'

She glanced at the window—the clouds had blended into a uniform white vista of nothingness and she saw a few snowflakes flutter past. The snow that had threatened all morning as she had travelled deeper into Kent had finally begun to fall.

'I should like to leave before the weather takes a turn for the worse. *If* you would be so kind.'

Benedict bowed, and gestured towards the door. 'Your wish is my desire, my lady,' he said, his words flat and emotionless.

'Thank you.'

She stalked to the door, passing close by him…

too close… His scent flooded her senses…triggering such memories, arousing emotions she had never thought to feel again. His unique maleness: familiar, even after eleven long years, spicy, heady…and…brandy. Brandy? This early in the day? He was a Poole through and through. Nothing had changed.

'Come, Janet.'

Harriet swept into the spacious inner hall, from which the magnificent polished oak staircase swept up to the first floor. The evidence of Sir Malcolm's wealth was everywhere, from the exquisitely executed landscapes hanging on the walls to the elegant Chinese porcelain vases and bowls that graced the numerous console tables to the magnificent crystal chandelier that hung over the central circular table complete with its urn of jessamine, lilies and sweet bay. *In February!* For all his wastrel tendencies, Sir Malcolm had clearly not exhausted his vast wealth. And, presumably, Benedict would inherit it all. Plus the title. No wonder he was here, with his cousin at death's door. He deserved none of it, but she would not allow him to sour her. Never again.

They spoke not another word as they climbed the stairs side by side, and walked along the upper landing, Janet on their heels. Harriet told herself she was pleased. She had no wish to exchange forced pleasantries.

They reached a door, which Benedict opened.

'Lady Brierley, to see Sir Malcolm,' he said, before ushering Harriet and Janet through, and closing the door firmly behind them.

It was baking hot in the room, which was not the master bedchamber, as Harriet expected, but much smaller, and decorated—tastelessly, in her opinion—in deep purple and gold. The fire was banked high with coal, blazing out a suffocating heat, and Harriet felt her face begin to glow. With an effort, she refrained from wafting her hand in front of her face. It was so airless and the stench caught in the back of her throat. How could anyone get well in such an atmosphere?

The huge bed dominated the room, the level surface of its purple cover barely disturbed by the wasted form of the man lying there. It was hard to believe this was the same man she had always known as strong and vital. He looked ancient but— she did a quick mental calculation—he could not be much more than eight and forty. Sir Malcolm's face was skeletal, the bloodless skin slack, and yet his eyes were still alert, dominating his shrunken features. Those eyes appraised Harriet with the same cold speculation she remembered from both her childhood and from the times her path had crossed with Sir Malcolm's during her marriage to Brierley. Disgust rippled through her.

'Heard I was dying, did you?' The voice was a dry, cracked whisper. 'Thought you'd have another shot at snaring Benedict's inheritance?'

'I have no interest in your cousin,' Harriet said. 'I am sorry to find you in such circumstances, but I have come on a quite different errand. I did not know you were ill, and I certainly did not know Mr Poole was here, or I would have thought twice about crossing your threshold.'

He croaked a laugh. 'That's as well for you. His opinion hasn't changed since the first time you tried to trap him. Even as a youngster, that boy was no fool. A Poole through and through. He could see straight through you then and he'll see straight through you now. He'll look higher for a wife than Brierley's leftovers, that I can promise.'

Harriet bit her tongue against rising to his provocation. It seemed even the imminent judgement of his maker could not cork Sir Malcolm's vitriol. She cast around for the appropriate words to ask him about Felicity's sister. When she'd decided to come to Tenterfield, she hadn't anticipated trying to persuade Sir Malcolm to tell her the truth on his deathbed.

'Well, girl? What d'you want? I haven't time to waste pandering to the likes of you. Tell me what you want and be gone. You hear, Fletcher?' He addressed the servant standing by the window. 'This *lady* is not to spend a minute more than necessary beneath my roof.'

The man bowed. 'Yes, sir.'

Harriet tamped down her anger. 'I wish to ask you about something that happened in the past. Do you recall Lady Emma Weston? She attended Lord Watchett's house party at the same time as you, in the summer of 1802.'

Sir Malcolm's lids lowered to mask his eyes. 'How do you expect me to remember one chit out of so many?'

'She was Lady Baverstock's daughter. It was the year following Lord Baverstock's death.'

His thin lips parted and Harriet recoiled as his tongue came out to touch his lip. 'Ah. Yes, indeed. The golden angel.'

Nausea churned Harriet's insides. Time had softened the memory of quite how contemptible Sir Malcolm had always been, despite his wealth and his handsome face. He had, however, been irresistibly charming to the young innocents he had targeted, and Harriet quite understood how a naive young girl could fall for his silver-tongued lies.

She had been fortunate to be immune from his attempts to seduce her when she was young enough to appeal to his tastes. She had resisted, thinking herself in love with Benedict. Time had proved she was just as naive as poor Lady Emma, whom she was now convinced Sir Malcolm had seduced and impregnated and abandoned. Emma had escaped by taking her own life. Harriet had not been so cowardly—or, mayhap, so brave—when *her* heart had been broken, although…there were times during the years following her marriage to Brierley when suicide had seemed an enticing option.

'So it *was* you,' she said to the man in the bed. 'She wrote to you, after the summer you met. She was in love with you.'

His head twitched to one side. 'I said I met her. I admitted to nothing else.'

But Harriet knew, without a shadow of doubt, that Sir Malcolm was the man who had despoiled Felicity's sister. He had been a rake of the very worst kind; she did not need his confession. She leaned in close, breathing through her mouth to avoid the sour smell emanating from the bed.

'She *killed* herself! You seduced her and abandoned her, and she killed herself because she was carrying *your* child.'

He looked at her, his slitted eyes glinting. 'Best

thing for her. One less fatherless brat to worry about. Isn't that so, my *lady*? Although *you* could not even manage that, could you? Lost it, as I recall. Careless of you.'

Harriet reared back, pain ripping at her heart. She must get out. Now. She should never have come. She suddenly realised this trip hadn't just been about Emma but about her, too—an attempt to make sense of the path her life had taken since she had fallen in love with Benedict. And she saw that she and Emma were the same: gullible victims of men who used and abused them and abandoned their responsibilities.

'I hope...' The words dried on her tongue. No, she would offer no comfort to this loathsome man, dying or not. She marched to the door.

Outside, the door firmly shut again, Harriet leaned against the wall, dragging in deep, shuddering breaths. Janet fumbled in her pocket and offered smelling salts. She had been with Harriet since the very early days of Harriet's marriage to Brierley, and had proved herself a loyal and protective friend to the young, bewildered bride. Harriet had long blessed the day the older woman had been appointed as her maid.

She waved the salts away. 'No. I will not faint,

I promise you. I am trying to calm my anger,' she said, forcing a smile to set Janet's mind at rest.

She glanced back at the closed bedchamber door. How could such a man have lived with himself all these years? She pushed upright and shook out her skirts, smoothing them.

'Come. Let us go. We must get back to the Rose as soon as we can in case the snow begins to drift.'

She had reserved accommodation at the Rose Inn at Sittingbourne, a bare four miles from Tenterfield Court, on their way through from London. The plan was to stay there the night and return to London the following day, when Harriet would tell Felicity what she had discovered. She must hope the news would not prove too upsetting for her friend, who was now with child herself. Harriet ruthlessly quashed her ripple of envy that Felicity would soon be a mother.

She was thankful there was no sign of Benedict as they descended the stairs and went through the door to the panelled Great Hall with its ancient blackened stone hearths at either end. The butler sent word to the stables for their hired chaise and four to be brought round to the front door, and a maid ran to fetch their travelling cloaks, muffs and hats. It was cold outside and they had prepared well for the journey from London, with blankets and furs piled in the carriage.

'The chaise is outside now, milady,' the butler said. 'Take care, it might be slippery. Cooper here will help you.'

A footman, well wrapped up, stepped forward and Harriet took one arm whilst Janet took the other. They emerged into a world transformed. The air swirled white and she could barely make out the trees that lined the sweeping carriageway that led from the house to the road. The easterly wind had picked up, gusting at times, and blowing the snow horizontal, stinging Harriet's cheeks. The waiting horses stamped their feet and tossed their heads, blowing cloudy breaths down their nostrils as the hapless post boys hunched on their backs. Harriet hoped they had been given a warming drink in the kitchen; she did not doubt they, like her, would be glad to reach the inn where they were to spend the night.

Harriet clung tightly to the footman's arm, feeling her half boots slide on the stone steps as they descended warily to the waiting chaise. She looked across at Janet at the very same moment the maid released Cooper's arm to hurry down the last few steps, presumably to open the door ready for Harriet.

'Janet! No!'

It was too late. A shriek rose above the howl of the wind as Janet missed her footing on the second to last step. Her feet shot from under her and she fell back onto the steps, one leg bent beneath her.

'Oh, no!' Harriet hurried as best she could to where the maid lay. 'Janet? Are you all right?'

'Yes, milady. I—' Janet screamed as she tried to rise, a high-pitched, sobbing scream. 'Oh, milady! My back! It—aargh! My leg! I can't move it!'

'Oh, good heavens!' *What if it is broken?* Harriet remembered only too well the pain of broken bones, a pain that, in her case, had been numbed by a far greater agony. She thrust those memories back down where they belonged. In the past. 'Can you carry her to the chaise, Cooper?'

The footman bent to lift Janet, but the maid batted him away. 'No! Don't touch me. It hurts!'

Harriet crouched down next to Janet, taking her gloved hand. 'We cannot just leave you here in the snow. You'll freeze to death.'

'I can't bear to move, milady. I can't bear it. And I can't go in that yellow bounder, not the way they drive. I cannot.' Her words ended in a wail.

Now what was she to do? Harriet stared through the driving snow to where the chaise and four still waited. It was barely visible now. The weather was worsening. She must move Janet somehow.

'Allow me.' A hand gripped her shoulder as the deep voice interrupted her inner panic.

Benedict.

Her instinctive urge to shrink from his touch battled against her relief that help was at hand. She glanced round, taking in his hard eyes and tight-lipped mouth, and she clenched her jaw. Janet must be her only concern.

'Thank you,' she said.

Chapter Two

Benedict Poole had returned to the library after escorting Harriet to the bedchamber where the last remaining member of his family, other than himself, lay wasting away. He poured himself another measure of brandy and settled by the fire, broodingly contemplating the woman he had never thought to see again. He gulped a mouthful of the spirit and grimaced. She'd driven him to drink already and she'd been here, what? Half an hour?

A bustle of movement in the Great Hall some time later interrupted his thoughts—the unmistakable sounds of departure. He would not say goodbye. She had not afforded *him* that courtesy, all those years ago.

One last look. That's all.

He crossed to the window and positioned himself to one side, shielded by the curtain, in order that a casual glance would not reveal him. Snow drove horizontally across the front of the house and he was all at once aware of the howl of the wind. He had been so lost in his thoughts he had not even noticed the deterioration in the weather. Three figures, well wrapped against the cold, appeared at the top of the steps, the smallest two clinging on to the arms of the taller central figure, presumably one of the footmen. That was Harriet, huddled in a hooded cloak of deep, rich blue, trimmed with fur. As he watched them gingerly descend the steps, the second woman—Harriet's maid—suddenly let go of the footman's arm and appeared to hurry ahead. Benedict jerked forward, ready to shout a warning even though there was no chance she would hear him, but, before he could utter a sound, the maid's feet shot from under her and she fell.

He didn't stop to think but ran to the door, through the hall and straight out of the front door. The cold air blasted icy spikes against his face as he hurried down the steps, almost slipping in his haste. The maid's leg—it could be broken. She mustn't be moved. Maybe he could straighten it... He had helped more than one ship's surgeon set broken bones during his travels. He thrust aside any nerves, any doubts.

Harriet was crouching by the maid, who was shaking her head, her tearful voice begging no one to touch her. He reached for Harriet, who seemed about to try to pull her maid upright.

'Allow me,' he said.

Harriet turned and gazed up at him, her expression inscrutable, those eyes of hers, once so expressive, guarded. Her nose and cheeks were bright red but her lips, when she spoke, had a bluish tinge. 'Thank you.'

'Go inside and wait,' he said. 'Get yourself warm and dry. We'll deal with your maid.'

'Janet,' she said. 'Her name is Janet. It's her back, as well as her leg. You…you won't hurt her?'

'I can't promise that. We must move her but we must first straighten her leg. Ask Crabtree to bring some brandy and something to bind her leg. He's the butler,' he added as she raised her brows. 'But be careful how you—'

She speared him with a scathing look. 'I am not likely to risk falling, having seen what happened to Janet,' she said.

The panic had melted from her voice, which now dripped contempt. Benedict mentally shrugged. Her moods were none of his concern. Harriet stripped off her cloak and laid it over her stricken maid before picking her way back up the steps.

Benedict glanced at the footman—Cooper, it

was, he now saw. 'That leg could be broken. Have you ever helped set a leg before?' he asked.

'I have,' a new voice interposed. One of the post boys had dismounted and had joined Benedict standing over Janet, who was shivering violently. 'I'm used to it,' he added with a grin. 'Always someone breaking somethin' when horses are involved.'

'Tell your mate to take the horses back to the yard and bed them down for the night,' Benedict said. 'The ladies will be going nowhere.'

'Right you are, sir,' the post boy said, signalling to his partner, who waved an acknowledgement before kicking his horse into motion.

Benedict crouched beside the stricken maid.

'Don't touch me!' she shrieked. 'It's my back! I can't stand it!'

'Hush, now,' Benedict said as the maid subsided into sobs. 'We must find out if your leg is broken. It will have to be straightened before we can move you.'

The butler appeared at the top of the steps and gingerly made his way to where Janet lay.

'Ah, Crabtree. Thank you.' Benedict took the glass and held it to Janet's lips. 'Drink.'

Janet shook her head. 'I never touch—'

'*Drink*. It will help dull the pain when we straighten your leg. You need to be moved.'

Benedict tipped the glass up, pinching her chin to force her mouth open. This was no time for niceties. The cold had seeped through his clothes, chilling his flesh already. Janet must be in an even worse case, lying on the snow-blanketed stone steps.

'What are you doing? How is she?'

His head jerked round. Harriet was back, peering over his shoulder at her maid.

'I thought I told you to stay inside.'

'Janet is my responsibility. I can help.'

'If you want to help, go back inside.'

Her stare might have frozen him had he not already been chilled to his core.

'Don't leave me, my lady. Pleeeease.'

Harriet crouched by Benedict's side and gripped Janet's hands. The length of her thigh pressed briefly against his and he was aware she shifted away at the exact same time he did, so they no longer touched. Another footman appeared, carrying lengths of cloth and a wooden board, with the information that the doctor had been sent for.

Benedict pushed Janet's cloak aside and raised her skirt, Harriet's soothing murmur punctuating Janet's whimpers. A close look at the bent leg raised Benedict's hopes. The foot looked twisted, making a broken ankle a distinct possibility, but the leg itself appeared intact. A pink stain in the snow, however, suggested it was cut.

Benedict spoke to Cooper and the post boy. 'If her back is damaged, we must move her carefully.' He directed the men on how to tip Janet sideways, keeping her back as straight as possible whilst he moved her leg from under her, silently blessing the time he had spent with Josiah Buckley, the ship's surgeon, on his recent voyage back to England from India. He might not know how to help Janet, but he did know how not to make things worse.

The next few minutes were hellish. Benedict gritted his teeth and forced himself to continue, gently straightening Janet's leg and then, using a knife proffered by the post boy, cutting off her boot. Another snippet of knowledge gleaned from Buckley—that an injured foot or ankle will swell, making boots hard to remove. Not that the sailors wore footwear aboard the ship, but their discussions had been wide-ranging. Benedict distracted his thoughts from Janet's screams by thinking of that voyage but then the shrieking wind recalled the storm that had almost foundered the ship, and he found his heart racing and hands shaking with the memory. He hesitated, squeezing his eyes shut as he gulped down his fear—*It isn't real. I'm here at Tenterfield, not on board*—then jerked back to full awareness as a gloved hand covered his. He glanced round into familiar violet eyes.

'You're doing well,' she murmured. He focused on her lips: too close…sweetly full…so tempting. 'Do not lose your nerve now.'

Benedict dragged in a jagged breath and the icy air swept other memories into focus with a vicious stab in his temples. Not life-threatening memories such as that storm, but soul-destroying nonetheless. Memories of Harriet and her betrayal. His hand steadied and he continued to cut Janet's boot until it fell apart.

They slid the maid onto the board then and, between them, Benedict and the post boy used lengths of linen to bind her to the plank and keep her still whilst they moved her to a bedchamber. Benedict rose stiffly to his feet as the two footmen lifted the board and carried Janet up the steps and back into the house. Benedict clasped Harriet's elbow, resisting her attempt to tug free, and supported her up the steps and into the hall.

'Why have you dismissed the chaise?' she demanded as soon as the front door closed behind them, shutting out the swirling snowstorm. 'I have accommodation bespoken at the Rose Inn.'

'You will stay here tonight.'

'I most certainly will not!' Her voice rang with outrage. 'Stay overnight at *Tenterfield Court*, with no chaperone?' Harriet marched over to Crabtree, about to mount the stairs in the wake of the footmen carrying Janet. 'Send a man to the stables, if you please, with a message to bring the chaise back round.'

'Your maid cannot travel.'

Harriet pivoted on the spot and glared at Benedict. 'I am well aware Janet must remain here,' she spat. 'I, however, am perfectly fit and well, and I will not stay where I am not welcome.'

'I thought you were concerned for your reputation?' Benedict drawled, the drive to thwart her overriding his eagerness to see her gone. 'Yet you would stay in a public inn without even a maid to lend you countenance? My, my, Lady Brierley. I have to wonder if your reluctance to remain here at Tenterfield owes less to concern over your reputation and more to fear of your own lack of self-control.'

'Oh!' Harriet's eyes flashed and her lips thinned. 'How *dare* you?' She spoke again to Crabtree, waiting patiently at the foot of the staircase, staring discreetly into space, the epitome of an experienced butler. 'Is there a maid who might accompany me to the inn?'

Crabtree's gaze slid past Harriet to mutely question Benedict, who moved his head in a small negative motion.

'I am sorry, my lady,' Crabtree said, 'but with Sir Malcolm so ill and now your maid to care for, I am unable to spare any of my staff. And I am persuaded it would be unwise to venture on even such a short journey in this weather.'

The satisfaction Benedict experienced at frustrating Harriet's plans glowed for only a brief few seconds. Her presence could only reopen old wounds. Why had he been so insistent that she stay?

'Inform me when the doctor arrives,' he bit out over his shoulder as he took the stairs two at a time, silently cursing himself for a fool.

In his bedchamber, he stripped off his wet clothes and shrugged into his banyan, then paced the vast room, his thoughts filled with Harriet.

The announcement of her arrival had nearly floored him. His heart had drummed against his ribs as his palms grew damp. She could not have known—could she?—that he was here, attending his dying cousin. That leap of hope, swiftly banished, had angered and unsettled him. Whatever her reason for visiting Malcolm, he didn't want to know. He was only here himself from a sense of duty to his erstwhile guardian. He had no affection for Sir Malcolm but he was indebted to him for supporting him financially ever since the death of Benedict's parents. Malcolm had ensured Benedict attended the best schools, followed by Cambridge University, and, for that, Benedict owed him some consideration.

He hadn't *needed* to meet with Harriet at all—he could have relegated the task to one of the servants. He *should* have relegated it but, dammit, that would be tantamount to admitting he still cared. Besides—and he might as well be honest with himself—curiosity had got the better of him. He'd wanted to see what she had become, this jade who had so thoughtlessly betrayed him and his heart: who had pledged her love for him and then coldheartedly wed another man for the sake of a title and wealth.

Before facing her, he'd gone to the library to fortify himself with a glass of brandy from the decanter there. *She* hadn't appeared to need any such additional support. He walked into the drawing room to find her—cool and elegant, an utterly gorgeous woman, with the same abundance of lustrous moon-pale hair he remembered only too well. His fingers had twitched with the desire to take out her pins and see her tresses tumble over her shoulders again. She was more voluptuous than he remembered, but then she had still been a girl when they had fallen in love. Correction, he thought, with a self-deprecating sneer, when *he* had fallen in love. And those eyes—huge, violet blue, thickly lashed; they were as arresting as ever. He had always thought of them as windows to her soul. He snorted a bitter laugh at his youthful naivety. Now, with the benefit of eleven more years' experience, he could see that those eyes had lied as easily as that soft, sensual mouth with its full pink lips.

Such a pity so perfect an exterior disguised such a mercenary bitch.

Later, before dinner, Benedict visited Malcolm in his bedchamber, as had become his habit in the seven days since his arrival at Tenterfield Court. Malcolm's breathing had grown noticeably harsher in the past week and Benedict was conscious that the air now wheezed in and out of his cousin's lungs faster than ever, as if each breath failed to satisfy the demand for oxygen. He pulled a chair to the side of the bed and sat down. Malcolm's eyes were closed, the thin skin almost translucent. A glance at Fletcher elicited a shake of the valet's head.

Benedict placed his hand over the paper-dry skin of Malcolm's hand where it lay on the coverlet. The flesh was cool to his touch, despite the suffocating heat of the room. Sweat sprung to Benedict's forehead and upper lip, and he felt his neck grow damp beneath the neckcloth he had tied around his neck in deference to his dinner guest.

Damn her! Why did she have to come? And now she would be here all night, a siren song calling to his blood as surely as if she lay in his bed beside him. He forced his thoughts away from Harriet as Malcolm stirred, his lids slitting open as though even that movement was too great an effort for his feeble energy.

'Water.'

Fletcher brought a glass and held it to his master's lips, supporting his head as he sucked in the liquid. As Fletcher lowered his head back to the pillow, Malcolm's eyes fixed on Benedict.

'Going out?'

Benedict fingered his neckcloth self-consciously. Malcolm still had the ability to reduce him to a callow youth with just a single comment. He had been a careless guardian with little interest in Benedict, who had been a mere eight years old when he was orphaned. As Benedict had matured and developed more understanding of the world, Malcolm's behaviour and reputation had caused him nothing but shame. Now, although he found it hard to feel any sorrow at Malcolm's imminent death, he could not help but pity the man his suffering.

'I dressed for dinner before visiting you tonight.' The lie slid smoothly off Benedict's tongue. He kept forgetting that, although Malcolm's body had betrayed him, his mind was a sharp as ever.

'Has that harlot gone?'

'Harlot?'

'The Brierley woman. She's no business here… I told her… Fletcher? Has she gone?'

Fletcher glanced at Benedict, who gave a slight nod of his head. 'Yes, sir,' he said. 'She left the house straight after she saw you.'

'Good. Good riddance. Have nothing to do with her, you hear, boy?'

Benedict bit back his irritation at being addressed in such a way. He was a successful businessman. Yes, he was Sir Malcolm's heir and would inherit both the baronetcy and Tenterfield, but he had no need of the man's support or wealth. Not any longer. He was his own man.

It was strange to think he would soon be master of Tenterfield. When he had arrived a week ago, he had gazed up at the red-brick Jacobean manor house with a sense of disbelief that, soon, this place of so many memories would be his. He already felt the pride of ownership and had vowed to restore both its reputation and that of the Poole family name after the years of damage caused by Sir Malcolm's disgrace.

'I have no intention of having anything to do with her, you can rest assured on that,' Benedict said. Then, curious, he asked, 'What do you have against her? I thought Brierley was a friend of yours.'

'That's got nothing to do with it. I saw what her fickle behaviour did to you. She's not to be trusted.'

Benedict felt his eyes narrow. *Now* Malcolm cared about his feelings? Or perhaps he knew more about Brierley's marriage than he was saying. Had Harriet played Brierley false, too? He shoved his chair back and stood up.

'You should rest,' he said. 'I will see you in the morning.'

He went downstairs, Harriet and the evening to come playing on his mind and churning his gut.

Chapter Three

Crabtree appeared, seemingly from nowhere, to open the drawing room doors for Benedict.

'Has Lady Brierley come downstairs yet?' Benedict asked the butler.

'Not yet, sir.'

Benedict was conscious of a sweep of relief. At least they would not have to make small talk before their meal—that would be strained enough, he was sure.

'Please impress upon the rest of the staff that they must not reveal the presence of either Lady Brierley or her maid to Sir Malcolm,' he said. 'It will only agitate him to no purpose.'

'Indeed I will, sir.' Crabtree bowed.

Benedict entered the room to await his dinner guest. Moodily, he poked at the coals in the grate, stirring them to life, pondering this spectre from a past he had long put behind him. He had been caught on the back foot—his feelings tossed and tumbled like a ship caught in a squall. Surely his reaction to Harriet was merely shock and, like a squall, it would soon pass. After all, what was she to him? She was just somebody he used to know a long time ago, when she was a girl. She must be all of seven and twenty by now, by God. Her betrayal—her marriage to Brierley—was ancient history. He was confident he would soon recover his equilibrium, and then he could treat her with the same detached courtesy he would employ towards any unexpected guest. Perhaps he should look upon this unexpected trial in the light of a rehearsal—an opportunity to put their past into some sort of reasonable perspective. In the future, should he happen to see her around town, maybe he could remember their shared past with dispassion and not with this angry bitterness that was eating away inside him.

Voices from outside the door roused him from his thoughts. He turned as Harriet entered the room, his breath catching in his throat at her stunning beauty. She wore an elegant lilac gown that accentuated the violet of her eyes and the fullness of her breasts, despite the neckline not swooping as low as some of the more daring fashions Benedict had seen. Her blonde hair was pinned into a smooth chignon, exposing the creamy skin of her neck and décolletage.

Battening down his visceral reaction, Benedict bowed.

'Good evening, Mr Poole.'

He straightened. Her gaze was both cool and distant, stoking his resentment. The grand society lady: graciously poised and certain of her superiority regardless of the circumstances. Had she forgotten her humble beginnings?

'Good evening, my lady.' His voice was smooth and assured—a stark contrast with his inner turmoil. 'I trust your bedchamber meets with your approval?'

'Thank you, it does indeed.'

The door opened again, and Crabtree announced that dinner was served. Benedict gestured for Harriet to precede him to the dining room.

'How is your maid?' Benedict asked, once they were seated and the food had been served. 'Janet, is it not?'

'Janet, yes,' Harriet said. 'I'm afraid her ankle is broken. Dr Green has set the bone and seems optimistic it will heal well. I do hope that is true and she does not end up with pain or a limp. Her back is very painful, too—the doctor cupped her and will examine her again tomorrow, when he visits Sir Malcolm. He did warn me, however, that she should remain in bed until the bruising comes out and he can see if there is any further damage to her back.'

'How long is that likely to take?'

A faint crease appeared between her brows. 'He did not say. A few days at the least, I should imagine, so I am afraid I shall have to impose on your hospitality a little longer.'

A few days? With her *as a house guest?* Benedict clenched his teeth against a sudden urge to laugh. *What a fool!* He was aware Harriet lived in London and since his return to England from India, he had taken care to avoid any risk of bumping into her. His efforts had been in vain; fate, it would appear, did not like to be thwarted.

'She may stay as long as proves necessary,' he said with a shrug of indifference, determined to give her no reason to suspect he could care less how long she stayed.

Harriet studied him for a long moment as she sipped her wine. She then put her glass down and leaned forward, trapping his gaze.

'In order there is no misunderstanding between us, sir, I should clarify that I will not leave Janet here alone. I intend to remain with her until she is fit enough to travel to Brierley Place. It is only eight miles away, and she can remain there until she is able to undertake the journey to London.'

'As you wish,' Benedict said. 'Heaven forfend your maid should be forced to undergo the privations of recuperating in *these* miserable surroundings.'

A flush lit Harriet's cheeks. 'The point is that she will be happier surrounded by people she knows,' she said. 'And I shall not hesitate to leave her *there* whilst I return to London.'

'Your maid will be perfectly safe here without your protection,' Benedict said, smarting at yet another reminder of the past scandals that had tainted both Tenterfield and the Poole name. It would take time to restore the reputation of both but he was determined to do so, and the sooner the better.

Harriet's words prompted another thought: he had forgotten Brierley Place was quite so near. 'I wonder, though, that you did not plan to stay with your family at Brierley Place, rather than at a public inn, after your visit to my cousin. Why?'

Her gaze lowered. 'I wish to return to London as soon as possible, and if I stayed with my stepson and his family they would expect more than an overnight visit.'

Her hand rose to her neck, and she began to twirl a lock of hair that curled loose by her ear. That achingly familiar habit catapulted Benedict back in time. She was hiding something. It was the first reminder of the girl he'd once known. He studied her, wondering what currents were masked by that calm, ladylike exterior of hers.

'Besides,' she continued, 'my stepson is always up and down to London in his carriage. He will return Janet to me as soon as she is well. The carriage will be far more comfortable for her than a hired chaise.'

'Indeed it will,' Benedict said, 'and, with that in mind, I shall arrange to pay off your post boys in the morning.'

'Thank you. I shall, of course, reimburse you.'

'Of course,' he agreed smoothly. 'And, when you are ready to leave, I shall put my carriage at your disposal.'

Her brows rose. '*Your* carriage? Do you not mean Sir Malcolm's?'

Benedict's anger flared in response to that challenge but he battled the urge to vent his feelings, telling himself that anger came from caring, and he did not care.

'I am not so devoid of feeling as to step into my kinsman's shoes whilst he is still alive,' he said, careful to keep his tone neutral. 'I have my own carriage. It is the use of that I offer to you.'

A delicate flush swept up from her chest to tint her cheeks as she turned her attention to her food. 'Of course. I apologise. I should not have cast such aspersions.'

The conversation faltered, and the silence accentuated the lonely wail of the wind outside. The windows rattled with every gust, the wind forcing its way through the gaps in the frames to cause the red velvet curtains to billow into the room from time to time.

'How long have you been here, at Tenterfield?'

Benedict finished chewing and swallowed his food before answering, 'A week. My cousin's solicitor sent for me on the doctor's advice.'

'So there is no hope of a cure?'

'None.'

He read sympathy in those glorious eyes of hers. He had no need of it. She, of all people, should know he had no fondness for Malcolm. He would be no loss to humanity and Benedict would not pretend a grief he did not feel. His predominant emotion was impatience to return to London. His business—importing goods from the Far East—needed his attention and he had matters to discuss with his partner, Matthew Damerel, who was due back in town again shortly.

They finished eating and Benedict stood, saying, 'Serve the brandy in the drawing room, will you please, Crabtree?' He caught Harriet's eye and added, 'Would you care to join me?'

'Thank you.' She rose elegantly to her feet. 'I shall wait for the tea tray and then I shall retire. It has been a somewhat exhausting day.'

Benedict had not proffered his arm to Harriet before dinner but now, mellowed by wine and bolstered by the certainty that he was in control of his temper, he waited for Harriet to round the table and reach him, then crooked his arm. She halted, her gaze fixed on his arm, then raised her eyes to his. She seemed about to speak, but then merely laid her gloved hand on his sleeve and allowed him to lead her from the room.

Every muscle in his arm tensed, even though her touch was feather-light. Her scent, sophisticated, floral and quintessentially feminine, assailed his nostrils and he found himself swallowing hard, trying to ignore the unaccustomed flutter of nerves in his belly. He gritted his teeth. He was a grown man, for God's sake. This ridiculous reaction meant nothing; it was merely the spectre of the past playing games with him. Maybe he should take advantage of the circumstances that had thrown them together like this. Lay her and those ghosts at the same time.

'Would you care for a glass of brandy?' he enquired when Cooper, the footman, followed them into the drawing room carrying a silver salver, complete with decanter and two glasses.

'Thank you, but I have no taste for spirits. A cup of tea will suffice.'

Cooper handed a glass of brandy to Benedict, then bowed to Harriet. 'I will hurry the maid along with the tea tray, milady.'

She smiled at him. 'Thank you.' She settled on the sofa opposite the hearth and Benedict noticed her shiver.

'Are you cold?' He poked the fire, which had recently been refuelled and was therefore not emitting much heat.

'Not really. It is the sound of that wind.' When he turned to look at her, she was staring towards the window, one hand playing with the pearls at her neck. 'I had forgotten, living in London, quite how desolate it can sound. Like a lost soul, crying into the void.'

'Like a lost *soul*?'

She started, and then laughed a little self-consciously. 'Oh! I do beg your pardon. I had quite forgot…that is…' Her voice tailed away and her cheeks bloomed pink as her lips quirked in a wry smile. 'I did not mean to spout such poetical nonsense. Please do forgive me.'

'There is nothing to forgive. I confess there have been times, usually aboard ship, when the wind has conjured many superstitious imaginings in my own mind. I generally avoided voicing them out loud, however, for fear I might be thought to run mad.'

She laughed, a genuine laugh this time. 'Goodness, sir. You put me quite out of countenance. You imply that I might be thought mad.'

Not mad, but bad. Why did you deceive me, Harriet?

The words pummelled his brain and battered at his tightly closed lips. It was a question to which he had long yearned for an answer. But he would never ask. What would be the point? She could mouth all the excuses in the world but she could never deny the truth. She simply had not loved him enough. She had broken her pledge of love for the promise of status and riches.

One of the maids came into the room at that moment with the tea tray. Relieved by the interruption, Benedict gestured at her to make the tea and he then crossed to the table to fetch a cup for Harriet. As he handed it to her he took advantage of her distraction in handling the delicate china to study her at close quarters.

Maturity had added to her beauty, not detracted from it. Her thick blonde hair was pinned up, exposing the long, vulnerable line of her neck and that sensitive spot below her ear where he had taken a lovesick youth's delight in kissing her and teasing her with his tongue. With her eyes lowered, he could count every one of the long lashes that swept the peaches and cream of her skin. He committed to memory the faint fan of lines radiating from the outer corner of her eye; they only served to render her more enticing, more beautiful...vulnerable, even.

He was so very close he could even see the soft, fair down that coated her cheek. Against his will, his gaze drifted—sweeping again to her shoulder, where pale skin skimmed delicate bones, and then to her chest, to delight in the flesh that nestled within the neckline of her gown. His pulse leaped in response to the shadowy valley between her breasts and saliva flooded his mouth as he recalled the glory of her naked flesh.

Her scent enveloped him, leading him to wish the impossible...leading him to wish the past had been different.

With a silent oath, Benedict straightened abruptly

and moved away to sit in an armchair, dismissing that momentary weakness. He crossed his legs to disguise his growing arousal, furious that he had allowed the fascination of the past to intrude upon the present. It was many years since he had believed a woman's appearance was an indication of her true worth, and he would never forget that, however beautiful Harriet might be on the outside, she was rotten and mercenary to her core.

Bitterness still lurked deep inside him. It was under control for now, but it would not take much for it to break free—for him to fling accusations at her and to demand explanations. He would not visit that time. He must allow those memories to fade away, and only look forward. Never back.

'Do you stay at Brierley Place often?' he asked, needing the ebb and flow of conversation to distract him, afraid of where his fixation with the past might lead.

'No, not often since I was widowed.'

'Does the new Lord Brierley not make you welcome?'

'He is very supportive in many ways.' One hand lifted to toy again with that loose curl by her ear. The repeat of that girlhood habit made him frown.

What is *she hiding?* The thought prompted a desire to dig further; to discover the real woman behind that cool civility. He dismissed that desire with an impatient inner snarl.

'What are your plans, Mr Poole? Will you remain here after…after…?'

'After Sir Malcolm dies?'

She blushed. 'Yes. I am sorry if that was an insensitive question.'

'There is no need to apologise. I have a business to run, so I shall spend much of my time in London once my cousin's affairs are in order.'

It was a prospect he viewed with little pleasure, but in the week since his arrival at Tenterfield—when he had realised for the first time exactly how little time Malcolm had left—Benedict had come to accept he would have no option but to enter society if he was serious about restoring the family name. He was aware he was unlikely to be welcomed into the top tier, but his title and the vast fortune he would inherit would be enough for many to overlook his links to trade.

He had travelled the world these past eleven years and thought of himself as having permanent wanderlust in his blood, with no urge to put down roots. He never dwelt on the past. The past was done. It couldn't be changed. Since his return to England, however, the time he had spent with Matthew and his new bride, Eleanor, had awoken something deep inside him—the urge for a family to call his own.

Benedict's memories of his early life, before his parents' deaths, were hazy. Seeing Matthew and Eleanor together, however, had gradually recalled those happy years and his plans for his future had changed. He and Matthew already had a trusted agent in India who would arrange shipments to England. There was no necessity for Benedict to return to India if he chose not to.

Silence settled over them as Harriet sipped at her tea and Benedict finished his brandy, then Harriet placed her teacup and saucer on a side table. She rose to her feet and he followed suit.

'I shall retire,' she said. 'It has been a long day. Thank you for your hospitality, Ben... Mr Poole.'

'You are welcome, my lady.'

Their gazes met, her violet eyes dark and unfathomable. Benedict stepped closer. Was it his imagination, or did her lips tremble? He saw the convulsive movement of her throat as she swallowed. Then she straightened and drew in what seemed to be an interminable breath.

'Goodnight.' With a swish of skirts she passed him by and headed for the door.

Benedict moved quickly. 'Allow me,' he said, reaching the door before her.

He grasped the handle but then hesitated. Slowly, his hand slipped from the handle and he turned to face Harriet, his back against the door.

Chapter Four

Harriet had halted a few feet away.

'Please let me pass.'

Her voice was low. She searched his face, her gaze uncertain.

'Harriet…'

'Mr Poole?'

But what could he say that would not risk unleashing all that anger and bitterness that scoured his insides? The past had happened. No amount of wishful thinking could change it and no good could come of stirring up all those raw emotions.

He spoke from the heart, but he spoke only of the present. 'You are a very beautiful woman, Harriet.'

His voice had grown husky; blood surged to his groin; he took a pace towards her and breathed deep of her scent. She was close. So close. He reached out and fingered that errant curl and revelled in the whispered sigh that escaped those full,

pink lips. He narrowed still further the gap between them, relishing the flush that suffused her
skin. Molten-hot currents burned deep within him,
making his skin tighten and his breath grow short.

He opened his fingers and released her curl, lowering his hand to his side.

He would not detain her. Her escape was clear,
if she wanted it. She had only to step away—walk
around him to the door. She did not. Her eyelids
fluttered and lowered as her lips parted. He tilted
his head, feathered his lips at the side of her neck,
savouring her quiet moan, satisfied by the leap of
her pulse as he laved that sensitive spot.

'No,' she whispered. 'Please…I…'

'Tell me to stop, and I will,' he murmured as he
licked at her lobe.

He blew gently across the moistened skin and
she shuddered, swaying, her full breasts and peb-
bled nipples pressing into his chest for one brief,
glorious moment before she jerked away.

'No!'

Benedict, grown hard with desire, reined in his
urge to grab her and kiss her anyway. He forced
himself to remain still.

'Why?'

'I do not need to give you a reason.'

Head high, she met his gaze. He recognised the

flash of vulnerability in her eyes…and something else. Fear? Of him?

'What are you afraid of?'

With his attention fully upon her, he sensed the shift under her skin as she drew her defences in place. 'I am not afraid.'

He wanted to doubt her. He wanted to believe her lips were saying 'no' when she meant 'yes'. But he could not. She—for whatever reason—really did mean 'no'.

He moved aside and watched as she left the room. His feet moved of their own volition, following her out the door into the hall to watch as she climbed the stairs.

Who is she? Who has she become?

He had no wish to revisit the past, but he could not help but be intrigued by the present-day Harriet. Her outer shell was well crafted: sophisticated, ladylike, at ease. And yet she had revealed some of her true spirit in that snowstorm, after he dismissed the post-chaise. Benedict suspected her calm exterior concealed hidden turbulence, much as the smooth surface of the ocean might conceal treacherous currents.

He wandered back into the drawing room to stand and stare into the fire, his mind whirling. He wanted to dig deeper, to find out more about her. Curiosity. It was dangerous, but that was no reason to retreat. She would be here for a few days yet—time enough to find out more. Perhaps testing those suspected undercurrents was risky, but he had never yet backed down from a challenge. And he wasn't about to start now.

The following day was grey and cold, the land still dusted white. No more snow had fallen, but the weather did nothing to tempt anyone out of doors. Harriet spent some of her time sitting with Janet, and the rest of the day exploring Tenterfield Court. Despite growing up in the area, she had never set foot inside the house until today and she had not realised its true magnificence.

Sir Malcolm had lived, for the most part, in London. He would descend, with guests, for a few days of wild, disruptive parties—the kind that fuelled horrified gossip in the local community—and then would disappear again for months on end. He avoided all interaction with local society on the rare times he visited on his own and, as his dissolute reputation spread, the people in the surrounding area—including Harriet's father, who was the local vicar—had in turn shunned Sir Malcolm.

Benedict, as his ward, had spent most of the school holidays alone at Tenterfield Court, mixing with the local children, including Harriet. Memories tumbled into her brain. He had been so tall and handsome—someone she'd liked and looked up to—and, as they had grown, so had their feelings. Now, looking back, Harriet knew those feelings to be a lie—the fanciful wishes of a naive young girl and the lustful desires of a boy on the verge of manhood.

As she changed her dress for dinner early that evening, she diverted her thoughts away from those past innocent—and not so innocent—pleasures and into the present. She was a woman grown now: experienced, wise in the ways of men, no longer a believer in love. The love she had once felt for Benedict Poole was no more, but she could not deny he was an extremely attractive man.

How would it feel to lie with him now?

That errant thought shook her. How could she even wonder such a thing after the way he had deserted her? Or was it natural to be curious about this past love of hers? Last night—and her blood heated at the memory—he had woven a spell of such sensuality around her that the temptation to succumb to him had near overwhelmed her. Thank goodness she had come to her senses in time.

A restless night had seen her up early in the morning with a vow to avoid Benedict as much as possible during her enforced stay at Tenterfield Court. Thankfully, Benedict appeared to share her reluctance for another encounter; according to Crabtree, he had spent the entire day holed up in the study with Sir Malcolm's bailiff, and that suited Harriet perfectly. The less time they spent together the less likely she would be to reveal too much. Her pride would never allow him to know how much he had hurt her with his brutal rejection eleven years before.

Her customary calm had already deserted her once since her arrival. That he had been right to dismiss the post-chaise yesterday had not even entered her thoughts, and she had allowed her anger and her resentment of him to show. She must ensure such a lapse did not recur, and she vowed to redouble her efforts to stay in control of her emotions.

She delayed coming downstairs until one of the maids came to tell her that dinner was ready to be served. She headed straight for the dining room, and Benedict joined her a few minutes later.

He strolled in, supremely confident and at ease, starkly handsome in his evening clothes. He gave her a lazy smile. 'Good evening, my lady. I trust you have occupied your time pleasantly today?'

Harriet ignored the tiny flutter of nerves deep

in her belly. *Don't allow him to fluster you. Stay in control.* After all, she was well practised in the art of concealing her feelings and opinions. Her late husband had schooled her well.

'Yes, most pleasantly, thank you,' she replied. 'And you, sir?'

He grimaced. 'I have been familiarising myself with the estate accounts,' he said. 'My head is reeling with facts and figures.'

He pulled out a chair for Harriet. As the night before, two facing places had been set, halfway along the long sides of the table. As Harriet sat down, Benedict's hand brushed her upper arm, sending a shiver of awareness dancing across her skin. He rounded the table and sat opposite her.

'Did you gain any experience of agricultural matters whilst you were overseas?' Harriet asked as Crabtree served her a slice of roast beef and a spoonful of glazed onions.

'No. My experience is all in trade. This is all new to me.'

Benedict fixed his green eyes on Harriet. 'Tell me—'

'How long have you been back in England?' Harriet asked hastily, keen to keep the focus of the conversation away from her own life.

'Three months.'

'Was Sir Malcolm's health the reason for your return?' She then took advantage of Benedict's distraction as Crabtree offered him a dish of potatoes in hollandaise sauce to say, 'You mentioned before that you are the only family he has left.'

Benedict captured her gaze and quirked a brow, as if to say, 'I know what you're up to,' and Harriet felt her cheeks heat. He took his time in finishing his mouthful of food before answering her.

'No. I had no idea his health was failing until I landed in England.'

'This food is delicious,' Harriet said, somewhat desperately.

Benedict might be answering her questions, but he was doing nothing to ease the evening ahead with the light, inconsequential conversation that any gentleman accustomed to society would employ. But what else could she expect, she thought irritably, when he had spent half his life in foreign climes? His manners were bound to be rough compared to the gentlemen of the *ton*.

'It is indeed,' he replied. 'Malcolm engaged a French fellow a few years ago—I suspect he relishes the opportunity to practice his art.'

He sipped his wine, studying Harriet over the rim of his glass as she cast around for another safe subject of conversation—in other words, anything that did not involve their past.

'Do you enjoy the theatre?'

He grinned openly. 'Yes,' he said. 'Now, tell me, what happened to your father? I understand the Reverend Twining has been the pastor here for a number of years past.'

She'd known it was only a matter of time before he started questioning her. Her stomach knotted with guilt, as it always did whenever she thought of her father.

'He died six years ago.'

Oh, Papa! Parson Rowlands, deeply shocked by his only daughter's fall from grace, had barely spoken to Harriet during that dreadful time leading up to her marriage to Brierley. His disappointment in her would have broken her heart had it not already been in pieces after Benedict's rejection. Then, after her marriage, she'd had no opportunity to heal the breach with her father because Brierley had discouraged—most strongly and very effectively—any interaction between Harriet and her parents. The mere thought of her late husband and his despotic ways prompted a swell of nausea and she forced it back down. She pushed her plate away, her appetite gone.

How she regretted that she'd had no chance to

reconcile with her father before his death. She gripped her hands tightly together under cover of the table, willing her voice to remain steady as she continued, 'After he died my mother moved to live with her sister in Whitstable.'

There was no security of tenure for the widow of a vicar. The rectory had been needed for the next incumbent. She risked a glance across the table. Benedict looked thoughtful, his green eyes locked onto her face.

'She does not live with you?'

'No.' After Brierley's death Harriet had rekindled her relationship with her mother, but Mrs Rowlands had declined to leave her ailing sister. 'My aunt Jane suffers from ill health. She benefits from the sea air and Mama felt her duty was to stay and care for her.'

'I am sorry to raise what is clearly a painful subject.'

'You were not to know.'

Silence reigned once again. Benedict continued to eat and Harriet fixed her gaze upon her half-eaten plate of congealing food. Her emotions were rubbed raw; everything...*everything*...was this man's fault. How she wished she could just leave the table and return to the privacy of her bedchamber. Good manners, however, dictated she must remain. She must distract herself somehow—her mind was as brittle as ice, ready to splinter into a thousand sharp accusations at the wrong look, the wrong word. She cast around for a topic of conversation.

'You mentioned yesterday that you intend to spend much of your time in London in the future,' she said. 'Is it your intention to take your place in society?'

She prayed the answer would be no. How could she bear it, knowing she might bump into him at any time? How could she endure the constant reminders of all that had happened?

'Yes, it is,' he said. Harriet's heart sank. 'I intend to restore the reputation of the Poole family name after Malcolm's depredations.'

'And how do you intend to do that?' Even to her own ears, the question sounded waspish.

Benedict's lips thinned and he frowned. Then he gestured at Harriet's plate. 'Have you had enough to eat? Might I pass you any fruit or sweetmeats?'

'No. I have had sufficient, thank you.'

Crabtree and the footman in attendance began to clear the dishes.

Benedict waited until they left the room, and then continued, 'To answer your question, I shall do it by example. I am conscious that my cousin made no provision for the future of the title and the estate but I shall not make that mistake. I will not allow the baronetcy to fail, nor do I relish the idea of the Poole estates reverting to the Crown to help fund the profligate lifestyle of Prinny.' He pushed his chair back, then rounded the table to draw her chair out to enable her to stand. 'I need an heir. I shall marry a respectable girl from a good family and have a family.'

His words stabbed at her heart. *An heir! How can he be so cruel?* How could he speak of having a child and not even show a flicker of interest in what had happened eleven years ago? Harriet tamped down her fury and distress as she rose, schooling her expression into one of polite disinterest before facing him.

'I wish you well in your endeavour.'

He stared at her for a long moment before speaking again. 'Perhaps you might help me in my search for a suitable wife?' He searched her face, his eyes intent. 'You must be acquainted with a number of young ladies.'

What does he want from me? Proof of the pain he caused? Tears? Harriet steeled herself to show nothing of what she felt.

With an effort, she raised her brows in a coquettish fashion. 'Perhaps you might furnish me with a list of your specific requirements, sir?'

His laugh sounded forced. 'Oh, I hardly think—'

'But I insist, sir! How else am I to help you?'

She was beyond taking pleasure at his look of discomfort. He had clearly not expected her to react in kind.

'Harriet—'

'Or perhaps you have not yet considered the precise qualities desirable in your wife, sir,' she rushed on. 'That is a mistake, I assure you. Allow me to help.'

She faced him, one arm crossed at her waist, her other elbow propped on it as she tapped one finger to her lips.

'Your bride... Now, let me see... You will require a girl of impeccable breeding. Her father should be no less than a viscount, I would suggest, in order to add to your consequence. She must have a substantial dowry, preferably of land, to increase your estates and wealth. What else?' She tipped her head to one side. 'She should be elegant, obedient, schooled in all the ladylike accomplishments. Oh! And, of course, it goes without saying she must be an *innocent*.'

Without intent, her voice had risen until she spat out the final word and Harriet silently cursed herself for rising to Benedict's bait.

Chapter Five

There was a beat of silence following Harriet's outburst.

'Harriet?' Benedict put his hand on her shoulder, curling gentle fingers around it. 'Why are you so upset?' He crouched slightly to gaze into her face and cradled her cheek with his other palm.

How fickle could one woman's body be? How treacherous? In the midst of her distress, she felt the undeniable melting of her muscles, the tug of need deep, deep inside and the yearning to lean into him and to feel his arms around her. To take his comfort.

She kept her gaze lowered. She could not bear to look at him, lest her weak-willed craving shone from her eyes. Harsh breaths dragged in and out of her lungs, searing her chest. What had she done? What would he think? Her mind whirled, looking for anything to excuse her behaviour.

'It was the memory of Papa. I must be overtired, to allow it to upset me so. I am sorry if I have embarrassed you. Goodnight, sir.'

Harriet jerked away from Benedict and swept from the room with her head averted, blinking rapidly to stem the tears that crowded her eyes. She climbed the stairs on legs that trembled with a need that both shocked and dismayed her.

'Harriet?'

She heard him call her, but she kept going. Then she heard the feet pounding up the stairs behind her. Coming closer, ever closer. Memories—dreadful, heart-wrenching memories—crowded her mind. Her heart beat a frantic tattoo and bile burned its way up her throat.

'No!' The breathy scream forced its way out of her lips as she scurried up the last few stairs, clutching at the banister for support. She reached the top. *Not safe. Not here.* Panic swarmed through her veins.

She stumbled across the landing and then spun round—panting in her distress—her back against the wall, well away from the wide open, threatening head of the stairs.

It's Benedict. You are safe. He would never attack you.

It was his fault. It wouldn't have happened if he had—

Harriet cut off that inner diatribe, but other random thoughts still hurtled around inside her head. She hauled in a deep breath, desperate to calm her terror, desperate to think straight. Benedict paused a few feet from her, his face flushed, his chest rising and falling.

'Harriet? Why did you run? What is it? What are you afraid of? Me?'

Harriet shook her head. She did not want his pity; she did not even want his guilt for what he had put her through. 'I am not afraid.'

'That is what you said last night, too, but your eyes tell a different story,' he growled as he stepped closer. She flinched and he moved back, frowning. 'What kind of a man do you think I am? I might be my cousin's heir, but I have not inherited his tendencies, you may rest assured of that.'

Harriet swallowed, her pulse steadying. 'I know,' she whispered. 'I never thought you had. But...'

But it was complicated. She *was* afraid. Still. Oh, not in the way she had been afraid on the stairs, hearing those feet thundering up the stairs behind her. Chasing her. *That* had been blind panic. Her current dread, though... Words she could hardly bear to think, let alone speak, crowded into her mouth and she barricaded them behind clenched teeth and pursed lips.

What she feared, almost more, were the memories Benedict had awakened. She was afraid of her own body's treacherous clamour for his embrace. She was terrified of where her weakness might lead.

She wanted him. So much. Even after everything.

But she could never forgive him.

'But...?'

Harriet sucked in a deep, deep breath, noticing Benedict's hot green gaze dip to her décolletage as she did so. That brought her to her senses enough to say, 'But I believe the past should stay in the past. Last night...you would have...*we* would have... if I had...' She swallowed. 'I have no wish to revisit our childish indiscretions,' she said firmly. 'I shall bid you goodnight, Mr Poole, and I trust I shall have no need to rely upon your hospitality for much longer.'

She turned and walked away, another rush of tears blurring her vision. She did not allow herself to think. Like a wounded animal, she craved a dark corner and her instincts led her straight to her bedchamber, where she shut the door behind her. There was no key, no bolt. Desperate, Harriet grasped hold of the heavy wooden chest set at the foot of the bed and tugged it, inch by inch, until it was set in front of the door. She cared not what the maid might think in the morning, when she came to light the fire. All she wanted was to feel safe but, as she collapsed onto the bed and allowed the hot flood of tears free rein, she acknowledged it was not Benedict she feared.

It was her own weakness that terrified her.

The next morning, Harriet woke late after a restless night. She arose and tugged on the bell rope to summon hot water before crossing to the window and twitching the curtain aside. The day was bright and clear and the snow that had clung tenaciously to the ground throughout the previous day might never have been.

The bedchamber was cosy, courtesy of the fire lit by a chambermaid earlier that morning. Harriet wondered what the kitchen gossips had made of the fact that the maid had to knock on the door and rouse Harriet before she could gain admittance. Together they had dragged the chest back to the foot of the bed, Harriet excusing her odd behaviour by saying she was scared of ghosts. The maid's sceptical look had seemed to say, 'But everyone knows ghosts can travel through doors and walls. A barricaded door is no protection.'

A tap at the door revealed a different maid carrying a pitcher from which steam spiralled.

'I've been sent to help you dress, milady, if you are ready now,' the girl said. She told Harriet her name was Annie. 'Breakfast is set up in the morning room for you.'

'Thank you,' Harriet said, turning to the washstand to wash whilst the maid pulled back the covers to air the bed and then waited until Harriet was ready to don her dove-grey carriage dress. 'Is Mr Poole... Has Mr Poole breakfasted yet?'

Please say yes. She could not face him after last night. When he had followed her up the stairs, the sound of his footsteps behind her had brought the terror and the anguish flooding back. What must he think of her? Had she managed to misdirect him with her talk of the past and their childish indiscretions?

And earlier, in the dining room—dear heavens, *how* she had been tempted, once again, to lose herself in his embrace, even after her loss of control over his provocation. How she had yearned for him, her body melting with desire. And that, she had thought, as she'd tossed and turned in her bed last night, her mind whizzing, was a near miracle considering how she had grown to abhor the marital act—she would not dignify it by thinking of it as making love—with Brierley. As recently as one year ago, her body might not have responded so readily to Benedict. But then she had set out to erase the memory of Brierley and his vile ways from her mind and her heart and…yes…her body. And she had succeeded, when she had, after great consideration and much soul-searching, taken a lover. And, with his help, she had overcome her fear.

'Oh, yes, milady. Mr Poole is ever an early riser. Comes from living in foreign parts, Mr Crab—' The maid stopped, her hand to her mouth, eyes rounded. 'Beg pardon, milady, if I'm speaking out of turn. My mum always said I never know when to stop.'

Harriet laughed at the girl, relieved to learn she would not meet Benedict at the breakfast table. 'That is quite all right, Annie. Now will you show me to the morning room, please?'

She had taken breakfast on a tray in her bedchamber yesterday and the house was so vast she had no confidence in finding her way on her own. Before they reached the morning room she had discovered that Mr Poole was once again perusing the estate ledgers with Sir Malcolm's agent in the study.

The morning room was a beautiful sunny room with a view to the east, over lawns that curved away, down into a valley that Harriet remembered from her childhood. In her mind's eye she saw happy, carefree days when the sun seemed to be forever shining and adults and their complicated world and rules barely existed, other than to provide food and shelter. Memories were strange things, she mused. From her adult perspective, she knew her childhood had also consisted of lessons and church, duty and chores, but those untroubled sunny days playing with her friends—and with Benedict—eclipsed all else. She pictured the shallow stream that gurgled along its stony bed at the bottom of the slope, with the choice of a wooden footbridge or stepping stones to cross it. As children, of course, they had always chosen to cross via the stepping stones, jostling and daring each other and, inevitably, someone had ended up with wet feet.

The opposite slope of the valley was wooded and stretched up in a gentle curve until, just beyond the far edge of the wood, a grassy hillock, bare of trees, jutted skywards. At the top of the hillock was the folly, modelled upon a ruined medieval castle complete with tower. Harriet's stomach knotted. Here were memories she had no wish to dwell upon.

She finished her breakfast of toast and coffee and then went upstairs to visit Janet, to see how she fared. Janet was sleepy but out of pain; the housekeeper, Mrs Charing, had been dosing her with syrup of poppies in accordance with the doctor's instructions.

After sitting with her maid awhile, Harriet decided to leave her to sleep. She would go for a walk, to blow some of the cobwebs from her brain. She wrapped up well in her travelling cloak, pulling the fur-lined hood over her head. It was a beautifully bright day, but there was still a cold easterly wind. Harriet strode out briskly enough to keep herself warm.

Almost without volition, her steps took her along the path to the valley where she had played as a child. The path down the slope was wet and rather slippery, but she negotiated it without mishap, right down into the valley and to the stream, which she crossed, by the bridge this time, as befitted a grown woman. She smiled at the thought of presenting herself back at Tenterfield Court with her half boots waterlogged.

She followed the course of the stream a short

distance and then struck off up the lightly wooded far slope of the valley, driven by the urge to see if the folly had changed. Just to look at it from outside, she assured herself, as the slope steepened and her breath shortened.

At the top, she paused to rest, gazing up at the stone walls of the folly tower as they reared into the clear blue sky. The curved walls were broken by a single Gothic-style arched window on each floor. The door—solid oak, massive, punctuated by wrought iron studs—was closed. She wondered if it was now kept locked. It hadn't been, back when she was young. Such memories. On the brink of walking on, she hesitated.

It was a foolish whim; one Harriet regretted the moment she entered the folly and realised she was not alone.

Chapter Six

Harriet could feel Benedict's gaze boring into her as she paused on the threshold, giving her eyes time to adjust to the gloom inside the tower.

'This is the last place I expected to see you.'

Benedict spoke the words, but they could as easily have been spoken by her. The memories evoked by this place swirled around her, almost a physical presence. Did he feel them, too? Was his mind also bursting with images from the past? This had been their trysting place: the place where they could be alone, out of sight of prying eyes or wagging tongues to cry scandal.

Silly, trusting girl—thinking she was in control of her life when, in reality, all control lay with others. See where her trust had led her—to marriage with a man who disgusted her, and to unimaginable heartbreak as a consequence of his temper. She had vowed, after Brierley's death, that she would never pass control over her life to another man.

'I am not one to sit in idleness. I felt in need of fresh air and exercise, after being cooped up indoors yesterday.' Harriet strolled with as much nonchalance as she could muster into the centre of the room. 'And why should I not visit here? It was on my walk and I was curious to see if there were any changes.'

He moved too, giving Harriet a wide berth as he crossed to gaze out of the window. 'For a medieval castle, it is in remarkably good repair,' he said, his tone light and unconcerned. 'But, then, it *is* only several decades old rather than several centuries.'

It had been a source of wonder and imagination when they were children and, with Sir Malcolm so rarely at home, they had played at knights and maidens and dragons and swordfights with other local children. Gradually, though, the other village children visited less and less frequently as the reality of their lives—the need to supplement their parents' income by working—had intruded. But Benedict and Harriet had continued to meet here. And their play had, in time, taken a serious turn.

Her head had been full of love; his, full of lust. It was the way of men. She knew that now.

'I am pleased Sir Malcolm has maintained the

estate, despite his…' She hesitated. It was not her place to criticise his kinsman.

'Despite his notorious ways? I have scant respect for Malcolm, as you know, but he was no spendthrift. His proclivities veered more towards the flesh than gambling.'

Harriet suppressed her shudder. Her late husband had been cast from the same mould.

'As you are here, it would be a waste not to go upstairs and admire the view.' Benedict stood aside, indicating the studded door that led to the spiral stairs. The tower was cylindrical, built over four floors, and the view from the top, she remembered, was spectacular.

She said nothing, merely inclined her head, and walked past him to the door. It opened easily. Whoever cared for the estate must take their work seriously, to include greasing the hinges to a door in a folly that served no purpose. She paused.

'I understood you to be in a meeting with Sir Malcolm's agent,' she said.

He huffed a laugh. 'And so you thought yourself safe from encountering me on your walk? I regret disappointing you, my lady, but I, too, felt in dire need of a good dose of cleansing fresh air. Do you need any assistance on the stairs?'

'Thank you, no.'

Harriet lifted her skirts high and climbed the stone stairs to the top floor. Here there were wooden benches, but she resisted the urge to sit and catch her breath. She would continue up to the battlements, admire the view over the Kent countryside and then be on her way.

Being here at the folly brought all those memories flooding back to Harriet. Knowing he still wielded that kind of power over her emotions and her body—despite the best efforts of her brain to stay in control—had kept her awake half the night. She had been oh-so-tempted by him. His lovemaking in their youth had been unpractised, as had hers. Now he, like she, would possess a certain skill. She wondered again how it might feel to lie with him, but did not dwell on the thought. It would surely bring regret. He had blood on his hands. Innocent blood. No matter how she might desire him, she could never forgive him.

She gazed across the landscape, dazzling in the sunlight—seeing it, but barely paying it the attention it deserved, all her senses straining for an awareness of Benedict's whereabouts. After several tense minutes she heard the door that led onto the roof open. She had no need to look to know that Benedict had followed her: the rising hairs on her nape confirmed his presence, and the gooseflesh that skittered across her arms wasn't purely caused by the chill wind. She sensed the gap between them narrowing, until she could hear the quiet sound of his breathing and she could feel the heat of his body warming the air between them and she could smell...*him*. Still familiar, after all this time.

She swallowed. A maelstrom of emotions buffeted her this way and that but she strove to stay calm, to stay in control.

'It is as beautiful as I remember,' she said. 'I count it as fortunate the weather is so good today—it has afforded me the opportunity to see the wonder of the countryside again.' She hugged her cloak around her as a gust of wind attempted to tear it open.

'It is a spectacular sight,' Benedict said, his deep voice close by her ear, raising another shiver. 'But it is very cold up here. Come, you must not catch a chill, or you will be forced to endure even more of my company.'

She could hear the effort he put into that light-hearted remark. His tone did not quite ring true and it forced her—for the first time—to consider how her presence was affecting him. Did he feel guilt over his betrayal? Was there a pang of conscience over the death of the baby, born too soon, who'd never had the chance to draw breath? Was there *any* regret—a tiny speck, even if it was well buried? He had not even mentioned the child, seemed uninterested in whether it was alive or dead. Had he wiped his memory clear of the fact she had ever been with child?

Would that she could so easily forget. Her empty arms still ached, as did her heart, at the knowledge that she would never now experience the joy of motherhood, for never again would she risk marrying and placing such power over herself and her body in any man's hands. And she resented—deeply—the fact that Benedict not only felt no guilt and had experienced none of her grief, but also that he was now poised to become a wealthy powerful man—and marry and have a family—whereas she…she was destined to remain loveless and childless for the rest of her days.

She swung away from the view and sidestepped around Benedict to head for the door but, as on the previous evening, he was there before her.

'Allow me to go first,' he said. 'In case you miss your step.'

At Benedict's words, an image rose to tempt her: that of her stumbling…of him catching her in his arms…of him lifting her chin and lowering his head. Her heart pounded and her breathing quickened as she took especial care in descending the spiral stairs, clutching with gloved fingers at the thick rope that looped from bracket to bracket all the way down. Back on the ground floor without incident, her breathing eased and her racing heart steadied as she straightened her cloak in readiness for the walk back to the house.

'Harriet...'

Her name hung in the air.

Slowly, she raised her eyes to his. She could not read his expression in the dim light that filtered through the window, but she did see the muscle leap in his jaw. The air between them crackled with intensity and her pulse responded with a lurch and a gallop. All moisture seemed to have been sucked from her mouth, and she licked at her dry lips as he moved closer. His gaze fastened on her mouth, sending desire sizzling through her. Pure instinct tilted her head, lifting her lips to his.

Aah. The most delicate of touches. Lip to lip... sweet, gentle, almost worshipping. Memories of love and laughter and pure joy. They had been so young. A shared future planned. They had followed the instinctive desires of their youthful bodies. She had felt so secure in his love for her. Before...

Harriet switched her thoughts away from the past

and into the present. A kiss. Why should they not? It was just a kiss.

She leaned into him, raising her hands to his shoulders, broad and strong. A man's body, reminding her he was no longer a youth. A silent sigh for what might have been echoed through her, and tears sprang to her eyes.

He deepened the kiss, his arms coming around her, moulding her to him as his tongue swept into her mouth and tangled with hers. His groan vibrated through her core and she could feel the steady thump of his heart as he tightened his hold, raising her onto her toes. His arousal pressed against her, and anticipation tugged deep inside her. Her own heart thudded in tandem with his as she explored his shoulders and back. She stroked his neck and threaded her fingers through his hair, knocking his hat to the floor. The thought surfaced that her gloves must go but, before she could act on that thought, he changed, urgency taking control.

Her toes barely scraped the floor as he lifted her higher, and backed her against the wall. She couldn't breathe. Panic mushroomed out of the past, bringing it all back—the pain, the disgust— and she swung her head in denial, wrenching her lips from his, grabbing his hair to jerk his head away. He grunted a protest, seized her wrists and raised her arms, stretching them up, above her head, trapping her between his body and the wall, and tasted her again, invading her with his tongue.

She could not move. She was trapped. A scream built inside. She had learned to submit, but this was not Brierley. He was gone.

Harriet twisted her head to one side. 'No!' She panted with the effort not to scream. 'No!' Louder. More forceful.

Benedict stilled. Raised his head to look at her with dazed eyes. 'What...?'

'Let go of me.'

He released her. Stepped back. Frowned. 'Why?'

Harriet stared at the blurry floor. Wiped her mouth with a shaking hand. 'I cannot. I am—'

'Don't say you're sorry,' he said in a savage voice. 'I don't want to hear your excuses.'

He swung away and slammed through the door, crashing it shut behind him, leaving Harriet alone, trembling with the memories that she had tried so hard to put behind her.

Benedict strode down the hill, away from the tower, his blood pounding with fury and un-quenched desire. How weak-willed could a man be? After her rejection—*twice*—still he had left himself wide open for another blow. His brisk pace did little to assuage the urge to lash out and, as he entered the Home Wood, on the path that led back to the house, he snatched a fallen branch from the ground to slash at last season's dried-up undergrowth as he passed.

His instinct was to leave. Return to London. Bury himself in his work and his plans for the future or jump on the nearest ship and seek out new adventures. Anything rather than stay here and suffer any more of her games, leading a man on and then freezing him out.

The house came into view. He slammed to a halt. Considered. Then changed direction.

He strode into the barn, then slowed so as not to spook the horses in the stalls. Heads turned enquiringly to watch his progress along the passageway, and he breathed in the familiar, calming smell of horses, leather and hay, pausing to pat one or two gleaming rumps as he passed.

A groom's head popped out from the end stall. 'Morning, sir,' he called. 'Was you going out?'

'Yes.' The question spurred him into a decision. 'Saddle the bay, will you, Tom?'

A long, fast ride would do him the power of good. It would douse both his temper and his lust and, hopefully, blast away the confusion that had beset him ever since Harriet had reappeared in his life. He swept his hand through his hair, realising he had lost his hat somewhere. No matter—his appearance would make no difference where he was going.

It was dark before Benedict returned to Tenterfield Court, weary and slightly foxed after an afternoon spent in the Crossways Inn in the village. He left his horse at the stables and walked towards the house, conscious that his steps were beginning to lag. He entered through a side door and met Cooper, the footman, in the passage. He must ask. He had no wish to bump into her unprepared.

'Where is she?' *Hellfire!* That didn't come out as he intended. 'Lady Brierley,' he added. 'I'm late. Has she eaten?' It was past the customary time for dinner in the country. With any luck she had already gone upstairs, as keen as him to avoid another encounter.

Cooper frowned. 'She's gone, sir. Lord Brierley came and took her off in his carriage.'

Benedict felt himself sway. *Must've drunk more than I realised.* He inched closer to the wall and propped his shoulders against it.

'When?'

'Soon after her ladyship came back from her walk, sir. His lordship was already here. He'd had her bags packed all ready, and been up to see Sir Malcolm and then, when her ladyship arrived, he dragged her off to his carriage.'

Dragged? The image unsettled him, but it also raised a hope he didn't want to feel. 'Lady Brierley didn't want to leave?'

'No, sir. First she said she wouldn't leave without her maid...'

Ah, of course. Her maid. Janet. She was the cause of Harriet's reluctance. Stupid to imagine it could be anything else. Benedict shook his head, trying to clear it and order his thoughts.

'And then,' Cooper continued, clearly relishing being the one to tell him the story, 'his lordship said Janet must go, too, and the doctor was here and *he* said as how she shouldn't really be moved, and his *lordship* said he wouldn't leave her here in this den of...den of...*something*...'

Iniquity, Benedict thought, his head reeling as his temples began to throb.

'...so we had to carry Janet downstairs and prop up her leg on cushions and all the while his lordship was looking like thunder—'

'Had he come to visit Sir Malcolm?'

'No, sir, but he did go up and pay his respects. He said something about a letter, sir, and *more* scandal, sir. Just like that. *More* scandal!' Cooper paused for breath.

'And her ladyship was happy to go?'

'Well, yes and no, I should say, sir.'

Benedict bit down the urge to bark, *Get on with it, man.* 'I'm waiting, Cooper.'

'Well, she seemed happy enough to go, but she wanted to go back to London, she said. Only his lordship wouldn't budge, even when her ladyship pleaded with him. He said as how she was to come home with him and explain herself properly if she knew what was good for her.'

What was good for her? She's his stepmother, for God's sake. What the blazes did he mean by that?

'And then he said as how he would stop her allowance if she didn't do what he said.'

'And so she went with him?'

'Yes, sir. But she wasn't happy.'

Benedict told himself it was for the best. He told himself it was a relief, but then why did his throat ache and why had his stomach twisted into knots?

'Thank you, Cooper. That will be all.'

Benedict levered himself away from the wall and headed towards the back stairs on decidedly unsteady legs.

'Please inform Sir Malcolm I am unwell and unable to pay him my usual visit. I am going to bed.' He flung the words over his shoulder at the footman.

'Her ladyship found your hat, sir.' Cooper's words floated up the back stairs after Benedict. 'Mr Crabtree brushed it and put it away.'

His hat! A vague memory surfaced of Harriet dislodging it during that kiss. Benedict stumbled as he reached the top of the stairs and turned in the direction of his bedchamber. He cursed under his breath, praying he would not meet any other servants in his current state.

Never again would he touch the ale at the Crossways. It was clearly tainted.

Chapter Seven

Edward's carriage bowled through the elaborately crafted wrought iron gates that marked the entrance to Brierley Place, and Harriet gazed from the window as the familiar manor house with its mullioned windows and ornate chimneys came into view. It had been her home for more than seven years, but she had left it with no regret when Brierley had died three years ago, and Edward, as the fourth Earl of Brierley, had moved his family in.

The journey—slow in deference to Janet's injuries—had been interminable, the silence heavy with Edward's unspoken fury, punctuated only by the occasional moan of pain that escaped Janet despite the clear effort she made to be quiet, biting at her lip and squeezing her eyes shut. Edward had spent the entire journey glowering at Harriet, arms folded across his barrel-like torso. Clearly he could not wait to rip into her, but Harriet knew he would never do so in front of a servant.

Physically, he was just like his father—no more than medium height, light brown hair, inclined to stoutness—but in his character he was the complete opposite. His chief concern, as ever, was for appearances, and he took himself and his duties with the utmost seriousness since inheriting the earldom. He sat as magistrate in the petty sessions whenever required, and he prided himself on his firm but fair judgement; he attended the House of Lords on a regular basis and spoke—according to the newspaper reports that Harriet had read—with authority and gravity on important matters of state; and he expected his family, including his late father's widow, to behave with the utmost propriety at all times.

If only, Harriet had often thought to herself, *he knew what his father was truly like.* Or perhaps he did know—at least some of it—and, like many men, he believed that what went on between husband and wife was nobody's business but their own.

The lack of conversation had given Harriet time to think…time to remember…time to relive. *That kiss!* Shivers rippled down her spine and spread beneath her skin. It was surely the shock of seeing

Benedict in such familiar surroundings that had provoked her into behaving so out of character. She determined to put her entire visit to Tenterfield behind her—going there had been a colossal lack of judgement on her part and she could not wait to return to her familiar, humdrum life. Benedict's intention to take his place in society had been a shock, but it should be easy enough to avoid him—he had been overseas for years and they would be unlikely to have friends in common. And once he married and had a family, the dangerous attraction he had awakened within her would be banished.

But first… She sneaked a peek at Edward, sitting opposite her. He caught her look and scowled. Harriet swallowed. First she must placate Edward.

After Benedict had stormed away from the folly, Harriet had retrieved his hat from the floor and carried it back to the house, where she was swept up in the whirlwind that was her stepson. He refused to listen to reason. Janet couldn't be moved? Nonsense. If she was able to sit up in bed, she could sit in a carriage for a couple of hours with her leg propped up and well padded. He would instruct the coachman to keep the horses at a walk. Harriet wished to return to London? Certainly. He would put his carriage at her disposal. *After* he had spoken to her about her behaviour, as was his duty as head of the family. And he would do that at Brierley Place. Not in this—Edward had looked around, his top lip curled—not in this den of iniquity.

A footman hurried from Brierley Place, ready to lower the steps of the carriage after it drew to a halt outside the front door.

'Lady Brierley's maid has a broken ankle,' Edward said as he clambered from the carriage. 'Find someone to help you carry her upstairs, will you?'

The footman hurried back to the house, and Edward turned to hand Harriet from the carriage. 'I will see you in my study, madam.' He released her hand as soon as she reached the ground and stomped into the house, leaving Harriet to follow in his wake.

Smithson, the butler, was in the hall, giving orders to more footmen about Janet and the luggage.

'Good afternoon, my lady.' Smithson bowed. He directed a passing maid to take Harriet's cloak, hat and gloves. 'Would you care for tea? Her ladyship is in the drawing room with Lady Katherine. They have asked you to join them on your arrival.'

Thank goodness Fanny and the children were as welcoming as ever, despite Edward's strong but unexplained discouragement of her visits to Brierley since his father's death. Harriet had become used to his frostiness and had merely avoided him as much as possible—she had her own life to lead—but this fury and disdain was something new.

'Thank you, Smithson, but his lordship has asked that I attend him in his study.'

'I will inform her ladyship, my lady. If you would care to follow me?'

For all the world as if I did not know the whereabouts of Brierley's study, Harriet thought, biting back her smile as she followed the butler. Edward insisted on the correct procedure being followed at all times. She was a guest; therefore Smithson must announce her.

'Lady Brierley, my lord.'

Smithson stood aside and Harriet walked past him into Edward's study with a smile of thanks before focusing on Edward, standing before the window, hands behind his back. He maintained his silence until the door closed behind Smithson.

'What the *blazes* were you doing at Tenterfield Court?'

She stared at him a moment. 'May I sit?' Her tone was icy. It did not hurt to remind him that she was a lady and his stepmother and that he was, supposedly, a gentleman.

'Of course.'

Edward tilted his chin to indicate the visitor's chair set in front of his vast mahogany desk and then rounded the desk to stand on the opposite side. Harriet sat with a twinge of disquiet, tucking her feet under the chair and loosely clasping her hands in her lap.

Very formal. I feel like a child about to be scolded.

Edward sat down, then frowned at her, his fingers drumming on the desk. 'Well?'

Harriet blinked, taken aback by the contempt conveyed by that one word. 'Why, I wished to make some enquiries on behalf...' She faltered as his expression blackened. She gripped her hands together and drew a steadying breath. 'On behalf of a friend of mine.'

'A likely tale, madam.'

Harriet stiffened. 'I can assure you I am speaking the truth,' she said with as much calm as she could muster. 'Why would you think otherwise?'

'You stayed for two days and nights. With no chaperone.'

'I had no choice. Janet slipped as we were leaving, and she was unable to travel.'

Edward surged to his feet and leaned towards her, fists propped on the desk, eyes boring into hers. 'But you, madam, were uninjured. *You* were fit enough to travel, were you not?'

'I could hardly stay at a public inn without even my maid to accompany me.'

'You could have come *here*.'

'Of course I could. After all, you have never left me in any doubt about my welcome here, have you, Edward?' She had never been able to bring herself to call him Brierley.

Edward's gaze flickered.

'Besides,' Harriet continued, 'there was a snowstorm. It was not safe to travel. Or am I to understand you would prefer the thought of me trapped overnight in a snowdrift to spending time unchaperoned at Tenterfield Court?'

'If you had heeded my advice the last time we met, you would not have been without a chaperone.'

Edward's bluster had started to fade, as it so often did in the face of calm, considered responses.

'And which advice might that be, Edward?' Harriet smiled sweetly at him.

'To accept my aunt Smallwood as your live-in companion.'

'But I have explained before, Edward, that I do not wish to have a live-in companion.'

'You do not care for your reputation?'

'I did not say that, Edward. Of course I care for my reputation. I would never do—'

'And yet you travel to a place like Tenterfield and remain *two nights*, with no other lady present and…and…'

Edward's chest swelled and Harriet eyed his straining waistcoat buttons with concern. He spun round and stalked over to the window.

'Have you so little pride? Was one rejection not enough?' he ground out, his back to Harriet.

She felt a dropping, curling sensation in her stomach. 'I do not know what you mean. Of whom do you speak?'

He whirled to face her. 'Poole! Of whom do you think I speak? Or have there been others? By God, madam, you are not fit to be a member of this family.'

Sick dread welled up to clog Harriet's throat. Only Sir Malcolm, her late husband and her papa had known. No one else. He could not possibly be talking of Benedict.

'S-Sir Malcolm is gravely—'

'Do me the honour of speaking the truth, now you have been found out. Did you think me unaware of your sordid secret? You may think yourself fortunate I have maintained your lies since my father's death.'

At last, the mystery of why Edward had changed towards her after his father died. Up to that point, he had always been respectful but, since then, he barely seemed to tolerate her, treating her much as an inconvenient liability.

'Fortunate, you say, when you have treated me with nothing but disdain since I was widowed? Why have you maintained those lies, if you have such a disgust of me?'

He cast her a look of contempt. 'I will not risk speculation over a family rift to bring your disgrace to public attention. I will not allow your lax morals to cast a stain upon my family name.'

Hysteria bubbled up and Harriet swallowed it down. He had the temerity to accuse *her* of lax morals? When his father… Anger bit at her insides at the injustice of life. What had she ever done but believe the honeyed lies of Benedict Poole when she'd been barely out of childhood?

'How do you know?'

He sat again behind his desk. His eyes narrowed. 'My father's affairs are now mine to deal with. Surely you realised that?'

'He swore… He would not have kept any papers… There *were* no papers…'

'And yet I do know. How do you imagine I felt, to learn that my own father was deceived into raising another man's bast—?'

'He was *not* deceived! He knew I was… He knew

everything. That is the reason I had to marry him! Did you think I—?'

Her words ended on a sob. No matter the truth of her married life, she could not bring herself to tarnish Edward's memory of his father with the reality of the man who had been a monster behind closed doors. Despite his pomposity, she knew he was a good husband to Fanny and a kind, if strict, father to his children. Besides, how could she ever discuss such shameful, intimate matters with *anyone*?

Brierley's voice sounded again in her head. *Now look what you made me do. Go and clean yourself up, you disgusting little whore.* Had it been her fault? Had she, somehow, been responsible for his violence, as he had claimed? *It's your own fault. You asked for it.*

Desperately, she tried to bury those memories and to silence his hated voice. She had sworn never to think of him again. It was Benedict's fault— coming back, bringing all those memories to life again. Her hands were shaking, and again she gripped them together as she forced herself to meet Edward's scathing look.

'At least you lost the baby,' he said, as though he were discussing a matter of no more importance than the loss of a handkerchief. 'That makes it—'

Harriet leaped to her feet and glared at her stepson. 'Don't you *dare* say such a thing!' Edward's words, on top of her already fragile state, were too much. 'How would *you* feel if Fanny had lost Kitty? Or James? Or even little Sophie?'

Edward's jerk of surprise was swiftly controlled. He sat back, his expression impassive. 'That is entirely different. They were conceived and born in wedlock. You, madam, are a disgrace.'

Shocked as much by her own behaviour as by Edward's words, Harriet sank back onto her seat. She must not push Edward too far. Although their relationship teetered ever precariously on the verge of estrangement, she loved Fanny and the children and she would be heartbroken if Edward were to ban her from seeing them. As for Edward's warning at Tenterfield that he would stop her allowance... Surely that must be an empty threat? He had not repeated it, and she was sure he did not have the power to do so. If he did... She concealed her shudder. Her widow's jointure was all she had to survive on. If she lost that, she would lose that which she held most dear—her independence. She would have no choice but to remarry.

Harriet studied her stepson, sitting stolidly in the chair opposite. How a man such as Brierley had spawned such a pompously superior son she could not fathom. It could only, surely, have been the influence of Edward's mother—Brierley had constantly held his first wife up to Harriet as a model of rectitude, an example of a perfect wife. It seemed that Harriet had somehow brought out his basest nature.

Edward shifted in his chair and, when he spoke, his tone was calmer. 'Do you still hanker after that rogue? Is that the truth?'

Harriet swallowed her pain at his words. She had not thought so. And yet…

'I did not know Benedict was at Tenterfield,' she said. 'I did not even know he was in the country. I would never have gone there had I known. I told you, I went on behalf of a friend, to talk to Sir Malcolm.'

A muscle leaped in Edward's jaw, his brows still drawn low. 'Hmph. The deed is done now. We must hope news of your visit alone to that place does not become public knowledge.'

'I was not alone. I had my maid with me.'

'Your maid! You know as well as I that—'

'How did you know I was there?' Harriet interrupted. 'Was it just a coincidence that you came to Tenterfield today?'

'Lady Marstone had it from the doctor,' Edward said, his shoulders slumping. 'She could not wait to tell me when I saw her in Sittingbourne this morning. I believe I convinced her it would not be in her best interests to spread such gossip around, but I am not certain.'

'Lady Marstone? Oh, no.' Sir Walter Marstone's wife was the worst tattletale in the district, and one of the worst in London, too. 'How on earth did you manage to convince her?'

'Her daughter, Bridget, is about to embark upon her second Season and she is quite desperate to get her married off. I hinted that their invitation to Kitty's come-out ball was in the balance, and that I *might* use my influence to persuade Lady Castlereagh to blacklist Bridget from Almack's.'

Lady Castlereagh was one of the powerful patronesses of Almack's, and it was well known that Edward was a political ally of Lord Castlereagh, whose return to government was rumoured to be imminent, three years after his resignation as secretary of state for war and the colonies, following the disgrace of his duel with foreign secretary George Canning. Harriet smiled at the chagrin Lady Marstone must have felt.

'That was quick thinking, Edward. Thank you.'

'Do not think that absolves you, madam, for it does not. I did that solely to protect my family name. But you...you do not appear to believe you have done anything wrong. Are you truly so lost to all propriety? Did you even stop to consider that Kitty is due to make her come-out this spring? I expect her to make a very good match. Do you not care if you sully her reputation with your scandals?'

'That is unfair. I have created no scandals—'

'What about that house in Cheapside? Oh, yes, madam, do not think I am unaware of your involvement with such women. I tell you now, if you wish to continue to be part of this family I suggest you look to your behaviour and ensure no further whisper of impropriety, past or present, reaches my ears.'

Harriet studied his resolute expression and her heart sank all the way to her toes. She set herself to placate him.

'Of course I wish to remain a part of this family, Edward. You know how much I love Fanny and the children. And as for the house in Cheapside... They are young girls—servants who have been despoiled by their masters and then cast out without a penny. Do you condone such behaviour by those men?'

'Of course not. A gentleman has a moral duty of care towards his inferiors,' Edward said, pompous as ever. 'But that does not make your involvement acceptable. I understand you appeal for donations from amongst your friends—'

'*And* from the *gentlemen* responsible,' Harriet said, her passion rising. 'I write to them to give them an opportunity to contribute, and most do eventually pay up, for fear of the slur on their reputations. You surely agree that a gentleman should take responsibility for his actions by supporting his by-blows—' she ignored Edward's wince at her use of the term '—but I am afraid some do not see it that way initially. They cast these girls, and their babies, aside as though they are less than human. With the money I raise, I offer those girls a roof over their heads and the opportunity to learn a new skill.'

She had set up a sewing room and a small bakery in the house, where the girls who chose not to have their babies fostered out could work together whilst caring for them. It was a cause very dear to Harriet's heart after her own experiences, and also since her late husband had violated two such girls—the youngest barely thirteen years of age—who worked in their household and thus had no choice but to succumb to their master's demands. He'd cast them out without a qualm, and Harriet had been helpless to either stop him or to help those two girls.

'No wonder you are so keen to help these young girls after your own lapse from grace,' Edward said. 'At least you had my father to rescue you.'

'*Rescue* me?' Harriet leaped to her feet. She took a hasty turn about the room, dragging in deep breaths in an attempt to calm herself. She returned to the desk and propped her weight on her fists as she leant across it. 'If you *knew*—'

She was interrupted by a knock.

'Hush!' Edward's eyes flashed a warning as the door opened behind Harriet. She straightened.

'Grandmama!' There was the sound of rushing feet, and Harriet turned to find herself wrapped in a tight embrace. 'Smithson said you had come. I didn't believe him.'

Harriet hugged her step-granddaughter hard before holding her away and looking her up and down. It never failed to amuse her to hear this lovely young woman, just ten years her junior, call her *Grandmama*.

'Well,' she said, smiling at Kitty, now fully as tall as Harriet. 'What have we here, Edward? She has every appearance of a young lady, but that behaviour... Was that not more reminiscent of an impulsive child?'

Both she and Edward had become adept at concealing their differences from the rest of his family.

'Oh, phooey!' Kitty's pale cheeks took on a rosy hue.

'Katherine!' Fanny, Lady Brierley, had come into the study in time to hear her daughter's exclamation. '*Such* a vulgar expression.'

Even as Fanny chastised her daughter Harriet could see the twinkle in her eyes. Harriet embraced Fanny with genuine pleasure.

'It is lovely to see you, my dear,' Harriet said. 'It was *such* a pleasant surprise when Edward arrived and *insisted* on escorting me here for a visit.' Harriet shot a mischievous glance at her stepson, knowing he would not retaliate in front of Fanny and Kitty. 'My maid and I were caught in a snowstorm, you know, and poor Janet slipped and broke her ankle. I do hope she may stay here to recuperate? I fear she is not strong enough to attempt the journey back to London.'

'Of course she must stay,' Fanny cried. 'And you, too, Harriet. We do not see nearly enough of you. We go up to London ourselves next week, to prepare for Kitty's come-out. You can travel back with us.'

The thought of spending time with Fanny and

the children was too good to resist, even though she knew Edward would disapprove.

'Thank you, Fanny. That would be perfect.' Harriet closed her eyes to Edward's black scowl.

Chapter Eight

Mid-April 1812

Sir Benedict Poole rested his head against the cushioned backrest of his carriage. He stretched his legs, propping his booted feet on the seat opposite, crossed his arms over his chest and closed his eyes—it would be close to five hours before he reached London. The minute his eyes were shut, however, his thoughts turned inexorably to Harriet and that kiss. Two months ago now… Two long, frustrating months in which he had striven to banish her from his mind, an endeavour that seemed doomed to failure.

Damn her, damn her and damn her thrice!

Since Sir Malcolm's death seven weeks ago Benedict had remained at Tenterfield Court, occupied in dealing with both the legalities and the practicalities of inheriting not only the baronetcy but a wealth he was still scrambling to comprehend. But through all those weeks, like an insistent drumbeat that only he could hear, Harriet called to him.

Now, the closer they got to London, the louder her allure rang out—*Harr-i-et, Harr-i-et, Harr-i-et*—marking time with the rumble of the coach wheels and horses' hoof beats. She was an itch he could not scratch. He did not want her in his head, and he did not want this battle whenever she stole into his thoughts—the battle between his distrust and his urge to understand. And, underlying it all, his greatest fear—the knowledge that, despite everything, he *still* wanted her.

He wanted to return to normality…whatever that might be. He suspected his life would never be the same again.

The carriage drew up outside the Poole residence in Grosvenor Street just after midday. Benedict stirred, stretched and leaped to the pavement, gazing up with a sense of wonder: this magnificent house now belonged to him. He was proud of the business he had built up with his partner, Matthew Damerel, since he had left England to seek his fortune abroad, but he could never have aspired to wealth and position such as this.

The door was opened from within by a solemn-faced butler with a black armband on his sleeve.

'Good afternoon, Sir Benedict,' he said, bowing. 'Welcome home. I am Reeves.'

'Good afternoon, Reeves, and thank you.'

Following a tour of the house—which was every bit as impressive as he remembered from the few times he had visited in his youth—Benedict settled in his library to read the letters that were piled on his desk. Recognising the bold writing on one sheet, he broke the seal and began to read. It was from Matthew, his business partner, announcing his arrival in town and asking Benedict to call upon him as soon as he arrived.

Benedict leaped to his feet, eager to see both his old friend and Matthew's wife, Eleanor, Lady Ashby, again. A good dose of business talk was just what he needed to distract him from the fact that Harriet lived a mere few streets away.

'Good afternoon, Sir Benedict.' Matthew and Eleanor's butler stood aside to allow Benedict to enter the hall of their newly leased house in Cavendish Square.

'Good afternoon, Pacey. Is Mr Damerel at home?'

'I shall go and enquire, sir.'

Minutes later, Pacey showed Benedict into the

library. Matthew, blue eyes bright with pleasure, strode forward to clasp Benedict's outstretched hand.

'Well, well,' he said, laughing. '*Sir* Benedict. Must I bow to you now? Pacey, brandy, if you please—we must celebrate!'

Benedict grinned and allowed Matthew to usher him to a wing chair by the fire whilst he sat opposite.

Several toasts later, Matthew leaned forward, suddenly serious, his piercing gaze direct. 'I have a proposal to put to you, Ben.'

Benedict sat up, his attention caught. 'Go on.'

'With our new responsibilities, neither you nor I will be in a position to travel far from England in the future, so… I've had Carstairs making enquiries about a ship for us to purchase, and I think he's found just the one. What do you say to establishing a merchant fleet of our own?'

Carstairs was a former customs officer they had employed to manage the London end of their importing business. Benedict felt a stirring of excitement deep in his gut. Although he knew his future must now lie in England, he also knew he would miss the cut and thrust of the business he and Matthew had set up together. His estates and investments might be vast but so, also, was the army of bankers, solicitors, clerks and stewards who had run them on Malcolm's—and now his—behalf.

'I say—' Benedict raised his glass '—it is a first-rate idea. I'll drink to that.'

Their glasses clinked in salute.

'Excellent!' Matthew said. 'We'll go and see Carstairs tomorrow and then we'll see the solicitor and instruct him to draw up a new partnership agreement. And, in the meantime...' He paused and his rugged features softened. 'In the meantime, I have one more announcement to make.' He grinned, stood up and spread his arms wide. 'I am to be a father.'

Benedict surged to his feet and gripped his friend's hand. 'That's splendid news, by God. Congratulations, Matt. How is Eleanor? She is well, I hope?'

Matthew headed for the door, eager as a schoolboy. 'Come and see for yourself,' he said. 'She is in the drawing room. She made me swear I would not allow you to leave without first paying your respects.'

The door to the drawing room was ajar, allowing chattering female voices to drift across the hall as Benedict and Matthew emerged from the library.

It was the time of day for the ladies of the *haut ton* to pay visits and Benedict tamped down his sudden attack of nerves. This would be his first venture into polite society. How would he be received? He was conscious of the need to make a good impression from the start if he were to restore the Poole name and overcome his own links to trade. He was fortunate to have Eleanor—a baroness in her own right—and Matthew as friends.

'That sounds like Lady Stanton,' Matthew whispered to Benedict as they approached the door. 'Eleanor only made her acquaintance recently, but they have become bosom bows already.' He lowered his voice still further. 'They have much in common.' He used his hands to mime a swollen belly. 'Not that you can tell yet,' he added with a wink, 'so be discreet.'

Benedict grinned at him, though he was still on edge. 'I won't let on that you've told me,' he said as he followed Matthew into the room.

He heard her voice before he saw her—low, warm, melodic—and his gut clenched. Somehow his feet kept moving and he concentrated on locating Eleanor, with her glossy mahogany locks and her wide welcoming smile, ignoring the clamour of every one of his senses to drink in Harriet, only Harriet.

* * *

She was at the edge of his vision: blonde hair sleek in a chignon, poised, controlled, politely smiling as Matthew first greeted the third occupant of the room—a slight, elegantly dressed lady, presumably Lady Stanton—and was then introduced to Harriet by Eleanor.

How could Matthew and Eleanor behave so normally? How could they be unaware of the fire raging out of control in his gut? How could *anyone*? That thought steadied him. Of course no one would know. Not unless he gave himself away, and that he would not do. He stepped forward to greet Eleanor, raising her hand to his lips as he caught her eye and mouthed the word *Congratulations* to her. Her eyes sparkled as her smile widened even more, her excitement clear. She tucked her hand beneath his arm and tugged him round to face the two seated ladies.

'Allow me to introduce my husband's business partner,' Eleanor said. 'Felicity, Lady Stanton—Sir Benedict Poole.'

'Delighted to meet you, my lady.'

Benedict dipped his head and when he raised it he found himself the recipient of a tight smile and a searching stare from a pair of clear amber eyes.

He had no time to ponder the meaning of that look, for Eleanor began to introduce Harriet.

Before he could think through the consequences, Benedict said, 'We have met.'

The room seemed to still for a moment, then Harriet inclined her head graciously. 'Indeed we have. How do you do, Sir Benedict?'

Benedict managed to voice a polite reply.

Harriet then focused on Matthew. 'Lady Ashby was telling us of your time in India. Is that where you and Sir Benedict met?'

'It was,' Matthew replied. 'It is quite a coincidence, you two knowing each other.' He studied Benedict, who battled to keep his feelings from showing. 'Did you meet recently, or is it an acquaintance of longer standing?'

Benedict smarted at his friend's innocent tone— a tone completely at odds with the knowing smile that played around his lips.

'We were neighbours in our youth,' he growled.

A devilish glint lit Matthew's eyes as he said, 'Then I shall leave you to renew your acquaintance.'

He sat on the sofa next to Lady Stanton and engaged her in conversation, leaving Benedict no choice but to sit on the only remaining seat—the chair next to Harriet.

A sizzle of awareness sped through his veins, fuelling his anger that Harriet's mere presence could affect him in such a way. Conscious of Eleanor watching from her chair at the far end of the sofa, Benedict thrust aside his shock and focused his mind on his goal—making a good first impression on Lady Stanton, and society in general, with a view to building his own reputation and allowing Malcolm's libertine past to fade in people's memories.

He would not allow Harriet's presence to deflect him from that goal, and he must strive to treat her as he would any other society lady.

'I trust you are well, my lady?' he said.

'Thank you, yes.'

To the others in the room, it would look as though Harriet was giving him her full attention, her head turned in his direction. Only Benedict was able to see that her gaze was fixed on a point somewhere beyond his right ear and that her cheeks were pink. She was, perhaps, not quite as calm as she wanted him to think. Despite his best intentions, he soon found himself trying to penetrate her outer shell of indifference.

He kept his voice to a murmur. 'You left without saying goodbye.'

Just like before. The old anger and betrayal swirled through him.

'I could say the same to you.'

'It is not the same. I came home and you had gone.'

Harriet shifted a little in her chair. 'I could not say goodbye to someone who was not there.'

'You could have written a note.'

'To what purpose?'

'To explain. To tell me why.'

Benedict was no longer sure if he meant two months ago or eleven years ago. Or both.

'It would have changed nothing, and you were no doubt told why. I had no choice.'

'Why Brierley?' His voice had dipped, his whisper fierce.

She stared at him now, her violet eyes narrowed, wary. 'What do you mean?'

He rubbed the back of his neck, aware he was heading into deep waters. *Be careful. Stay in the present.*

'Why did you go with Brierley?'

'I had no choice,' she repeated.

'You do not have to answer to him.'

'Yes, I do. He is the head of the family...*my* family. He was concerned about my reputation.'

'A widow is allowed some licence. As long as she is discreet.'

'*That* is entirely immaterial if the widow has no interest in having such licence in the first place.'

'That is not the impression I got. You enjoyed that kiss.'

'You consider yourself a skilled reader of minds, do you, sir? I—'

Benedict leaned towards Harriet and lowered his voice further. 'I may not be able to read minds, Harriet, but the body speaks a very different language. One to which I am well attuned.'

Harriet's chin tilted. Just a fraction, but he knew he had touched on a nerve. Before he could respond, however, Eleanor rose to her feet, smiling apologetically at Matthew and Felicity, saying, 'Please do forgive me, but I really cannot allow Sir Benedict to monopolise Lady Brierley's attention like this.' She then treated Benedict to one of her most direct looks and continued, 'I know you will forgive me for ousting you from the lady's side, sir, but Lady Brierley and I have only just become acquainted and I am convinced we must discover more about one another, in order that we may determine whether our next meeting will be one of new friends or mere passing acquaintances.'

Benedict had risen from his chair when Eleanor stood up, and now he had no choice but to exchange seats. As a good hostess, Eleanor had clearly recognised the tension between her two guests, and had acted to intervene. Knowing Eleanor, Benedict could foresee some probing questions about that tension. He diverted his thoughts from that awkward conversation to come.

Before he could join Matthew and Lady Stanton, however, the lady rose from the sofa, saying, 'I fear Harriet and I shall outstay our welcome if we remain very much longer—we have been here close on an hour already. My apologies for running away before we have had an opportunity to become properly acquainted, Sir Benedict. I should like to remedy that very soon.'

'As would I, my lady.' Benedict bowed. Had he imagined that slight edge to Lady Stanton's words? He watched as she walked across to speak to Harriet.

'Are you ready to leave now, my dear?'

'Yes, indeed,' Harriet said. 'It was a great pleasure to meet you, Lady Ashby, and you, Mr Damerel.'

'I am delighted to have made your acquaintance, Lady Brierley,' Eleanor said. 'And, please, call me Eleanor. I have heard much about you from Felicity and confess I am intrigued by your charity work. I am very much interested in finding out more about it.'

'That is splendid, for we have need of all the patronage we can muster.' Harriet's voice rang with enthusiasm. 'And the school for orphans that Felicity champions is most worthy, as well.'

Benedict's interest was piqued by Harriet's obvious passion. *What charity work?*

Don't ask her. The less you see of her and the less you know about her the better.

'I am eager to visit both places,' Eleanor said. Then, her eyes on her husband, she added, 'As long as *you* have no objection, my love?'

Benedict bit back a smile. Matthew had told him all about Eleanor's independence as a wealthy peeress in her own right before she'd met him and they'd fallen in love. She was clearly trying her utmost to adapt to taking his opinion into account when making decisions.

Matthew smiled at his wife. 'I have no objection, my dear.'

The love that shone in the look they exchanged stirred both envy and yearning in Benedict's heart, as it had since the moment he had first seen them together. Would he ever find love that special?

More to the point, will you ever find love you can trust?

He must believe he would.

'Splendid,' Eleanor said, beaming. 'We will make arrangements soon, Felicity. In the meantime, Harriet, I shall send you an invitation to our musical evening a fortnight today. I do hope you will be able to attend.'

'Thank you. That is most kind.'

'Felicity and Lord Stanton have already accepted, and you will come as well, I hope, Benedict?' Eleanor continued with an eager smile. 'It will be our first ever party since our wedding, so I am praying for it to be a success.'

Benedict's heart sank. It sounded deadly dull to him. He exchanged a look with Matthew, whose glum expression suggested he was no more enamoured at the prospect.

But he was fond of Eleanor, and it behoved him to support Matthew, so… 'I shall look forward to it,' he said with a bow.

'Richard and I are very much looking forward to it, too, Eleanor,' Lady Stanton said. 'And you have reminded me of something I meant to ask Harriet. Are you invited to the Cothams' masquerade ball next week?'

'I have been invited, but it is out of town and—'

'But that is why I am asking, you goose,' Felicity said. 'You shall come with us in our carriage. You cannot miss such an event.'

'It does sound like fun,' Harriet said. 'Thank you.'

'Oh, but how delightful,' Eleanor said, her glowing eyes wide with excitement. 'Matthew and I are attending, too. And Benedict as well, I hope. I happened to mention to Lady Cotham that you were coming up to town, Benedict, and she included you on our invitation. I have plenty of garments you can choose from for your costume—I had so many ideas, I hardly knew which ones to pick for Matthew and me. *Do* say you'll come.'

Benedict grinned at her. 'You try to stop me.'

'Indeed,' Matthew interjected. 'Give this man a chance to dress in some outlandish costume and he is as happy as a sailor in a—'

'*Mat*thew...'

They all laughed at Eleanor's warning and Lady Stanton tucked her arm through Harriet's, saying, 'Come, my dear, it is time we left.'

Unanswered questions swarmed through Benedict's head. This might be as good a chance as any to get some answers.

'I must also be on my way,' he said. 'Were you ladies accompanied by your maids?' He had seen no one waiting in the hall. 'Might I offer to escort you home?' He included Lady Stanton in his glance.

A flush washed Harriet's cheeks and a spark of irritation lit her eyes but he knew she could hardly refuse when he was so obviously a close friend of their host and hostess.

Chapter Nine

Once they were outside in Cavendish Square, Lady Stanton turned to Harriet and smiled. 'I shall see you very soon, my dear,' she said, and embraced her. She then faced Benedict. 'Thank you for your offer, sir.'

Once again, he felt the force of her clear-eyed appraisal, reminding him of the look she had given him when they were first introduced. Why did she appear wary of him? Had Harriet confided something of their past to her friend?

'My home is across the square,' Lady Stanton continued, 'and I have no need of company for that short distance. I venture to hope, however, that you will escort Lady Brierley to *her* home. She has developed a sad habit of walking around town unaccompanied now that her maid is indisposed.'

'Most shocking behaviour,' Benedict agreed gravely, wondering why, if she was chary of him, she would encourage him to escort Harriet. 'I shall be sure to see her safely home.'

It was another question to add to the list for Harriet to answer.

'It was only this once, Felicity, as you well know,' Harriet said. 'My footman accompanied me to Lady Stanton's house earlier,' she continued, in explanation to Benedict, 'but he had errands to run. And I am not a green girl who needs chaperoning everywhere. It is the middle of the afternoon, for goodness' sake. What possible harm could befall me?'

Benedict bowed. 'I shall escort you nevertheless. It was a pleasure to meet you, Lady Stanton.'

She nodded, unsmiling. 'Likewise, sir.'

Before they parted company, however, a shrill voice accosted them.

'My dear, dear Lady Stanton, how do you do? And, if I am not mistaken, it is Sir Benedict Poole, is it not? And…Lady Brierley.'

The fashionably dressed matron's voice noticeably cooled as she spoke Harriet's name. Benedict saw Lady Stanton bristle and he warmed to her. She was clearly a loyal friend.

'Good afternoon, Lady Marstone,' she said with the slightest of bows, and went to pass by the woman and her younger companion, a slim brunette with a pretty face somewhat spoiled by a petulant expression.

Lady Marstone added hurriedly, 'And of course you know my daughter, Bridget?'

Lady Stanton nodded at the girl. 'Yes,' she said. 'How do you do, Miss Marstone? Now, please do excuse me, but I am expected home.'

She smiled at the group and walked on, crossing the corner of the square, leaving Benedict and Harriet with Lady Marstone and her daughter, neither of whom Benedict could recall having met before.

The lady was eyeing him with an eager light in her eyes.

He bowed. 'My apologies, Lady Marstone, but have we met?'

'Oh, no, no, Sir Benedict, we have never been formally introduced, but I recognise *you*. Why, the whole district is agog with your return. We live not three miles from Tenterfield Court, so we are practically neighbours. So fortuitous, our bumping into you in the street just now—I hope you will forgive me for dispensing with the formalities?

'I recognised you the instant I saw you—*so* like Sir Malcolm…although no doubt of more…less… well, yes…' She faltered, but only momentarily, before charging ahead once again. 'And of course I am already acquainted with dear Lady Stanton and with Lady Brierley so there can be no real impropriety, can there?'

'Quite so.'

'As we are such close neighbours, you will of course attend our ball next month? I shall be sure to send you an invitation.'

'Thank you. I shall consult my diary as soon as I receive it.'

'Oh! Oh, yes of course. But…being such *close* neighbours, surely you must… Well, I shall leave it to you, sir, but dear Bridget was only saying yesterday how wonderful it will be to stand up with a gentleman of your considerable standing.'

Benedict managed to prevent himself frowning as Miss Marstone simpered at him. How had this conversation bounced from a chance meeting to the expectation he would dance with this woman's daughter? He suspected his *considerable standing* owed more to his wealth than to anything else about him. Was this what he must expect from society? The pitfalls in business were as nothing beside the perils of negotiating the hazards of the *ton*. He was encouraged, however, that his wealth appeared to override any scruples over Malcolm's past—at least, as far as Lady Marstone was concerned. Although it remained to be seen whether this particular lady was quite as finicky as others in the *ton* might prove to be.

Without volition, he glanced at Harriet, standing to one side. Her expression was neutral but his look resulted in a slight elevation of her brows. He suspected she was hiding a smile.

She addressed Miss Marstone. 'I do not doubt that Sir Benedict will prove a most accomplished dancer, Miss Marstone. I collect this is your second—'

'*Thank* you, Lady Brierley.' Lady Marstone placed herself firmly between Harriet and her daughter. She then turned her steely gaze back to Benedict. 'We have taken enough of your time, sir. I bid you good day. Come, Bridget.'

Benedict stared after them. 'She was intolerably rude to you. Why did you not give her a set-down?'

Harriet said nothing as she walked across the Square in the direction of Holles Street.

'Harriet?'

Benedict hurried to catch her up and then kept pace with her. How did she remain so composed? He could interpret nothing of what was going through her head from her expression or her demeanour.

'Lady Marstone is the person who informed my stepson that I was at Tenterfield,' she said eventually. 'She clearly believes that I am an unsuitable acquaintance for her daughter. And, if I am honest, I cannot blame her for that. She is being protective. It is what any mother would do.'

Benedict digested the implications of this.

'Is she likely to gossip about it?'

'I hope not. Edward threatened to prevent Bridget gaining approval for Almack's this Season—he is a friend of Lord Castlereagh.' She peeped sideways at him and he saw her lips twitch. 'You do not understand the gravity of such a threat, it is clear. Lady Castlereagh is one of the patronesses of Almack's—the group of ladies who preside over who is and who is not deemed acceptable to attend the assembly on a Wednesday evening during the Season. To have her name added to the approved list is the pinnacle of every young girl's ambition. To be denied that privilege would be enough to cast that same young miss into the depths of despair. The threat should be sufficient to ensure Lady Marstone's discretion.'

She then added, 'Almack's is also popularly known as the marriage mart. You will do well to cultivate one of the patronesses—it will be the perfect place to gain introductions to suitable young ladies on the lookout for a husband.'

There was nary a quiver of emotion in her

voice—maybe she *had* been telling the truth, back at Tenterfield Court; maybe it *was* remembering her father, and not Benedict's talk of finding a bride, that had so upset her. He had often wondered about that evening.

'And if I am deemed unsuitable? You will recall I have been in trade all my adult life.'

'Your new status and wealth might overcome *that* particular taint. If not, however, I am acquainted with a lady who undertakes to perform discreet introductions between suitable parties. I shall be happy to introduce you to her if you wish.'

'I should prefer to rely on my own instincts, thank you.'

And his instincts were, at that very moment, clamouring to take Harriet in his arms, despite his bitterness, despite his distrust, despite the deafening clamour of his common sense. The idea that had surfaced at Tenterfield re-emerged. She was a widow. They could be discreet. If he bedded her, he might rid himself once and for all of this nagging feeling of unfinished business. And then, when he took a wife, surely these muddled feelings she had awoken within him would disappear?

'Although,' he added, 'if I *should* need some help in the matter, I seem to recall *you* promising to help me with my search for a spouse.'

'I fear my time is already fully occupied in assisting the needy,' she replied.

Benedict stifled his laugh. *Cleverly done. Needy, eh?* Yes, he was needy, but not in the way Harriet had meant. Or—he sneaked a look at her serene profile—was her double entendre deliberate?

They walked side by side for several minutes in silence. As they reached Oxford Street and waited for a break in the traffic to cross the road, Benedict offered his arm. After a second's hesitation, Harriet laid her gloved hand on his sleeve. Something seemed to settle deep inside him at her touch. It felt right.

'I am curious about your friend, Lady Stanton,' he said, after they crossed and continued on their way towards Hanover Square. 'She seemed almost wary of me. I cannot think why as I have never met her before.'

Harriet remained silent for so long, Benedict feared she was not going to answer him.

'It is not you, personally,' she said eventually, 'but your name that unsettles her. It was on Felicity's behalf I went to Tenterfield Court, to discover the truth about a matter concerning her sister. Felicity has no cause to love the Poole name.'

The Poole name... How many others would be

of the same opinion? How many would judge him by the actions of Sir Malcolm?

'That is yet another reminder that I should lose no time in restoring good opinion of my family name,' he said.

'So you said before. Well, you might take heart from Lady Marstone. She showed no sign of disapproval but, on the other hand, she does have a daughter to marry off. A respectable marriage would go a long way to overcoming past scandals, and I am sure Bridget's dowry would add nicely to your wealth.'

'I have no need of more money.' Benedict shuddered inwardly at the thought of Lady Marstone as a mother-in-law.

He sensed Harriet's swift sideways glance, but he kept his gaze fixed ahead.

'Everyone always wants more money,' she said, 'or why would wealthy men baulk at providing for...? Besides, I was talking about land. The Marstone estate is not far from Tenterfield and, from what I have heard, it is not all entailed, so Bridget's portion would be likely to include some of the unentailed land. She only has the one brother. That must be an enticing thought to a bachelor considering marriage.'

'The enticement of more land is entirely immaterial if said bachelor has no interest in adding to his estates.'

Harriet halted, raising her violet-blue eyes to peer searchingly into his. 'Those are, almost, my words to you.' Her fair brows drew together, creating a crease between them. 'What is it you want, Benedict?'

He was vaguely aware of people passing them on both sides, but his vision was filled with only her. What did he want? The answer echoed through him, stronger than ever. He wanted her. Harriet. Fickle and untrustworthy as he knew her to be, still he wanted her.

'Let us keep moving,' he said. 'We are causing an obstruction.'

They walked on. Harriet was silent, awaiting his reply.

'It is obvious we are destined to see each other here in London,' Benedict said. 'What I should like is for us to meet and socialise without the past coming between us.'

'The past? Would that be the distant past or the more recent past? Or, mayhap, both?'

The first time either of them had touched upon that most contentious of subjects—the distant past. And yet that was what it was: distant. Those achingly raw emotions that had haunted him in the days, weeks and months following her betrayal should have no influence on the present. But they did, whipping into a frenzy the two contradictory emotions that had plagued him ever since Harriet's unexpected appearance at Tenterfield—bitterness and yearning.

'I meant the distant past,' he replied, thrusting aside the confusion of his feelings. 'Might we relegate it *to* the past? We both said things, made pledges...but we were so young. I was in the throes of calf love. I know better now. But I still... Harriet...'

Benedict took a quick look around. There was no one nearby. They had just left Hanover Square and were walking down St George Street, approaching the great portico of St George's Church, with its magnificent columns. He tugged Harriet to a stop and clasped her shoulders to turn her to face him. She looked up at him, wide-eyed, soft lips parted on an exclamation of surprise, and he battled the impulse to lower his head and to taste her lush lips there and then.

'Benedict...no... Do not...'

Had she interpreted his longing for more than mere words? He reined in that mad impulse to kiss her here, in the street, but—he *had* to remove this awkwardness between them…this feeling of unfinished business. Should he even contemplate asking her? If she refused him, how would he feel then?

'Harriet…'

Her violet eyes darkened as her pupils grew impossibly large, an involuntary sign of her arousal, whatever words she might say. His body reacted to that silent message, his loins growing heavy with desire.

'What I felt for you in our youth may have been calf love, but that does not stop me wanting you now. You feel the same. I know it. I can *feel* it.' He released her shoulder and traced the fine bone of her jaw with a gentle forefinger.

Dammit! Why not? It would draw a line under the past. Allow us both to move on with our lives.

'We are both adults. Will you—?'

'You! Sir!' A hand grabbed at Benedict's shoulder and wrenched him away from Harriet.

With a curse, Benedict spun round to face a spluttering, puce-faced gentleman about four inches shorter than him. Benedict shrugged the man's hand from his shoulder and thrust his face close to his assailant's. Before he could take further action or utter a word, Harriet was pushing between them, her back to Benedict.

'No! Edward, please. Benedict, no, I implore you.'

Her stepson, Brierley; he was called Edward. Benedict battled for control of his fury as Edward continued his diatribe over Harriet's head.

'You, sir, are a blackguard. I shall see—'

'Edward! No. Please...' There were tears in Harriet's voice and Benedict's heart squeezed.

How dare this pompous oaf upset her? Benedict grasped Harriet by her upper arms. She struggled, resisting his efforts to put her aside, panting with the effort.

'Do not, Benedict. I beg of you. You will only make it worse.'

Benedict released her but continued to glare at Brierley, wanting nothing more than to land his fist squarely on the other man's nose. He forced his clenched hands to remain at his sides.

'You will get into my carriage now, madam, and leave me to deal with this villain, if you know what is good for you.' Brierley grabbed Harriet's arm and pushed her towards a carriage that had drawn up by the kerb.

'*Deal* with me?' Rage roared through Benedict at the sight of Brierley's fingers digging into Harriet's flesh. 'Why, you—'

'*No!* Listen to me! Think of the scandal, Edward. Please. Someone will notice and the tale will be all over town in a trice. For Kitty's sake, if not for mine.'

Chapter Ten

'For *Kitty's* sake? It is a pity you did not consider her before wantonly throwing yourself at this… this no-good *merchant* in full public view.'

Frantic, Harriet scanned their surroundings. Edward's carriage effectively blocked them from the view of most of the street and the pavement on their side of the road was empty. Her relief was short-lived, killed off by one look at her stepson, his face deep red and bulging above his neckcloth. His fingers dug like claws into her upper arm.

'You are hurting her. Let go of her now, or I will not be responsible for my actions.' Benedict's voice was low with menace, his face taut with anger, as he stepped closer.

Edward tightened his grip, wringing a gasp from Harriet. 'I expected nothing more than such low threats from your sort, Poole,' he said with a sneer. 'A public brawl *would* be about your level. Now stand aside. This *lady* will do my bidding as head of the family.'

She had no choice but to go with Edward if she were to prevent the two men coming to blows or, even worse, flinging out a challenge to a duel— and she could not bear to be the cause of such a clash. She submitted to Edward's pull on her arm, turning to the open door of the carriage.

'I shall be all right,' she said to Benedict, looking over her shoulder at him with a silent plea.

'You do not have to go with him,' he said, holding her gaze with deep green eyes that sparked rage. He was bristling with controlled aggression, his jaw tight.

'I must. I—'

'Yes, she does,' Edward cut in as he almost shoved her up the step into the carriage. 'If she values this family, and her independence, she has no choice whatsoever.'

He clambered in behind her and slammed the door before rapping his cane on the roof. The carriage jerked into motion, Edward's bulk blocking Benedict from Harriet's sight.

'I am appalled by your lack of judgement, madam. Not only have you defied my clear instructions that you must have nothing more to do with that scoundrel but you appear to have taken leave of any sense you might once have possessed. I repeat what I said to you before. Was one rejection not enough? The man is a nobody and a merchant.'

'He is a baronet, Edward, hardly a nobody.'

'And where has he come from? Who were his parents? Although—' he cast her a scathing look '—I suppose I can hardly expect *you* to consider such niceties as being of importance.'

'My father was a gentleman, Edward, as was Benedict's.' His gibe against her parentage stung and, now that the immediate danger of the two men coming to blows had passed, Harriet's temper—usually so equable—began to simmer. 'And I happen to know that Benedict's mother was the granddaughter of an earl.'

'He is in *trade*. If nothing else, consider *my* position.'

'I have done nothing, Edward. I was walking along the road—'

'That is not what I saw,' Edward interrupted furiously, 'and I dare say a good many others also witnessed your disgraceful behaviour. You were nigh on *embracing* in the street. You are not to speak to him again.'

Harriet's stomach lurched as she realised that,

although his accusation was a gross exaggeration, he had a point. She *had* allowed her emotions to overcome her common sense, but that did not give Edward the right to control to whom she spoke.

'I am your stepmother, Edward, and a widow. I am perfectly capable of handling Sir Benedict.'

'Ha! You have proved that, have you not, madam? You were *handling* him, were you, when I came upon you just now? You were on the brink of a public show—a scandalous indiscretion. And he—baronet or not—thought nothing of subjecting you to such behaviour. But then, what can you expect from someone brought up under the influence of a libertine such as Sir Malcolm Poole?' His voice softened a touch. 'You might be my stepmother, but you are a female and you need protection. I am older than you and wiser in the ways of the world. You will do as I say.

'Poole is trouble. You are to have nothing more to do with him. Do I make myself clear?'

'And if I refuse?'

He regarded her thoughtfully. 'Then I regret but I shall have no choice but to banish you to Brierley Place for the remainder of the Season. There is an empty cottage on the far side of the estate you could live in.'

Harriet's mind reeled. His prompt response suggested he had it all worked out. 'Banish me? But… why? You cannot—'

'I think you will find that I can,' Edward said. 'Very easily. I shall stop your allowance and lock up the house in Sackville Street. You will have no choice. Your only other option will be to walk the streets.'

'But…Kitty's ball…'

He shrugged. 'The remedy is in your hands. My priority must be my daughter's reputation. I am in the process of negotiating a most advantageous match for her, one that is very important, politically and for the family. I will not allow you to ruin that.'

The carriage halted and Harriet saw her own front door through the window. She had been sure Edward would take her to his own house in Upper Brook Street first.

'I shall leave you to reflect upon what I have said. I shall return tomorrow and you may tell me your decision. Will you comply or will you rebel? Until I am satisfied, you are forbidden to contact either my wife or my daughter.'

Stevens, Harriet's butler, appeared at the carriage door and opened it, helping Harriet to the pavement.

'Tomorrow at two,' Edward barked. The carriage drove away.

Later, glass of wine in hand, Harriet fretted over Edward's demand as she relaxed on the green-and-cream-striped chaise longue in the small sitting room—her boudoir—that adjoined her bedchamber. She should be happy to have nothing to do with Benedict after his treatment of her so why did she hesitate to obey her stepson? Was it pure contrariness that made her baulk at doing as she was told? Was her hesitation solely due to her dislike of being told what to do and how to behave and to whom she might speak?

Her heart and mind still reeled from the shock of meeting Benedict today—he had been the last person she'd expected to see when Felicity had urged her to come and meet her new friend, Lady Ashby. He had walked into Eleanor's drawing room and jolted Harriet out of the dreamlike stupor that had assailed her ever since her visit to Tenterfield Court. Since then, she had gone about her daily routine as if in a daze, as though waiting for an unacknowledged dread to come to pass. And now the worst had happened. Benedict was here. In London. And it would seem that Harriet's life was about to become complicated. On the one hand, she could hardly avoid Benedict completely but, on the other, she must tread with care if she was not to completely antagonise Edward.

When Brierley died she had sworn she would never allow another man to control her, and yet here was Edward, intimidating her in an attempt to bend her to his will.

Can Edward really withhold my allowance? Am I not entitled to a pension, as his father's widow?

Without funds to live on, her only other option would be to remarry—a prospect that filled her with terror, for how could she know, before it was too late, if her spouse would have the same violent tendencies as her late husband? She had never questioned her rights, she realised. She had simply accepted what Edward had told her was her due. Mayhap it was time she found out, for if she did not look after her own interests, who else would?

The memory of Benedict facing up to Edward floated through her thoughts. She suppressed her *hmph*—maybe she had felt momentarily protected but when, in reality, had he ever put her interests first? She could not deny, however, that meeting Benedict today had again awakened some of her old feelings for him.

Are those feelings real, though, or merely an echo of the past?

What had happened between them—eleven years ago…two months ago…today—was not, none of it, complete. She resented how his return had stirred up long-buried emotions to disturb her peaceful life and yet she yearned for some kind of finality to the whole sorry story of their relationship.

But what good could come of raking over the past? Would it not be better to comply with Edward's wishes and have nothing more to do with Benedict? He was not even interested enough in what had happened to her to ask after their baby. Had she not sworn to never forget—nor forgive— the way he had so cruelly abandoned her?

Edward is right. Why risk yet another rejection? Her mind drifted back over her conversation with Benedict, the conversation Edward had interrupted. What had he been about to say? His deep voice sounded again inside her head.

That does not stop me wanting you now. You feel the same. I know it. We are both adults. Will you—?'

Harriet jerked upright, the heat of anger bubbling through her. *He was about to proposition me!* Or mayhap, she thought, swallowing down a bitter laugh, he had been on the brink of offering her *carte blanche*, which was even worse. He had contemplated setting her up as his mistress in the midst of all his talk of restoring the Poole name and finding a suitable bride to smooth his way in Society.

Hmph! Well, Sir Benedict Poole would find himself sorely disappointed. She would treat him with the same friendly courtesy she had afforded Stanton after their *affaire* ended when he had married Felicity last year.

Thinking of the Stantons reminded Harriet of the friends she now had in common with Benedict, and she realised it would be impossible to avoid him altogether. She vowed to hide her conflicted feelings about Benedict both from him and from their friends: not only her pain at his treatment of her in the past but also her curiosity about the man he had become and, most important of all, that tiny bud of desire deep inside her that, even now, she could feel stirring into life. She could not bear anyone to guess at her jumble of emotions but at least her marriage to Brierley had taught her the value of strict control.

Exhausted by the thoughts swirling around her

brain, Harriet relaxed back against the cushions and closed her eyes, drifting into sleep.

Harriet awoke with a start at the tap on the door. It could only be Stevens—the maids would not knock before entering her boudoir—and that could only mean a visitor.

'Yes?' she called.

The door opened to admit her butler. 'Sir Benedict Poole has called, my lady. Will you see him, or shall I say you are not at home?'

Benedict? Here?

On the brink of denying him, she hesitated, remembering the offer he had been about to make to her. Would this not be the perfect opportunity to remind him that she was a respectable widow who was content with her life? Future meetings, surely, would be less fraught if he knew she was not interested.

Harriet's heart quaked at the thought of Edward finding out about Benedict's visit. *Thank goodness dear old Stevens is loyal. It will be just this once, and then never again.*

'Thank you, Stevens. I will see him. Please show him into the salon and send Janet to me.'

It was time she put an end to this dithering and uncertainty.

Her nerve held until she descended the stairs, her hair tidied and pinned in place and her cheeks tinted with a dusting of rouge. In the hall, she hesitated. Stevens, about to open the salon door, paused and waited for her. Harriet drew in a steadying breath and smoothed her suddenly moist hands down the skirt of her pink sprigged muslin gown. She nodded to Stevens.

Benedict stood by the fireplace, tall and handsome. She steeled her heart.

'You should not have come here.'

'I wanted to make sure you were all right.'

It is a pity you didn't feel that way eleven years ago. The memory of his callous behaviour gave her strength.

'Edward is not a violent man. He blusters his way through his anger. I can cope with him.'

'And will you obey him?'

Obey. That word. 'I will do as he asks as it happens to be my natural inclination, too. As I said before, I have no wish to revisit our youthful indiscretions.'

Benedict crossed the room towards her, as lithe and graceful as a panther. Harriet stood her ground, holding his gaze.

'That is not the impression you gave earlier,' he growled.

'Then, you must learn to interpret a woman's behaviour with more accuracy,' Harriet said, lifting her shoulders in a shrug. 'Especially as you intend to look for a wife.'

He was close now. She could smell his cologne, subtle and spicy, feel his heat.

'What did he mean when he said, "If you value your independence"? It sounded very like a threat to me.'

'As I said, it is all bluster. He cannot withhold my allowance. There is no reason for you to be concerned,' she said, with a silent prayer she was right.

I shall make certain. I shall visit the solicitor tomorrow.

'But I am concerned.'

His voice had grown husky, triggering a tug of need deep inside her.

'There is no need. I have managed perfectly well these past eleven years without your concern. I am unlikely to disintegrate now that you have returned.

'However, our conversation earlier was unfinished,' she continued. 'I asked you what it is you want. Your reply was that you wanted us to be able to meet and socialise without the past coming between us. That is what I want, too. As we both want the same thing, our meetings henceforth will be that of casual acquaintances.'

'But…'

Harriet inhaled, and raised her chin. '*If* you are about to suggest some kind of liaison, sir, then I would urge you to resist the temptation to do so, for I shall only refuse and it can only cause more tension and discomfiture between us. I am a respectable widow and I guard my reputation with care, not because my stepson demands it but because *I* wish it.'

Benedict stiffened, his jaw muscles bunching as his brows lowered. He bowed. 'Pardon me for taking up your valuable time.'

Harriet waited until he had gone, then sat numbly on the sofa. She should be relieved. His reaction proved he was, once again, only interested in bedding her. She'd had a lucky escape.

Long-suppressed despair stirred, deep down inside the hollow shell she presented to the outside world. It welled up, invading her constricted throat, stinging her nose and eyes.

She. Would. Not. Cry.

Never again. Not over him. She slapped her hands over her eyes, rubbing furiously as she swallowed down the swell of misery.

Hide your feelings. Don't give in. He'll hurt you all over again.

Gradually, she brought her emotions under control. She stood, smoothed her hair back and crossed the room to the door. It was done. Look to the future.

But my baby... She paused, shuddering. Why did he have to return, bringing all those unwanted memories with him? She could still feel the fragile weight of her daughter in her arms before she had been whisked away, never to be spoken of again, as though she had never existed.

Harriet squeezed her eyes shut, swallowing down her pain. Only when she was certain she could maintain her poise in the face of her servants did she leave the salon and climb the stairs to prepare for the dinner and ball she was due to attend that evening.

Chapter Eleven

'I do not understand.' It was the following day, and Harriet gazed at Mr Drake, the Brierley family solicitor, with dawning horror. 'My stepson... Lord Brierley...I... *Surely* he cannot stop paying my allowance?'

The little man sighed and shuffled the papers on his desk. 'I am sorry, my lady, but I fear he can, if he so chooses.'

'You say there was a sum of money invested in funds at the time of my marriage—was the income not meant for my use? Is that not how it usually works?'

'Usually, yes, but there was an additional condition stated in this particular deed and Lord Brierley, as the primary beneficiary, has the right to withhold the dividends if he so chooses.'

'The primary beneficiary? Please explain.'

The solicitor's cheeks turned the colour of brick.

He cleared his throat. 'I recall these were not the usual circumstances.' He selected a scroll and unrolled it, smoothing it flat. 'This is the deed in question—it is not a standard form of settlement deed but I was present at the meeting where the details were agreed and I can assure you your father raised no objection.'

Harriet's stomach churned. How humiliating, to sit here in the full knowledge that this man knew about her sordid past. 'Pray continue,' she said, gripping her reticule tightly on her lap.

She listened as Mr Drake explained that Harriet's father, desperate to get his pregnant daughter a husband, had agreed she would forgo her dower rights over the Brierley estates, which were entailed for Edward, Brierley's eldest son by his first marriage. The sum of ten thousand pounds was settled on her as compensation, with the income intended to provide her with pin money during her marriage, and a jointure in the event she was widowed.

Pin money? Brierley had never paid her as much as a farthing. If she had needed anything, she'd had to go to him and ask. And there would always be conditions attached.

Always.

Harriet tamped down her disgust at those memories—her reluctance to ask him; her despair when she had no choice—and concentrated as Mr Drake continued to explain how her late husband had re-served the right to withhold the income from the funds—which was to be paid to Harriet, for life, through him and his successors in title—if Harriet did anything to bring the Brierley name into disrepute. A condition, Mr Drake said, that Lord Brierley insisted upon in view of—here he gave a delicate cough—Harriet's proved loose morals.

'And my house in Sackville Street?' A part of her thought, *Why ask? You know the answer.* But she needed to hear it spelled out in all its grue-some reality.

'It belongs to his lordship.' Sympathy gleamed in the little man's eyes. 'I am afraid he is correct. He can shut it up anytime he pleases. At least, from what you have said, he would offer you a cottage on the estate. You would not be homeless.'

Scant comfort. Harriet's world tilted on its axis. Nothing was as it seemed. She had—stupidly, blindly—believed she was safe. She had congrat-ulated herself on being an independent widow. But now… Brierley was still controlling her from be-yond the grave, she realised with a shudder that vibrated through her very bones. Her security and her much-valued independence had been a complete illusion. Edward could stop her allowance anytime he chose, and she would have no recourse whatsoever. What would her options be then? Sick despair rolled through her. Marriage. That would be her only option—to put herself, once more, at the mercy of a man.

'Why was I never informed of either the allowance or that condition?' Her throat had thickened and she had to strain to speak those words without breaking down in front of the solicitor.

Drake shrugged as he re-rolled the deed and placed it with the other documents at one side of his desk. 'I suggest you speak to Lord Brierley, my lady. It was he who made the decision not to apprise you of them after his father's death.'

Edward… The clock on the mantelshelf read half past twelve. Edward had said he would call at two for her decision.

'Thank you for your time, Mr Drake. Good day to you.'

Harriet stood and blindly headed to the door of Drake's office. How stupid had she been? How blind? Why had she never questioned any of this?

You were only sixteen. It was Papa's responsibility to get you a just settlement.

Her father had let her down, yes, but she was a

girl no longer. She should have asked. She should have questioned her position instead of merely trusting the existing state of affairs. Had she learned nothing? She was as naive now as that sixteen-year-old who had succumbed to a handsome youth's charms. As she walked through the outer office she could feel the curious gazes of the clerks burning into her, and she imagined what they must know about her, how they must despise her and laugh at her—a brainless female without a clue as to the ways of the world. She reached the door and stumbled into the street, where she stopped and sucked in several deep breaths.

Her mind would not stop spinning. She could not hold a single steady thought. Could not...could not... She felt her knees sag. Her vision greyed, and then turned black.

'Congratulations, partner.' Benedict clapped Matthew Damerel on the back as they emerged from the offices of Granville and Pettifer in the city.

They had spent a productive morning, first viewing the ship that they intended to purchase—the first of many, they hoped—and, second, instructing their solicitor to draft a partnership agreement for their new business venture.

'Let us go to the club and have a drink to celebrate,' Matthew said. 'I—' His mouth snapped shut.

Benedict turned to see what had caught Matthew's attention, and his insides turned a somersault. Harriet. Pale and trembling, standing on the pavement's edge, looking for all the world… He darted forward and caught her as her legs gave way. Her eyelids fluttered as a soft sigh escaped her lips.

'That is Lady Brierley,' Matthew said, peering under the rim of her bonnet. 'I wonder what—'

'I'll take her home,' Benedict interrupted. He hailed a passing hackney. 'I'll see you later at White's, Matt. We will celebrate then.'

'Shall I come with—?'

'No need,' Benedict said as he swung Harriet into his arms and carried her up the steps into the carriage.

'Do you know where she lives?'

'I know.' Benedict smarted as he caught Matthew's raised brow. 'I escorted her home from your house yesterday, if you recall.'

'Ah…yesterday. Of course. How *could* I forget?'

Matthew's knowing smirk provoked a swell of irritation in Benedict. 'Sackville Street,' he shouted to the driver, then slammed the door, leaving a laughing Matthew standing on the pavement.

Benedict kept his arm around Harriet and manoeuvred her so that she leaned against him and he could steady her against the sway of the hackney. She felt frail. She looked so vulnerable. A wave of protectiveness swept through him, leaving his resolve to stay away from her floundering in its wake.

He studied her... In comparison to her bloom when she had called at Tenterfield Court, she almost looked like a different woman. How had he missed the signs of strain when he had seen her yesterday? Was it, somehow, his fault for reappearing in her life and causing problems with that damned prig of a stepson of hers? Or... He recalled that she had come from a solicitor's office. Perhaps something had happened there to upset her?

The hackney turned into Sackville Street, and Benedict banged his cane against the roof as they reached Harriet's house. He tossed the driver a coin and carried Harriet to her front door, ignoring the curious stares of the few passers-by in the street. Harriet began to stir as he knocked on the door. The footman who opened it blanched when he saw his mistress cradled in a stranger's arms.

'What happened?' He flung the door wide and

ushered Benedict through, shutting it quickly behind him.

'Send for her ladyship's maid immediately.' Benedict flung the words over his shoulder as he strode into the salon, where he carefully laid Harriet on the sofa, then perched on the edge, by her side, facing her.

Within minutes Harriet's butler, followed more slowly by a hobbling Janet, joined him. Janet reached into her pocket, withdrew a small bottle, removed the stopper and waved the bottle under Harriet's nose.

Benedict rubbed Harriet's hand as she coughed, thrashing her head from side to side, dislodging her bonnet. Janet bent to untie the ribbons and remove it.

'Steady,' he whispered, stroking her hair back from her forehead. 'You're safe. You're at home.'

Her lids slowly lifted to reveal eyes of violet blue, dazed and confused.

'What...?'

'Hush. It's all right.' Benedict glanced round at the butler. 'Stevens, I think her ladyship would appreciate some tea.'

'Yes, sir.' Stevens hurried from the room.

Harriet's eyes widened. 'What are *you* doing here?'

'You fainted in the street. In Gray's Inn. I brought you home. What the blazes were you doing in a place like that, without even a maid or a footman in attendance?'

'I… Gray's…? Oh!' She hauled in a ragged breath. '*Oh!*' She struggled to sit and Benedict gently pushed her back. 'The solicitor… He told me… He *owns* me,' she continued disjointedly. 'He controls *everything.*'

'He…? Who owns you, Harry? The solicitor? You are making no sense.'

'Edward!' Her lips quivered as she clutched at Benedict's hand, despair in her eyes. 'Don't you see? *Everything.* And he can take it away at any time.'

'Edward? You told me his threats were all bluster.'

'I was wr—' Harriet stiffened, then struggled to a sitting position. 'What time is it?'

'It is half past one. Why?'

She almost threw his hand aside. 'You must not be here! You must go, before Edward comes. If he finds you here, he will stop my—'

She stilled, catching her lower lip in her teeth. Then, before his eyes, her expression blanked and she was the serene society lady he had encountered at Matthew's house the day before.

'I must apologise,' she said blandly. 'I am not quite myself. Thank you for seeing me home. I shall be quite all right now.'

Benedict felt his eyes narrow as he held Harriet's gaze. 'Tell me. Let me help.'

'Help? Why, sir, I have no need of help. It is merely an inconsequential family matter that I foolishly allowed to overcome me. Now I can think more clearly, I can see I have overreacted.'

Her tone was overly bright and, even as he watched, her hand crept up to play with a lock of her hair. 'Janet. Please show Sir Benedict out.'

He had forgotten the maid was present. He stood—now was not the time to probe deeper and, really, why should he care? She had made it clear yesterday that she viewed him as nothing more than a casual acquaintance. Any issues between Harriet and Brierley were entirely of her own making. He had offered his help and she had refused.

Despite those harsh thoughts, however, he found himself handing her his card and saying, 'You know where I am if you have need of me. I hope you will soon recover from your...from your *inconsequential family matter*. Good day to you.'

He bowed, thrusting aside the voice in his head that insisted Harriet was in trouble. Outside, he walked a short way down the street then, just as he was about to turn the corner into Piccadilly, he hesitated. Cursing beneath his breath, he looked back along Sackville Street. What was she hiding? And what was she scared of? Was Brierley, in some way, misusing her? But then, why would she defend him? It made little sense. That was twice— no, three times now—he had seen her afraid. He propped his shoulders against some railings and settled down to wait, his attention fixed on Harriet's house. He did not have long to wait. A carriage drew up at the kerb and a familiar stout figure trod up the steps to Harriet's front door.

Brierley.

Benedict roundly castigated himself for a fool, but he could not help himself—for all her betrayal of him, he still felt a sense of responsibility towards her. He *wanted* to protect her. He vowed to keep a close eye on Brierley. The man had taken an instant dislike to him for some reason that Benedict couldn't quite fathom. Was it merely that Harriet had been forced to stay unchaperoned at Tenterfield? That made no sense—the snowstorm had hardly been his fault. It hadn't helped that Brierley had caught that intimate moment between himself and Harriet in St George Street, but even that could not explain the extreme threat of cutting off his support of his stepmother. Besides, he recalled

Cooper, the footman, telling him that Brierley had threatened the same thing when he had collected Harriet from Tenterfield Court.

With a muttered oath, Benedict spun on his heel, crossed over Piccadilly and headed in the direction of St James's Street.

Harriet turned Benedict's card over and over in her hands.

Why is it always me who suffers? He left me without a backward glance eleven years ago, never caring what might become of me or our baby, and now he is back and stirring up trouble for me whilst he struts around, guilt-free, with a new title and untold wealth.

A maid came in with the tea tray, snapping her from her resentful thoughts. She thrust the card into her reticule and stood up to remove the spencer she still wore, handing both to Janet, who tidied and re-pinned Harriet's hair before taking her discarded outer clothing upstairs, leaving Harriet to settle on the sofa with her cup of tea to await Edward.

As the clock struck two, Stevens opened the salon door and announced Lord Brierley. Harriet placed her cup in her saucer and put them on the table, taking deep breaths as she strove to remain calm. She had made her decision or, rather, she had accepted that she had no choice. Being under Edward's control was surely preferable to another marriage, where the control would be of an entirely different kind. She stood to greet her stepson.

Edward strode into the salon, halted and bowed. 'Good afternoon.'

'Good afternoon, Edward. Thank you for being so prompt,' Harriet said. 'Stevens, a glass of Madeira for his lordship, if you please.' Her stepson's scowling expression prompted her to add, 'And bring a glass for me, too.' She might need a little fortification.

She sat again on the sofa and settled her skirts around her. Edward took a chair.

'Well, madam?'

'Goodness, Edward, you do come straight to the point. Are you in so much haste? Might we wait until Stevens has served our drinks?'

'You have reached a decision?'

Harriet inclined her head, watching Edward carefully. He did not quite meet her eyes and was fidgeting with his watch chain—something he often did when agitated.

'Good. Then we will wait until Stevens returns,' he said.

Their Madeira was served and Stevens left the

salon, closing the door behind him. Harriet braced herself, but Edward now appeared content to take his time, sipping at his wine as he studied her over the rim of his glass. His hesitation, rather than providing reassurance, shook her. Had he already decided to do his worst, whatever her answer might be? The fear that thought generated strengthened her confidence that she had made the right decision. She did not want to be cast adrift from Fanny and the children. They were her family, and she loved them all dearly. She was also now more certain than ever that she did not want to be forced to marry again simply in order to survive.

'I have decided I will comply with your wishes, Edward,' she said, unable to bear the silence a moment longer.

His relief was apparent and it made her wonder whether he regretted issuing such a drastic ultimatum to her in the first place. He might be stuffy and pompous, but he was not a cruel man. Unlike his father. Harriet did not believe he would take pleasure in either cutting her off from the family or in casting her into penury.

'Very well, madam. I am pleased you have come to your senses.'

'There is one difficulty I must draw to your attention, however,' Harriet continued.

'Difficulty?'

'Indeed, sir. You decreed yesterday that I must have nothing more to do with Sir Benedict Poole, that I must not even speak to him.'

'I did.'

'It occurs to me that it is inevitable our paths will cross from time to time. We have friends in common and—'

'Which friends?'

'Lord and Lady Stanton, for a start.' Harriet carefully hid her satisfaction. She knew Edward would never risk upsetting the Earl of Stanton. He was a member of a powerful clique of the aristocracy.

'Hmph! Continue,' Edward said.

'It would be rude if, on those occasions, I failed to even acknowledge Sir Benedict,' Harriet went on. 'And it would surely start people wondering why I never speak to him. That would not meet with your approval—it would surely cause that speculation you are so keen to avoid.'

'Hmm. Indeed. Very well. I shall concede that you may treat Poole as you might any casual acquaintance, for the sake of good manners.' He heaved himself to his feet. 'But be under no illusion, madam. If I hear of any further indiscretions on your part, it will be the worst for you.'

'And I may still visit Fanny and the children? And come to Kitty's ball?'

Edward hesitated, frowning at her.

'Come now, Edward. How shall you explain my absence to Fanny?'

'Very well. But make sure you heed my warning.'

Edward marched from the room, leaving Harriet unsure whether to laugh or to cry. At least she had wrung the concession from him that she might at least speak to Benedict without the risk of Edward's harsh penalties. That should at least make life less fraught.

A casual acquaintance. That should prove no problem at all.

Chapter Twelve

Benedict felt the stares burning into him as he followed the footman through the hall and into the morning room at White's. Speculative whispers faded into silence as he came within earshot. He ignored the blatant curiosity as he walked past several members—sitting in small groups or alone with their rustling newspapers or simply dozing, a glass of brandy by their side—to join Matthew, seated by one of the windows that overlooked the street, a glass of red wine in hand.

'Another glass for Sir Benedict,' Matthew said, half rising and reaching across to shake Benedict's hand. 'How is Lady Brierley?'

'She is fine,' Benedict said tersely. The speculative gleam in Matthew's blue eyes did nothing to placate Benedict's exasperation with Harriet and her secrets, and neither did the fresh wave of muttering from the other members when they heard his name mentioned. He sat down, saying, 'I seem to be attracting some interest.'

Matthew glanced round. 'Indeed,' he said with a quirk of his lips. 'For some, you will be the highlight of their day—a titbit to take home to their wives. Although, seeing who has just followed you in, I doubt you will remain the highlight for long.'

Benedict looked up to see a tall man with dark brown hair framed in the open doorway. He skimmed the occupants of the room, then turned and disappeared. The low murmur of conversation swept away the silence that had greeted the newcomer's appearance at the door.

'Who was that?'

'Stanton,' Matthew replied. 'Lady Stanton's husband.'

'Why would he cause such attention?' Benedict could understand a stranger such as himself causing ripples, but not someone like Stanton.

'A rumour is going the rounds,' Matthew said. 'There were whispers last summer that he was seeing someone—a widow—but no one could ascertain the truth of it. Then he married in September and the rumours died down. But someone has started them up again, and there is a rush to discover who she is and whether she is still under his protection. There's all kinds of gossip, including—

you might be interested to hear—speculation that it was your friend, Lady Brierley.'

Matthew's words hit as effectively as a physical blow, but Benedict quelled the anger that surged through him, determined to give his friend no cause to question his reaction. Was Stanton the reason Harriet had been so quick to forestall his suggestion they become lovers?

'Hmph,' he grunted. 'Have these people nothing better to do with their time?'

Matthew grinned. 'No. That is the point. For many, their interest is solely in what their friends and neighbours are up to, and if they can embellish the tale, so much the better. Plus, according to Ellie, there is a certain amount of jealousy amongst some ladies that a woman such as Felicity succeeded in snaring Stanton where all their efforts had failed. They, no doubt, are relishing their chance to stir the coals. Still—' his piercing eyes lingered on the empty doorway '—I find it hard to believe Stanton has a mistress. I've never seen a man more besotted with his wife.'

Benedict choked on his wine. He eyed Matthew, who was staring at him, clearly perplexed by his reaction. 'Have you taken a look in the mirror lately, Matt?' Benedict shook his head slowly at his friend. 'I'd wager that you'd see one there.'

As Matthew continued to stare blankly at him, he clarified. 'The only husband more besotted with his wife than *Stanton* happens to be you, you numbskull.'

Matthew smiled, his hard features softening, and Benedict felt again the solitude of his own life. He had not known love since his parents had died. He had watched Eleanor and Matthew together, and he was envious. He yearned to be the centre of someone else's universe, and to feel the same way about her. Harriet's face materialised in his mind's eye. Once he had believed that was what they shared. He had been wrong. That had not been love. Infatuation, lust, call it what you would, it was not love. He would be more careful this time.

'In fact,' he continued, 'your blissful contentment with married life has persuaded me it is time to take the plunge myself and find a wife. As soon as possible.'

Matthew frowned. 'Not every marriage is as happy as mine, Ben. It can take time to adjust to it. You'd be wise to get settled into your new life before marrying. Or have you already met someone?' He paused, then said, 'A certain widow, perhaps?'

Benedict clamped his lips against an angry retort and carefully kept his tone unconcerned.

'Not a widow, no,' he said. 'I have every intention of restoring the name of Poole to a place of pride. I am aware my trade connections will count against me, but marriage to a suitable well-bred girl will surely help. You saw the reaction when I came in here—I have the disadvantage of resembling my cousin, so my identity was guessed at the minute I set foot inside the door. I thought I might ask Eleanor for some introductions.'

Matthew's lips firmed in disapproval. 'I still think you should not rush into it, but if you are determined to go ahead, I am sure she will be pleased to help.'

'I did not expect to see you out and about this evening.'

The quietly spoken words prompted a lurch in Harriet's stomach, followed by a skip of her heart. Had she suspected Benedict would be here, she would not have come to the Barringtons' rout, not so soon after Edward's ultimatum. There was no point in going looking for trouble. She swallowed her regretful sigh at the sight of him, so tall and handsome in his beautifully tailored evening coat, his auburn hair burnished in the candlelight, and then chided herself for her inconsistency. It was no good deciding at one minute that she was happy to play by Edward's rules and treat Benedict as a mere acquaintance and the next minute hanker after him purely because she could not have him.

'I was overcome by the stuffiness of the solicitor's office today, that was all,' she said. 'Now, if you will excuse me, I—'

Benedict grasped her arm above the elbow, his fingers warm against her bare skin. Everything inside her clenched tight at his touch, and her heart beat faster.

'Not so fast,' he hissed. Then he raised his voice. 'Allow me to escort you to a chair and to procure you a glass of wine.'

He tugged her to his side, then crooked his elbow. A few nearby guests had turned to stare. Harriet raised her chin and placed her hand on Benedict's arm.

'Why?' Her voice shook despite her best efforts to control it. 'You will make things worse.'

'Worse? How so?'

They left the salon, which had been stripped of virtually every stick of furniture in order to accommodate the Barringtons' guests. As they passed through the hall, Benedict asked a footman where they might sit and they followed him to a smaller room where chairs were clustered in random groups. There were a few other guests in here, taking the opportunity to rest, but it was quiet compared to the babble of conversation in the salon.

Harriet sank onto a chair as Benedict asked the footman to bring them some wine. He pulled another chair round so he faced her. His intense scrutiny unnerved her but she was careful to show no sign, concentrating on breathing steadily and reciting a poem in her head. She had learned the trick in the early days of her marriage, in order to prevent reactions that might provoke her husband.

'How will I make things worse?'

'This!' Harriet gestured to the room. 'It is so *particular*. It is not how casual acquaintances behave.'

'I saw Brierley come to your house after I left. Is he still threatening you? I take it from what you said earlier that he is able to stop your allowance if he sees fit?'

'That is not your concern—my life is nothing to do with you.'

'We used to be friends. If you are in trouble... If there is anything I can do...'

'Trouble?' She laughed, battening down the anger and bitterness that roiled her stomach. She had been in trouble since the minute he had decided she was only good for sowing his wild oats. It was a little late for him to develop a conscience

now. She eyed him, envying the simplicity of his life. *He* could marry, secure in the knowledge that he would be the one in control. If *she* was forced to marry again, if Edward carried out his threats, she would be completely at the whim of her husband. 'My only trouble will arise from being seen with you.'

The footman brought two glasses of wine and Harriet sipped gratefully, grasping at this distraction from her negative thoughts and emotions.

'Why has your stepson taken me in such dislike?'

'I do not know. I suggest you ask him.'

His hand—large and warm—enclosed hers, where she had been fiddling with a tendril of hair, left to curl loose by her ear. She snatched her hand free.

'Stop it! What if someone should see?'

'What are you hiding?'

'Nothing.'

'Do you already have a lover? Is that the reason for your stepson's threats?'

She stiffened, aghast. 'I *beg* your pardon?'

'Oh, don't look at me with such innocent indignation.' He leaned towards her, lowering his voice. 'After all, you did not scruple to sleep with me when you were still a virgin. Why should you quibble over the suggestion of a lover here and there now you are a widow?'

Harriet shot to her feet. As quickly as she moved, however, Benedict's fingers encircled her wrist. Twist as she might, she could not break free of his grip.

'Why were you afraid of me, in the folly? Were you scared your lover would find out?'

'I do *not* have a lover,' she said through gritted teeth.

'I hear differently.' His rage was palpable. 'Why did you not tell me you already had a protector when you rejected me?'

She froze. *What has he heard?* But it was nonsense; she had only ever had the one lover, and that had ended months since.

'It is nonsense,' she said, out loud for his benefit. 'How could I tell you about something that does not exist?'

'But something terrified you, that day at the folly,' he went on relentlessly.

Why will you not just let it be? 'You are wrong. Your memory is wrong. I changed my mind.'

'What about the evening before? You ran up those stairs as if the devil himself was on your heels.'

He was...in the past. And, just like that, all of

her fight drained away. Times like that were hard to forget. Her knees trembled and she sank once again onto the chair. Benedict released her wrist.

'I was upset about my father, and also that you thought I would be so readily available, just because I am a widow.'

He cast a look of scepticism at her. 'And yet you kissed me at the folly.'

'I was confused.'

'Hmph.'

Benedict said no more, but his anger dissipated before her eyes, and she hoped that would be an end to his questions. She wished it was an end to her worries, but it seemed as though they might still be amassing. Fears gnawed away inside her until she felt near overwhelmed.

What had Benedict heard about her? Lately, her life appeared to consist of disaster after disaster, and now— Had news of her *affaire* with Stanton somehow got out? What if Edward were to hear of it?

Her vision swam. She would *not* give way to tears. She reached inside her reticule and found her fan. She opened and plied it in front of her glowing face and then picked up her glass to sip at her wine. Resentment simmered inside her, both at Benedict's unjustified interrogation of her—what business of his was *any* of her life?—and at the unfairness that dictated that *she* should suffer all the penalties of their young love and that he had emerged scot-free. The most wretched and terrifying time of her life had been a mere bump on his road to success and riches.

By the time she was composed enough to glance at Benedict, he had ceased studying her and was gazing around the room. *No doubt selecting the prettiest young ladies to make up to.* She followed his gaze and choked back a sarcastic laugh. He would not find any matrimonial candidates in *here*. There was not one person present under the age of at least fifty.

It serves him right for bullying me into coming in here with him.

He looked round then, as if she had spoken her words aloud.

'I am sorry you feel unable to confide in me, Harry,' he said. 'Whatever happened between us, you do know I would always protect you, don't you?'

A painful lump swelled in her throat. Why was he making this so hard? All she ever wanted was to feel safe and secure. She conjured up again the memory of Benedict standing up to Edward. He had made her feel safe then, protected and cared for. Except it was not real. It was an illusion. Besides, she didn't want him to be nice. She *wanted* to hate him. Her entire predicament was his fault. *Deep breaths. Take care.* She forced a careless shrug.

'You are imagining dramas where there are none. I am not hiding anything.'

'Yet you will not tell me why your stepson is prepared to resort to blackmail to keep you from associating with me.'

'Blackmail? I should hardly call it that.'

Although it was blackmail, wasn't it? And Edward had the power over her to force her to obey his wishes. Nausea clogged her throat. Power. All men used it, to keep women compliant. And Benedict—perhaps unconsciously—was using his power as a man to persuade her to confide in him. Well, she wouldn't do it.

'Edward is worried about my reputation, in case it harms his daughter's come-out,' she said. 'Any father would do the same and I do not blame him. He wishes to ensure that no scandal attaches to *any* member of his family. He was upset to find me at a place such as Tenterfield Court.'

'Scandal?' Benedict's growl was menacing. 'There is no scandal attached to *my* name. I'd better have a few words with that stepson of yours.'

Harriet swallowed. An argument between Edward and Benedict could only exacerbate matters. She drew on all her years of learning how to calm a fraught situation. At least with Benedict she need not fear raised fists or forced, unwanted intimacies.

'It will take time for people to forget the link between the Poole name and Sir Malcolm's behaviour,' she said soothingly. 'Edward is conservative. He doesn't like change. Give him time. Once Kitty is out, he will relax. He is in the throes of negotiating an advantageous match for her, one that is very important for both the family and for him politically.'

She raised her gaze to Benedict's, forcing herself to maintain eye contact. 'You have formed an entirely mistaken impression of my relationship with my stepson. That is no doubt my fault. When you saw me this morning I was upset with myself and my failure to ever ascertain my legal right to the allowance Edward pays me. Realising my own naivety was not pleasant, but it makes no difference whatsoever to my position and I most certainly have no need of protection from my own stepson.'

'Then, why say I will make things worse?'

'I have no wish for my name to be linked to yours for the reasons I have stated. It is acceptable for us to converse in the company of others, but you must understand that a *tête-à-tête* such as this will only raise speculation and, possibly, expectations. *That* will help neither of our causes. You wish to find a bride, do you not? Having our names bandied about together will not help.

'We were friends once, long ago, but we are different people now. I no longer know you, and you no longer know me or the person I have become. I fully understand you might gravitate towards me, as a familiar face in a sea of strangers—'

'*Familiar?* You think I suffer from *bashfulness*?'

'Are Lady Ashby and Mr Damerel present tonight?'

'No, but—'

'It is only natural you must feel your lack of acquaintance,' Harriet said, meeting Benedict's darkening expression with a kind smile, 'but you will soon find your feet, I promise. In the meantime, might I introduce you to anyone?' She couldn't resist adding, 'A suitable young lady, perhaps?'

His eyes narrowed. Then he smiled back at her, but his smile did not reach his eyes. He stood up. 'Thank you for your kind consideration, my lady, but I flatter myself I am capable of arranging my own affairs.' He proffered his arm. 'Might I escort you back to the salon?'

Harriet stood and shook out her blue silk skirts

before smiling and accepting his arm. 'Thank you, sir. I am so glad we had this little chat. I think we understand one another more clearly now, do you not agree?'

Chapter Thirteen

Benedict kept his answering growl hidden deep in his chest.

Infuriating…patronising…contradictory…*witch.*

They reached the salon and Harriet immediately left his side, heading towards a knot of people standing by one of the open windows. The salon was stiflingly hot, crammed with people, all of whom appeared to be talking at once. The room echoed with voices. How did these people tolerate it? Where was the pleasure in standing around in groups, shouting at each other and struggling to make sense of the conversation? A glance around showed not one familiar face and Benedict found himself wondering if Harriet had a point: had part of his reason for seeking her out been simply that he knew her?

He had become reacquainted with several old school and university friends since his return from

India, but he could see none of them in this crowd. He wended his way past various knots of people until he caught sight of a face he did recognise. He hesitated. Did he really want to encourage Miss Marstone's attentions? He deliberated a second too long; Miss Marstone caught sight of him and her eyes lit up as she glided in his direction.

'Sir Benedict! We meet again.'

She halted in front of him, standing too close for his liking. Her flowery perfume, heady and strong, wafted over him.

He bowed. 'Good evening, Miss Marstone. We do indeed. Are you here with your mother?'

'Oh, yes. She is around somewhere.' She raised her fan and fluttered it before her face. 'I declare, it is exceedingly hot in here with all these people, is it not? It is enough to make one feel quite faint.' Above her fan, she watched him through her lashes.

For his part, Benedict eyed Miss Marstone and decided she looked far too robust to swoon on him, but he nevertheless proffered his arm, saying, 'May I escort you across to the window, Miss Marstone? I am sure you will find it cooler over there.' He gestured to the window next to the one where Harriet appeared to be holding court in the centre of a group. He recognised Lady Stanton and, by her side, his large hand at the small of her back, the tall man Matthew had pointed out as Lord Stanton.

Benedict tore his attention away from that group and focused on the girl by his side.

'Such a gentlemanly gesture.' Miss Marstone dimpled up at him as she took his arm. 'Tell me, sir, is it hard to adjust to London society after spending so many years abroad?'

'There are many English people who live in India, Miss Marstone. I did socialise with them in addition to the natives.'

'Oh, yes, but they are *merchants*, surely? Oh... not that there is anything *wrong* with such people, oh, good heavens, no. But in London you can mix with the elite in society. You must, I feel certain, acknowledge the superiority of the company found here to that found anywhere. *This* is the pinnacle of civilisation.'

Benedict bit back his retort. She was young and innocent. She only knew what she had been taught and, with a mother like Lady Marstone, she surely could be forgiven her prejudices.

'I was, and still am, a merchant,' he reminded her.

'Oh, yes, I know. But you are a gentleman as well...a baronet. That makes all the difference.'

The difference to what? Are all young ladies as openly covetous of a title, as Harriet had once been?

He must hope not, or his search for a bride would consist of much biting of his tongue. Such superiority was not an admirable trait in Benedict's book. His head began to ache.

'And,' Miss Marstone added, 'you need no longer work, now you are a property owner.'

The inference being that it was socially acceptable for a gentleman to make his money from land, but not from trade.

Why her words, and the sentiment behind them, rankled he did not know. He knew full well that being in trade was deemed an unsuitable occupation for a gentleman of the *ton*, but he had not been prepared for it to be pointed out to him in quite such a brazen manner.

'Yes, I have property,' he said, 'but I happen to enjoy working, so I intend to continue to run my trading business. In fact,' he added, hoping to puncture her innate conviction that her view of the world was the only correct one, 'my partner and I have just purchased a ship so that we can increase our business interests.'

'Oh! Oh…yes…well…but…your partner?' Her white brow wrinkled, then she drew in a deep breath, and her lips were smiling again. 'Mr

Damerel is your partner, is he not? Mama told me all about him, and I make no doubt if that kind of work is suitable for Lady Ashby then *I* can have no objection to it.'

Benedict gave up, but made a mental note not to get trapped in Miss Marstone's company again, or he was likely to say something he regretted.

They had reached the window where there was, indeed, a fresher feel to the air. Miss Marstone released his arm and propped her hands on the low sill as she leaned forward to draw in a deep breath.

Perhaps not so innocent after all, Benedict mused, eyeing the bottom thrust provocatively in his direction.

'Do you need rescuing?'

At the exact time those quiet words reached his ears, Miss Marstone straightened and turned to him, her smile dying on her lips as she saw Harriet.

Laughter bubbled beneath Harriet's cheery, 'Good evening, Miss Marstone. How do you do?'

'I am very well, thank you, Lady Brierley.' Miss Marstone moved to stand beside Benedict and linked her arm through his in a proprietorial manner that made him stiffen. 'Sir Benedict and I were just enjoying a breath of fresh air. There is an uncomfortable *closeness* in the room tonight, do you not agree?'

'Oh, indeed,' Harriet replied. 'Almost suffocating, one might say. I wonder, sir, that you do not propose a walk on the terrace to allow Miss Marstone to cool off. She is looking somewhat flushed.'

Benedict felt Miss Marstone's fingers tighten on his sleeve. He frowned at Harriet, who returned his glare with one of limpid innocence. What the hell was she playing at? One minute she could not wait to get away from him, then she was all false sympathy, concerned that he was *shy*, for God's sake, and *now* she was affability itself. Her changes were mercurial and he did not understand her.

He resisted the urge to massage his temples and smiled at her instead. 'What a very thoughtful suggestion, Lady Brierley.' He peered through the open window. There were several people outside, taking the opportunity to cool off. 'Would you care to take a turn around the terrace, Miss Marstone?'

He did not miss the triumphant smile she directed at Harriet. Harriet, irritatingly, merely smiled graciously, seemingly unconcerned.

'Thank you, sir. I should like that very much,' Miss Marstone said.

Later that evening, Benedict strolled up the dark path towards the terrace. The crowds at the rout party had begun to dwindle and the evening air had cooled significantly, driving everyone else indoors. Benedict had taken advantage of the peace of the garden—large by the standards of most London town houses—and had escaped the throng to soothe his aching head and to mull over the young ladies to whom he had been introduced. Not one of them stood out as someone he would particularly care to share his life with. But it was early days, and he had only just begun looking for a bride, so there was no need to despair.

As he placed one foot on the bottom step up to the terrace, quiet voices reached his ears. Harriet… That was Harriet's voice—with a man. His temple began to throb again. Who was he? Taking care to tread silently, he moved up a couple more steps, keeping to the shadow at the side of the flight. There… A couple in the shadows, standing close, face-to-face. There was an intimacy about their stance that set Benedict's heart racing with the urge to charge up those steps and haul the man away from Harriet.

'We must hope Brierley doesn't get wind of these other rumours, as well.' A stranger's voice, deep and rich.

'Heavens, yes.' Harriet's reply was heartfelt. 'I cannot believe…after all this time…' There was a pause. 'Stanton…about Felicity… Are you sure? I mean, we have never spoken about—'

'Hush, Harry. It is all sorted. There is no need for you to fret. Your friendship means the world to Felicity. She will not jeopardise—'

Something pushed against Benedict's leg and he jerked it back. His foot slipped over the edge of his step to the one below with a loud scraping noise. He glanced down to see a pale-coloured cat slinking away down the steps, no doubt startled away by his reaction.

'Shh! I heard something.'

Hell and damnation. There was nothing for it; he must brazen it out. Benedict strolled up the remaining steps, making no attempt to conceal himself as he silently cursed the cat. He reached the terrace, rounded a pillar topped with a stone urn and saw that the man with Harriet was the Earl of Stanton, her best friend's husband.

Bloody hellfire.

Harriet's alarmed expression eased. 'Sir Benedict! It is you. You startled me.'

Benedict's mind whirled with the implications of the snatches of conversation he had heard. That their talk was clandestine could not be denied. Why else had they been standing out here, alone, in the dark? Were the rumours they had been discussing the same ones that Matthew had told him about?

Although he had nigh on accused Harriet of having a lover, he had not really believed it, but now— Were Harriet and Stanton involved? A hard ball of anger barrelled through his chest.

Virtuous widow indeed.

Harriet and Stanton were staring at him, awaiting his reply.

'My apologies for startling you, Lady Brierley. I felt the need to clear my head.' He eyed Stanton, who returned his glare with a hard stare and bunched brows.

'I understand you are an old…*acquaintance* of Lady Brierley's,' Stanton said. He thrust out his hand. 'Stanton.'

Benedict shook the proffered hand. 'I prefer to think of myself as a friend,' he said. 'A very *good* friend.'

Stanton turned from Benedict and took Harriet's arm. 'Come. Felicity will be wondering where we are.'

Benedict stepped sideways, blocking their path. 'Not so fast.'

Stanton appeared to grow taller and broader as he sized Benedict up. He manoeuvred Harriet so that he stood between her and Benedict, his hand clamped around her wrist.

'Is there a problem, Poole?' Stanton's voice was deathly quiet.

Benedict felt his rage grow. If this buffoon thought he could intimidate him, he was way off course. 'There is. Go inside, Harriet. I want a private word with *his lordship.*'

'Do not,' she said. 'Please.' She twisted free of Stanton's grip and tugged at him, her obvious familiarity with the earl doing nothing to calm Benedict's anger. 'There is no need for this. I do not want a scandal.'

'If you do not want scandal, what the blazes are you doing out here in the dark with a married man?'

'And why is that any of your business?' Stanton snarled. 'Harry. Go indoors. Now.'

'No! I will not leave you two here like this. This is madness. There is nothing—'

'Richard. There you are.' Lady Stanton was suddenly in their midst, chattering away, linking arms with her husband. 'I trust you managed to sort out that little misunderstanding between Harriet and me? Oh, you are here, too, Sir Benedict. Now then…what *will* you make of all this? *Such* a foolish thing…I did tell you, Harriet, not to pay attention to such silly talk. It is a good job, is it not—' she turned guileless eyes to Benedict '—that we ladies have you gentlemen to talk some sense into us when we are all ready to fly at each other, fluffing our feathers?'

She smiled and her rather ordinary features were transformed. Benedict felt his anger abate. Had he misinterpreted that conversation? Lady Stanton seemed relaxed about her husband and Harriet being out here together. He had at first wondered at the pairing of the handsome earl and his lady, but he now began to see the qualities that had attracted Stanton to his wife as she deftly defused the situation. Stanton, too, had relaxed his combative stance and was watching his wife with adoring eyes.

'It is all settled now, Felicity, dear,' Harriet said. 'There is nothing more to resolve, apart from asking these two to shake hands. Sir Benedict has done his own fair share of jumping to conclusions, when he discovered Stanton and me talking in the dark.'

'Really, sir? You have no need for suspicions in *that* direction, I assure you.'

Lady Stanton's voice rang with confidence and Benedict was left feeling rather foolish.

'And the rumours you were discussing?' He

could not shake the impression he was being mis-led, but he could not for the life of him work out why. If there was something between Harriet and Stanton, his wife would not be out here trying to smooth things over.

'Oh, that was just silly talk by somebody who passed on some scurrilous gossip to Harriet,' Lady Stanton said. 'I am exceedingly fortunate to have Richard to rely on, for he sorted it all out in a trice. He would make an excellent diplomat.'

'He would indeed,' Harriet said warmly. 'Now, will you two please shake hands? It is chilly out here and I am feeling the cold.' She slipped her arm through Benedict's and nudged him round to face Stanton.

'I apologise for jumping to conclusions,' Benedict said, holding out a reluctant hand.

Stanton's jaw remained set, but he took Benedict's hand and shook, for the second time that evening. 'Accepted,' he said. 'It was—perhaps—an easy mistake to make.'

'There,' Harriet said. 'Now we are all friends again.' She squeezed Benedict's arm. 'Relax,' she whispered. 'And thank you—I do realise you were trying to protect me but, trust me, it was not needed.'

Trust her? He looked into her violet eyes, reading nothing there but calm friendliness, knowing that underneath lurked secrets and unanswered questions. No, he did not trust her but the Stantons clearly did, so he would keep his own counsel.

They went back inside the house, but as Benedict began to take his leave of Harriet, she stayed him.

'Do not go. Please, Benedict. Not yet. I have something I wish to say.'

Benedict? Against his better judgement, he waited, suspicion niggling away deep inside. What *was* she up to?

Harriet's smooth forehead bunched in a frown. 'You were right, what you said earlier. We *were* friends and, despite Edward, I would like to be friends again. I do not like this feeling of being on edge whenever we meet. Might we start again, do you think?'

He would not refuse. How could he, when he wanted the same thing? But this change in her attitude to him had been prompted by something other than feeling uncomfortable in his presence.

'I would like that,' he said, but he silently reserved judgement.

She was up to something and, when she played her hand, he would be ready for her.

Chapter Fourteen

Harriet studied her reflection in the long mirror on her bedchamber wall. A stranger stared back at her.

'Tie on the mask, please, Janet.'

The black mask, decorated with silver stars and crescent moons, covered her face from above her eyebrows to the tip of her nose, from which point it swept out to follow the curve of her cheeks and then round to her ears, leaving just her mouth and jawline exposed. She felt the weight and worry of the past few days melt away. Tonight, she was not Harriet, Lady Brierley, widow, but Diana, Roman goddess of the hunt and of the moon, and she could relax and enjoy herself without wondering, every time anyone looked at her, whether they had guessed that it was she who had been Stanton's lover last year. The rumours had continued to build day by day and she knew it was only a matter of time before the truth was out in the open. What Edward would choose to do then was anyone's guess.

'Ooh, milady, even I can't tell it's you,' Janet said, grinning from ear to ear.

Harriet smiled at her maid. 'Thanks to you and your hard work, Janet,' she said. 'You have worked a miracle. I shall have to cultivate a foreign accent, so no one can discover me by my voice.'

She touched the delicate silvery gauze head-dress—like the mask, also enhanced with beautifully embroidered crescent moons and stars—that disguised her distinctive silver-blonde hair. Pinned securely in place, she was confident it would not be dislodged by dancing.

What costume will Benedict wear? Shall I recognise him? She must pray she would, for her plan depended upon it.

She had not seen him since the evening of the Barringtons' rout, where the sight of him in private conversation with Bridget Marstone had provoked such a white-hot spike of jealousy within her that she had been unable to stick to her resolution—made only minutes before—to avoid him for the rest of that evening. Now her resolve was for the opposite, and she shivered in excitement at the thought of seeing him again, and at what she was planning.

At the rout, the seed of an idea had taken root in her brain, and in the days since then, its tendrils had infiltrated her thoughts until it was all she could think of: if the worse should come to the worst, and she was forced to look for a husband, well…

Benedict wants a wife. Why should it not be me?

She knew he was not violent, and he had already shown by his reactions when they met at Tenterfield Court that he would not force himself on her. *He* would never punish her for a wrong look or a wrong word.

Her instinct to dismiss the idea as being unfair to Benedict had been drowned by a surge of resentful entitlement.

He owes me!

Her predicament was his fault. Actions had consequences, and his refusal to marry her when she'd conceived his child had resulted in her disastrous marriage, which in turn had driven her to take a lover to vanquish her terrible memories of her husband.

The consequences of Benedict's return, their past relationship and her *affaire* with Stanton had now combined until it threatened to leave Harriet destitute, with no income and no means of support unless she married again.

Besides, he owes it to me. He owes me peace of mind... He owes me respectability... He owes me a baby.

If you are still able to have a baby. She shook the errant thought away, determined to allow nothing to spoil the evening ahead. It was true she had not conceived during her marriage to Brierley, and she had counted that a blessing, but surely God could not be so cruel to deny her a child if she remarried.

She focused on her image in the mirror, spinning this way and that to examine her appearance from all angles. Her dress consisted of a length of fine silver muslin draped around her figure and caught at the waist with a woven silver-coloured belt, knotted to allow the ends to dangle free. A silver brooch, fashioned in the shape of a bow and arrows, pinned the fabric at one shoulder and, daringly, left the other shoulder bare, preventing the wearing of her shift. The fabric flowed over the roundness of her hips and bottom before spilling to the floor in shimmering waves. A silver-coloured quiver containing three 'arrows'—made from slender canes to represent the shafts, with white feathers stuck on the end to represent the fletching—was slung diagonally across her back, secured in place by a fine silver chain. The effect of that chain passing between her breasts, emphasising each full mound, was deliciously provocative.

Did she dare carry out her plan to seduce Benedict?

What if he shrugs his shoulders to the fact he has compromised you? He walked away from you before, and you were with child then.

He is older now. Surely he will be more responsible. Besides, I'll seduce him so thoroughly, he won't be able to resist me.

You know this is wrong. You are not being fair to Benedict.

She thrust aside her niggling conscience. What choice did she have? Anyway, when had Benedict been fair to her... When had *life* been fair? But that thought prompted the memory of all the servants she had given shelter to in the house in Cheapside. She pictured their innocent babies, and she felt ashamed. In comparison, life had been very fair to her. Those servant girls were, however, another reason why she must do something drastic to protect her future. The charity relied on donations. If it came out that she had been Stanton's lover, and Edward cut her off from the family, then those donations would surely trickle to a halt.

'Lord Stanton's carriage has pulled up outside, milady. Are you ready?'

Janet's voice jerked Harriet from her reflections. 'Yes. I am ready.'

The masquerade ball was a private party to celebrate the birthday of Lady Cotham, at her country house, north of Paddington village. A full moon lit the way, as did the coach lamps on the procession of carriages leaving London on the Edgware road. At Cotham Manor they were required to produce their invitations to prove they were invited guests. In the well-lit hall, Harriet got her first proper look at Richard and Felicity, resplendent in their costumes as a medieval nobleman and his lady. Studying the guests arriving at the same time as them, Harriet marvelled at the inventiveness of some costumes and realised that, as much as she had embraced the knowledge that she would be hard to recognise, she was less keen that she was unable to put a name to many of the other masked revellers. Anonymous eyes glittered through masks and she felt a shiver of apprehension descend her spine.

Thank goodness she was with the Stantons and had not ventured here alone.

There was no formal announcement of their

arrival. Lady Cotham had decreed nothing should spoil the fun of guessing the identities of her guests and, to that end, the only people whose costumes were known were Lord and Lady Cotham themselves. His lordship was Henry VIII—a role perfectly suited to his ever-expanding waistline—and her ladyship had let it be known that *she* was Boudicca, and that she would not be amused by any other warrior queens of ancient Britain who might presume to turn up.

The ballroom was already crammed with people clad in colourful and sometimes bizarre costumes, resulting in a great deal of hilarity as everyone circulated, making wild guesses. Stanton disappeared into the throng to procure three glasses of punch, leaving Harriet and Felicity by a window with strict instructions not to move.

'It is disconcerting not to instantly recognise the person to whom one is speaking,' Felicity whispered to Harriet.

'Indeed it is.'

Felicity threaded her arm through Harriet's and a nervy sensation stirred deep inside her as she realised it wasn't just her being prudish—Felicity was wary, too. Somehow, behind the anonymity of their masks, people had shed their inhibitions. Manners took second place to innuendo and—in some cases—out-and-out suggestive remarks, none of which were appropriate comments a gentleman should make to a lady. And, already, she had witnessed a passionate kiss and a sultan squeezing the ample breast of a giggling shepherdess. The atmosphere was reminiscent of some of the parties she and Brierley had attended when they were first wed, after she had lost her baby. Without volition, Harriet tensed, squeezing Felicity's hand against her ribs.

'I am certain there is nothing to worry about, Harriet,' Felicity said. 'We will look after you, and I make no doubt Richard will insist we leave if it gets too disorderly.'

Stanton reappeared, carrying, with some difficulty, three glasses of muddy-looking liquid. 'It's madness,' he grumbled. 'It's impossible to tell who is who.' He handed a glass to each of the women and sipped cautiously at his own. His lips turned down in a grimace.

'Is it horrid?' Harriet said.

'It certainly packs a punch,' Stanton replied, making them laugh as they, in turn, tried the punch. It was undoubtedly fiery, burning Harriet's throat as she swallowed, but the after-effect was a lovely warm glow.

'You had better not imbibe too freely,' Stanton

continued with a grin. 'I can't cope with two tipsy women on the journey home.'

Felicity had taken one sip, coughed and then passed her glass back to Stanton. 'You need not worry about *my* state of mind, my love,' she said, 'for I'm afraid I cannot stomach this. Do you think—?'

'I'll find you some lemonade,' Stanton said immediately, and disappeared once more.

He was soon back with a glass of lemonade for Felicity.

'It's no wonder everyone is so merry, with the strength of this stuff,' he said, gazing around at the revellers. 'Can't understand what Cotham was thinking,' he added in a mutter. 'He must have realised such a gathering would descend into chaos. But then, he always was somewhat buffleheaded.'

'He may not have realised what might happen,' Felicity said. 'After all, we did not guess, did we? Do you want to go home, Richard?'

He slipped one arm around her waist and dropped a kiss on her nose. 'I want to keep you and our baby safe,' he said.

The familiar stab of envy pierced Harriet, despite her love for her friend. Silently, she scolded herself, aware that if she did not strive to overcome her jealousy, she would struggle to properly rejoice with Felicity and Richard when the baby was born. Their friendship was far too precious for her to risk losing it because they had been blessed and she had not. *Maybe, if my plan with Benedict works…* Resolutely, she diverted those thoughts, stifling that same whisper of conscience that she was being manipulative and unfair.

'We cannot go home yet anyway,' Stanton continued, raising his voice to compete with the musicians, who had begun to play. 'Carriages are still arriving and it's chaotic out there. Besides, my man will never forgive me if we leave before he's had a chance to brag about his exploits with the other coachmen. And whilst we're here, we may as well have a dance. At least I shall avoid the accusation of being hopelessly unfashionable by dancing with my own wife. We'll give it an hour or so, and then I'll order the carriage round. Our hosts won't be too insulted if we make our escape then.'

'Felicity! Is that you?' A statuesque flower seller, her burnished mahogany hair threaded with flowers and carrying a basket filled with fresh blooms, appeared, followed by a powerfully built, scowling Roman centurion. 'I am relieved you told me what you would be wearing or I might never have found you.'

Harriet recognised Eleanor's voice.

'Yes, it is me,' Felicity said, 'and this is Harriet—she came with us in our carriage.'

Greetings were exchanged all round and, while the two men had a comfortable grouch about the masquerade shaping up to be an unsuitable place for the ladies, Eleanor said, 'It's a pleasure to see you again, Harriet. What a beautiful costume—I should never have known it was you had Felicity not said.'

She lowered her voice, continuing, 'Matthew is being most disagreeable, complaining about the *tone* of the party, but I must confess I have been happily diverted in trying to guess who is who. Benedict came with us, too, but heaven knows where he has disappeared to. He's gone off to find himself a mermaid, no doubt.' She laughed, adding, 'He has come as a pirate.'

So Benedict *was* here. Harriet skimmed the crowd of revellers closest to them, but could see no pirate. She sipped at her punch, watching the guests, the conversation between Felicity and Eleanor washing over her. Babies. Again. Could they talk of nothing else? She instantly castigated herself for her meanness. If she were in their shoes, would she not be the same? Excited, and wanting to speak of it every chance she got? She realised, with a lurch of guilt, that Felicity had not mentioned her baby, unless Eleanor was present, for a few weeks. Had she somehow guessed that Harriet was envious? Tears of self-pity prickled at Harriet's eyes and she drank some more punch, scanning the crowd again until—there he was.

Benedict: tall, lean and unbearably sexy, clad in an open-necked white shirt with full sleeves that billowed between shoulder and cuff; a red waistcoat, fastened by laces; loose-fitting calf-length striped trousers with a wide ragged hem and black shoes sporting large silver buckles. To complete his costume a red patterned sash was tied at his waist and a cocked hat completely covered his auburn hair. As with most guests, a mask covered his upper face, but she knew him in an instant by the line of his jaw and the curve of his sensual lips. He moved amongst the crowds, at his ease, a smiling bow here, a laughing shake of his head there.

As she watched, a buxom milkmaid clutched at his arm, up on tiptoe as she said something. He bent to listen to her, sliding his arm around her waist, then cocked his head to whisper in her ear. Jealous resentment squeezed Harriet's chest, making it hard to breathe, as he led the milkmaid into a set forming in the centre of the room.

Life is so easy for him. Why should he not pay a price for what he did?

She glanced at her companions. They were all preoccupied, taking no notice of her. She could not afford for Benedict to see her with his friends, for then he would guess her identity, so she slipped away and wended her way through the throng, fending off the clumsy advances that each man she passed appeared to feel obliged to make. In escaping her friends she had also lost sight of Benedict so she made her way to the side of the room, reaching the relative safety of a wall to await the end of the dance.

She gazed around, vulnerable and on edge. There must be over a hundred people here and, although the collection of invitations at the door was intended to prevent any uninvited guests from gaining access, the glazed doors along one side of the ballroom all stood open, making the house freely accessible from the garden. At that moment a chimney sweep and a Turkish sultan staggered in through the doors, arm in arm, and kissed passionately before disappearing into the crowd. Was one of them a lady? Or was…? Harriet swallowed, feeling suddenly very naive and very uncomfortable.

This was foolish. She must return to the Stantons. On the brink of plunging back through the crowd, she saw him again, walking from the dance floor, his erstwhile partner nowhere in sight. His gaze passed over her, halted and returned. She felt stripped bare by his perusal, but there was no spark of recognition in his eyes, and that gave her the courage to smile at him, hoping he might ask her to dance. He smiled in response, and moved on. To talk to Queen Elizabeth. Harriet felt the smile freeze on her lips. This was not going to plan. She should forget the whole thing straight away and return to the Stantons.

She had no sooner left the relative safety of the wall than a hand caught hers from behind. She whirled round, tugging her hand free as the Turk she had seen earlier swayed towards her, lips puckered.

'Come here, my little arch…archer…archer*ess*,' he slurred.

'No!' she gasped. 'I must go. My husband is—'

'Her husband is here, and is not amused,' interposed a deep voice.

The sultan took one look at the tall, dangerous-looking, stubble-jawed pirate who stood protectively by Harriet and staggered back into the crowd without a protest. A nervy sensation fluttered in Harriet's stomach. Should she? Shouldn't she? She gathered her courage in both hands. It was only a dance. For now. She need not commit to following her entire plan.

She remembered to disguise her voice, speaking with what she hoped was a passable Italian accent. 'Thank you, *signor*. Would you—?'

'You are very welcome,' Benedict said, cutting across her intended invitation to dance. 'I suggest you go and find your real husband if you do not wish to attract further unwanted advances.'

He melted back into the crowd. Indignation fired Harriet's blood. Did he not find her in the slightest bit alluring? She followed his path through the other guests, and was in time to see him disappear through the open garden door. Before she could talk herself out of it, she followed.

Chapter Fifteen

Outside, Benedict had crossed the deserted stone-flagged terrace and stood, tall and erect, at the top of a flight of steps that led down into a garden, criss-crossed by paths lit by flaming torches.

Harriet crossed the terrace to stand behind him. 'But why did you flee, *signor*?' Her voice low and husky, she slid one hand across his lower back. 'Are you pirates not bold adventurers, taking risks and facing danger as you seize and conquer?'

He tensed, then turned and smiled, slowly and sensuously, as he perused her once again from head to toe, lingering over her breasts, softly out-lined by the silky fabric of her dress.

'I was curious to see if you might follow,' he said. 'And now that we are here, allow me to haz-ard a guess.' His gaze roamed over her again, and then he leaned towards her. He pushed her gauze headdress aside and put his lips to her ear. 'If I am correct, you will owe me a forfeit.'

Shivers danced across her skin. Would he recognise her? 'What is this forfeit, *signor*?'

'Why, one that allows me to worship you, of course,' he breathed. 'What else would a poor pirate do when he meets the goddess of his dreams?'

His finger trailed from her neck to her shoulder and stroked the bare skin of her arm, barely touching her, raising gooseflesh in its wake. He circled the sensitive skin of her inner elbow and repeated the motion on her inner wrist, before taking her hand and raising it to his lips.

'The goddess of my dreams… Diana, goddess of the moon.' He fingered her headdress and she tensed, ready to whisk out of reach if he attempted to remove it. 'Tell me I am right.'

Harriet forgot to breathe, mesmerised by the magnetism of his eyes, glowing behind his mask. He moved closer, one arm encircling her waist, pulling her hard against him.

'Tell me I'm right.' Demanding now, staring down at her, so close she could feel the thunder of his heart as well as her own. They were in full view of anyone who ventured onto the terrace, but she found she did not care. No one would know her. She relaxed. She would enjoy this moment and her forfeit.

'Diana the huntress,' she said, lifting her chin, 'as well as goddess of the moon.'

'Diana the beautiful, a female deity of unfathomable depths and hidden talents.' His lips quirked. 'And were you hunting me, Diana?' His head dipped and he feathered kisses along the scant inch of skin between the top of her mask and the line of silver stars that edged her headdress. 'Was I your prey?' His lips moved on to her ear and he traced its rim with his warm tongue. 'Do you intend to slay me now that you have me in your power by moonlight?'

His lips were on her neck, tickling as he laved the sensitive spot beneath her ear. Before she knew it she was arching back over his rock-solid forearm, her entire throat exposed to the magic weaved by those lips. She clutched at his sleeves, aware of the weight of Diana's quiver as it swung free beneath her, the silver chain that crossed between her breasts taking its weight. He kissed and nibbled at her neck, then drifted down to her neckline. She gasped as he pushed aside the taut chain and probed the valley between her breasts with his tongue, desire sizzling through her.

Raucous laughter burst from the ballroom and

Benedict lifted his head to look back towards the house. Still arched over his arm, exposed to his view and to his touch, a feeling of defencelessness stole through Harriet and she battled to stop the memories of Brierley encroaching on this moment. She could not upright herself without Benedict's help and was completely at his mercy, and yet she was not afraid. And even if she *could* stand upright, she feared her legs—weak and boneless after so simple a caress—would never support her. But she had no urge to move. She wanted his hot kisses and caresses. She needed him to heal her invisible wounds. She yearned for his loving.

She ran her hands along the length of his arms and kneaded his hard biceps. Benedict's eyes glittered as his attention returned to her and a smile hovered around his lips.

'You wanted danger, my sweet goddess,' he whispered. 'You shall have it.'

He watched her intently as, slowly, he cupped her breast, rubbing her nipple with his thumb, then squeezing and kneading until moisture slicked between her thighs and her breath grew ragged.

'My goddess,' he whispered, his voice hoarse with need, then dipped his head to nip her aching nipple through the fine muslin of her gown, sending a lightning bolt streaking straight to her core.

'No corsets to contain such abundance—only the purest and silkiest of fabric permitted to caress her soft, moonlit skin.'

His arm tightened and he took her lips in a slow, drugging kiss that stole her breath. He slid his lips from hers to seek her ear.

'Will you follow, me, Diana?'

'Where?' she whispered. She would follow him anywhere. She vibrated with need.

'Wherever I choose,' he said. 'Will you follow my scent, hunt me down and slay me with the abundance and bounty of your charms?'

He caressed her breast once more, and her nipple ached for the touch of his lips. His hand slid lower, to her stomach; lower, to stroke her thigh through the sheer muslin. One finger pressed, a firm but fleeting touch between her legs, and scorching desire seared her veins.

'Yes,' she breathed.

He seized her lips again and then straightened, bringing her with him, holding her against the length of his hard frame until the strength returned to her legs. He stepped back then, and stared at her, a hint of a smile once again playing around his mouth. She absorbed his gaze, her blood racing. He backed away, down the steps towards the garden, one step at a time. He reached with one hand, long fingers beckoning, but when she went to take his hand, he backed down another step, always just out of reach.

Harriet stopped, uncertain what game he was playing. Did he want her, or did he not? Had he somehow guessed it was her?

He laughed up at her, teeth gleaming white as they caught the light from a lamp set on the terrace balustrade. 'What about your husband, goddess of my dreams?'

He does not know me. Emboldened, she descended another step. 'He…is beyond caring.' He was always beyond caring.

'Then, come, Diana—huntress, goddess of the moon, temptress and siren. Follow me of your own free will and together we will taste the ambrosia of the gods.'

He was at the base of the flight now, disappearing along a path flanked by rows of low-trimmed box. Harriet followed him, the lure of making love with Benedict—even if it turned out to be only this one time—too tempting to resist. He waited for her at a square stone-flagged area edged by taller hedges, with a raised circular pool at its centre, a place at which four paths converged.

'Look,' he whispered, glancing over his shoulder

as Harriet entered the square. 'She is beautiful, is she not? She is almost real.'

As if in a dream, Harriet crossed the square to stand by his side and they both stared into the dark, silent pool. The moon was mirrored in the water, the surface of which was so still the image seemed unlike a reflection, but real and solid, as if it had tumbled out of the sky and into the cold water where it waited, patiently, for the time it could rise again.

Benedict slid his palm to her cheek and nudged her to face him. He cradled her face, gazing deep into her eyes, his thumb tracing her lower lip. She felt a sigh escape her as he gathered her to him and claimed her lips, then his knees dipped and he scooped her up as though she were a baby, as though she weighed next to nothing. Eyes closed, she felt him move purposefully away from the pool. She stroked his jaw, his stubble grazing her palm as she pressed her mouth closer to his, her tongue probing at his lips, which parted at her prompt. She wound her arms around his neck as she melted into their kiss.

Even with eyes shut Harriet knew they were now under cover, shielded from the silver gaze of the moon and prying eyes. The noise of the ball had faded to a distant drone. She kissed Benedict fervently as he bent forward at the waist, and then he was sitting with Harriet on his knee, reclining against his arm, immersed once again in his kiss whilst his free hand roamed her body, stroking and caressing and exploring.

It wasn't enough.

She squirmed around, lips still locked to his, revelling in the hard length of his erection beneath her bottom. She pressed against it, trying to ease the ache that had been building deep inside her since the moment he had reappeared in her life.

Still not enough.

She straddled his lap—the hard surface upon which he sat unforgiving to her knees—and moulded her torso to his, cradling his face in her palms. His hands, large and hard-skinned but gentle, were beneath her skirts, skimming up her bare legs to her thighs...*there.* With an inner sigh, she tilted her hips to ease his access. Her need climbed.

It still wasn't enough.

She eased her upper body away, grabbed at the laces that tied his waistcoat, pushing it from his shoulders. She tore her lips from his to trace urgent kisses down the column of his neck to the open neck of his shirt, swirling his coarse chest hair with her tongue. Sliding back along his thighs, she reached for the fall of his trousers.

The buttons were the work of a few seconds, and she reached to set his erection free. Gripping his hard length, she bent her head. A loud groan reverberated in the night. Strong hands gripped her waist and lifted her, setting her on her feet, standing where she had just been kneeling.

She gasped, clutching at his head and sending his hat flying as she threaded her fingers through his hair. She cracked open her eyelids as Benedict snapped the chain holding her quiver and arrows and flung it aside. She could just make out they were on a bench inside a plant-festooned arbour with a thatched roof. Then all thought dissolved as a hand cupped each globe of her bottom, tilting her pelvis. Her knees trembled with the effort of keeping her upright as his hot tongue explored her moist folds, returning again and again to tease the swollen bud where frantic need burgeoned until finally overwhelming her in a starburst of ecstasy.

Her legs were made of rope. Her knees were jelly. She sank to his lap, panting, her head on his shoulder, clinging tight. But he had not finished and, as her breathing steadied and slowed, he again took hold of her by her waist and he stood up, setting her on the ground before the bench. He was bending her over, sliding her skirts up to her hips. The cool night air momentarily washed over her hot skin, then he was behind her, large hands on her hips.

Her flailing hands found the back of the bench and she gripped as her legs were forced wide, and then he entered her slowly, pushing, pushing until he was buried to the hilt and he filled her completely. He stilled. A groan whispered into the night. She waited, holding her breath, anticipating, impatient. She twitched her hips, and then he was moving with hard, powerful strokes. She braced her arms to withstand his onslaught, relishing every inch of him as she spiralled higher, racing for the moon and the stars and beyond.

As Harriet reached her second climax, Benedict abruptly withdrew to spill his seed. She slumped forward, panting, her head on her arms, knees propped against the bench seat, preventing them from buckling, every inch of her replete. Her thundering heart slowed and steadied as she drifted in a glorious haze of satiation.

Oh, how wonderful he had made her feel.

Reality intruded and Harriet's nerves began to flutter to life once more as the enormity of her deception pricked at her conscience. Would he propose when he discovered her identity? And yet… her confidence shattered as she suddenly saw, with hopeless certainty, that the only person she had deceived was herself. The plan she had agonised over was useless. How had she failed to see the flaws? Why should any man, offered sex so overtly, feel any obligation to the woman concerned? She was no virgin, and Benedict had even had the presence of mind to withdraw before his climax, ensuring that, this time at least, there would be no unwanted consequences.

Benedict. Where is he?

She peered back over her shoulder. Where had he gone? Hurriedly, she pushed herself upright and straightened her dress. Heavens, what if someone else had come and seen her there, her skirts bunched up, fully exposed? She blushed with the shame of it, and yet…there had been something gloriously wanton about the way he had taken her: controlling her and satisfying his need. But he had ensured her pleasure first—totally the opposite of the way her late husband had behaved and how he had made her feel despite, on the face of it, the acts being similar.

Had Benedict taken his pleasure and deserted her without a second thought, or would he return? Should she wait and reveal her identity, or should she melt into the moonlight? She had abandoned any hope of teasing a proposal from him. Perhaps she had not wanted to see the flaws in her plan.

Perhaps, if she was brutally honest, she had wanted an excuse to have sex with him again.

A noise alerted her a split second before a large shape appeared, silhouetted against the moonlit gardens outside the arbour. A lurch of fear gave way to relief. Benedict took her in his arms and kissed her, his lips soothing, caressing, and hope surged again, flooding her with anticipation. Would her sudden doubts prove fruitless? Did he still harbour feelings for her? Might he…possibly…offer for her after all? Her blood raced as she kissed him back, pouring her whole heart into it.

He lifted his lips from hers. 'Did you miss me?'

'Oh, yes.' She had missed him forever.

'I needed to make sure we were alone,' he said. 'I want to see you.'

Her heart rose to fill her throat. She gazed up at him, then raised her hand. She traced his lips with her finger, then slid it under the lower edge of his mask. 'And I, you.'

He clasped her wrist with gentle fingers, removing her hand from his face. 'Not that.' His voice was rough. 'Not your face. Not yet. Let us not destroy this magic yet. I want to see…'

His voice faded as he unfastened the brooch that secured her dress at her shoulder. He withdrew the pin and the fabric slipped down her naked breasts to pool at her waist, where it was held in place by the tie at her waist. With neither shift nor corset beneath her gown, her breasts were bared to him, and she revelled in the swell of his chest as he drew breath, and the way he moistened his lips as though he longed to feast. Her nipples hardened as he raised his hands almost reverently and cupped each mound, weighing them. His head dipped and he suckled first one, then the other, a deep groan rumbling in his chest.

Harriet stood still. Proud. Her head high.

As he pulled at her nipple with warm lips, his hands reached for the belt tied at her waist and loosened it. Then he put his hands to her shoulders and rotated her.

'Do not move,' he whispered in her ear, touching the tip of his tongue to her lobe, and she quivered as heady anticipation near overwhelmed her. *Again?* Her pulse quickened; her breath shortened. The belt was swiftly drawn away and her dress fell to the ground. She stepped clear, pushing it aside with her foot. He then set to work on the ribbons that fastened her petticoat at her waist, warm lips feathering the nape of her neck. Instead of allowing it to drop to the ground, he gathered her petticoat from the hem, baring her legs and her bottom.

'Lift your arms.'

She obeyed. His fingers brushed against her skin as he lifted the garment over her head and her raised arms.

'Hush. Don't move. Keep your arms like that.'

He reached around and cupped her breasts, squeezing, as he kissed and nibbled her neck and shoulder. Her legs trembled and the heat at the apex of her thighs flamed. Desperate need swept through her body again and she moaned.

'Hush.'

He swept his hands down the sides of her body, skimming the indent of her waist and the curve of her hips before returning to lightly settle at her waist.

'Turn to me now.'

His hands fell away. Harriet sucked in a deep breath and turned to face Benedict, her arms still above her head. She felt no shame. She felt no embarrassment. She felt…strong. His jaw was tight. His lips set in a firm line. He took his time, his hot gaze drifting over every inch of her exposed flesh, sparking trails of fiery need wherever it alighted, setting her pulse racing anew. Then he came to her, wrapped her in his embrace and kissed her, sensually and thoroughly.

She returned his kiss eagerly but, all too soon, he lifted his lips from hers, saying, 'I shall help you dress. You will never manage that gown by yourself.'

She was soon fully clothed and stood silently whilst Benedict straightened her headdress, awkwardness flooding her. Ought she to reveal herself, before it was too late? She dithered, unsure if it would serve any useful purpose. It had been a foolish idea, and she had not fully thought through the consequences. And she realised belatedly that he might—quite rightly—be angry with her for tricking him.

He did not speak, but she felt his fingers on the ribbons of her mask, and it loosened. She did not move, but she felt her muscles stiffen. He took the mask from her face and stepped back, the mask dangling from one finger.

There was no sharp intake of breath. No sudden tensing of his lean frame. No questioning lift of his brows.

'You knew,' she said.

'I did.' He paused, then touched her chin and traced the line of her jaw with one finger. 'And you knew, too.' He reached up and tore his own mask off. 'We both did.'

Harriet licked at suddenly parched lips. What would he do now? Was there any way to encourage him to propose? Did she have the nerve?

He leaned towards her and took her lips in a slow, thorough kiss but, other than where their mouths joined, he did not touch her. Harriet's arms lifted of their own accord to wrap around his neck, but he caught her wrists before she even touched him and gently forced her arms down to her sides.

He took his mouth from hers and stepped back, his eyes glinting with reflected moonlight. 'As the goddess of my dreams, you are perfection,' he said, his voice a deep rasp. 'But you are a mortal being, Harriet. With a mortal's weaknesses and desires. As am I. And we do not have the power to change the past.'

He bowed and walked away from her.

Chapter Sixteen

Harriet opened the letter that had just been hand delivered. It was the evening after the masquerade ball and she had neither seen nor spoken to a soul, other than her servants, since the Stantons had brought her home in the early hours. The letter bore Stanton's seal and was addressed to Harriet in Felicity's handwriting.

Dearest Harriet,

I trust your headache is much improved—I missed your company in the Park today. Eleanor and I have planned a jaunt to Richmond tomorrow! Do say you will come—it won't be the same without you. We shall travel in our carriage and the men have agreed to escort us on horseback. We leave at ten o'clock, and will drive round to collect you unless you tell me you cannot come.

Be forewarned, though, that I shall expect an unassailable excuse if you refuse!

Your friend,
Felicity Stanton
PS: I shall arrange enough food for everyone, so there will be no need for you to bring anything.

Harriet folded the letter and sighed. *The men...* Did Felicity mean just Stanton and Mr Damerel, or was Benedict included? How could she face Benedict after last night when, by the time she had followed him from the arbour and re-entered the ballroom, he had vanished? But, then again, how could she not?

The longer she left it, the more difficult it would become.

They were not even halfway to Richmond Park before Harriet deeply regretted her decision to accept Felicity's invitation. The party consisted of two carriages that conveyed those ladies who chose not to ride, plus several gentlemen and ladies on horseback, Benedict amongst them. She had thought seeing Benedict in company with others would ease the awkwardness of the situation.

Instead, for her, it had heightened her discomfort. She noted, however—whenever his horse ranged within sight of the carriage window—that it appeared to affect him not one jot. He had greeted her pleasantly, with not even a flicker of awareness of what so recently had passed between them, and had ridden for much of the journey in company with Barbara Barrington and one of her daughters.

Flames of jealousy had licked through Harriet's veins until she was on fire with the need to jump out of the carriage and confront him. But of course she could not. She would not. She must just swallow her disappointment and her hurt and continue with her life as she had always done. Then Felicity and Eleanor started to talk—again—about children. And, once again, Harriet had battened down her anguish, smiling and nodding in the appropriate places in the conversation. The journey seemed to last for six hours, let alone two.

Servants had been sent ahead of the main party and, by the time they arrived, had set out chairs, rugs and blankets and were ready to serve refreshing drinks and snacks. The sun beat down from a cloudless sky and most of the ladies settled in the shade, under the spreading branches of three huge oaks, whilst the gentlemen dismounted, handed their horses to the care of the three grooms who had also ridden ahead, discarded their jackets in deference to the heat and threw themselves down onto blankets.

Harriet had always loved the easy, informal atmosphere of picnicking but was quite unable to relax today, particularly with Benedict in her direct line of sight, sprawled at his ease next to Matthew and Eleanor. At least, now that there were others within hearing, Felicity and Eleanor had ceased to chatter about babies but for Harriet the damage had been done—the memory of her daughter and her despair at her loss were firmly centre stage amongst the countless issues that buzzed unendingly through her thoughts.

She sipped her lemonade and tried to join in the general chat, her eyes burning with the effort of stemming her tears. Benedict's occasional deep rumble vibrated through her until every nerve in her body felt as tightly strung as a piano wire. Her gaze kept wandering to him, despite her efforts to concentrate on others. His chiselled jaw, clean shaven today...those broad shoulders...his trim waist and those long, lean legs encased in skin-tight buckskin and highly polished top boots.

'Are you all right, Harry?'

Harriet jumped at the quiet question. Stanton had

moved to sit next to her without her even noticing. She felt a flush rise from her neck to heat her face.

'Yes, of course I am,' she replied, a little sharper than she intended. She *would* be all right, as long as nobody offered her any sympathy.

'Hmm, if you say so. Would you like some more lemonade?'

'Yes. No. Thank you, but I think, if you will excuse me, I shall take a short walk. Sitting in the carriage for so long has turned me into a fidget.' She smiled at him, determined to allay any concerns he had about her.

'Would you like some company?'

'I think that would be a bad idea, in view of those rumours,' Harriet said, keeping her voice low in case anyone should overhear. 'Have you heard any more?'

'No, but no one is likely to say anything to my face, are they? Don't fret about them, my dear. They will soon die down.'

Stanton's contented gaze was on Felicity as he spoke. Clearly the rumours gave him no cause for concern, but then *he* had no need to worry— a man of his power and connections could not be harmed by rumour and innuendo. Unlike Harriet. She longed to believe him but she knew the workings of the *ton*. People wanted to winkle out the truth, and some people would not rest until they did.

Harriet bent her knees, ready to stand up, and Stanton rose smoothly to his feet and offered his hand to help. Once upright, Harriet shook out her skirts and then, about to thank him, she caught the significant look that passed between Lady Fenton and Barbara Barrington. The meaning of that look was simple to interpret, their interpretation of Stanton's gentlemanly gesture all too clear. If she had been Felicity or Eleanor, no one would think twice about him assisting her but, because she was a widow and therefore always viewed with some suspicion by married ladies, they would happily think the worst of her, despite her best efforts to keep scandal from her door.

'Thank you,' she murmured to Stanton, careful not to meet his gaze in case he recognised her distress.

'If you will not allow me to escort you, please ensure you do not wander out of sight,' Stanton said. 'Better still, take a maid with you.'

'I shall only walk down to the brook,' Harriet said. It was only about two hundred yards away. 'I promise I shall not go out of sight.'

She opened her parasol, angling it to shade her head from the sun, and walked down the slope towards the stream, feeling the tears come, helpless to stop them. Despite her friends—and she knew how lucky she was to have them—and despite Fanny and the children, she had never felt more alone in her life. She had no one to confide in. No one, apart from Janet and Edward, even knew about her baby. And even if they did know, surely they would think her mad for still grieving when so many babies and children tragically died in infancy. Her baby hadn't even taken one breath.

She had always prided herself on her self-control and yet lately it appeared to have deserted her. She sniffed, then reached into her reticule for a handkerchief, blew her nose and dabbed at her face, sucking in deep, calming breaths. She must tuck those horrid memories away again and be happy for her friends and their families. And she must continue to hold her head high, or those blasted rumours would keep gaining momentum, Edward would eventually hear them, and then being childless would be the least of her worries. She was sure she hadn't imagined that exchanged look between Lady Fenton and Barbara Barrington when Stanton had singled her out. Sick apprehension churned her stomach. All she could do was continue to ignore the gossip and hope people soon moved on to the next *on dit*.

And as for Benedict… A self-deprecating laugh huffed from her lips. How foolish and how naive she had been to think he might provide the answer to her prayers. He had not done so in the past and he appeared disinclined to do so now. The trouble was…she still wanted him. How would she bear it when he found a wife? But yet again, bear it she must. She hauled in a shaky breath, crouched down on the bank, dabbled her fingers in the cool, clear water of the brook and then patted her face with her wet hand.

There. That is better. I must stop all this self-pity. I shall return—

A shadow fell across her and she looked round and up, startled but not scared, for she was still in sight of the rest of the party. Benedict. Somehow she had known it would be. She straightened, and he cupped her elbow to steady her as she did so.

'This is a pleasant spot, is it not?' he said. 'It is most refreshing to get out of London. I had an urge to explore. As did you, I see.'

'Indeed.' She gestured in the direction of the picnic party, avoiding his gaze. 'I must return to the others.'

'Harriet…?' Benedict nudged her chin up with one finger. His eyes grew intent as they explored her face. He frowned. 'Have you been crying?'

'I… No! Why should I cry?' Something akin to panic coursed through her. He must not guess how vulnerable she felt. She could not cope with probing questions right now. 'If my eyes are red it is because they watered in the sunlight.'

Benedict rubbed at his jaw, glancing back to the trees where the others rested and then down at Harriet's open parasol, lying on the bank where she had placed it when she'd crouched to reach the water.

'Is it because of what happened the other night?'

'No! Why should something so trivial cause me to cry?'

She could not bear for him to think she was upset over him. She tilted her chin and started to walk back to the oaks.

She's lying. She has to be lying. Trivial indeed.

As Benedict watched Harriet walk away she paused, glancing back over her shoulder.

'Well?' she said. 'Are you going to offer me your arm up the hill?'

He retrieved her parasol—white with a blue ribbon trim to match her muslin dress and her bonnet—caught up with her and proffered his arm. Her eyes, their violet colour accentuated in the sunlight, exuded nonchalance and her brows were raised in haughty entitlement. But the still-pink tip of her nose and her puffy lids told their own story, and his gut clenched at the thought of her going off on her own to cry but he quelled his natural sympathy. Her tears could only, surely, be that her plan to shame him into offering for her had not worked. He understood enough about her situation to know that if Brierley carried out his threat to stop her allowance she would have no choice but to remarry. And he also understood that he would prove a familiar and convenient choice for that role.

She had wanted nothing to do with him—they would be casual acquaintances, she had said—until those rumours had begun to circulate in earnest.

He could see it with absolute clarity, looking back. She knew there was a risk Brierley would hear the stories sooner or later so she had considered her options and seen Benedict as her best bet. He could pinpoint the moment her attitude had changed—at the Barringtons' rout party, after he had challenged her about having a lover and had then come across her and Stanton out on the terrace. He had suspected at the time that she was up to something. And he had been right.

Then…at the masquerade…*she* had pursued *him*. He had known her at first glance, and he knew she had recognised him. She had deliberately pursued him and allowed herself to be thoroughly seduced. His anger and his jealousy had driven him to ignore his conscience and take what she had offered, after which, no doubt, she fully expected him to make an honest woman of her. She had been mistaken. He was not so green, nor so soft, as to fall for her game. He had taken her and then he had walked away, vowing to have nothing more to do with her.

His every instinct had rebelled against being used in such a way and even though, having tasted her again, he still wanted her—desperately—he could never, ever trust her. She had married for riches before, and now she had targeted him for his wealth. Whilst he knew his wealth would be a lure for any girl he courted, with Harriet those old wounds ran too deep. He could not live every day for the rest of his life with the knowledge that he was only good enough for her now that he had wealth. Her betrayal would eat away at him and they would never be content together.

'Why are you upset, if it is not about the other night? Is it Brierley? Has he threatened you again?'

'I have not seen Edward. He is out of town on business and not due back until Kitty's ball next week.'

'That doesn't answer my question.'

Her lips firmed and she remained silent, her nose in the air, face averted.

Anger made him rash. 'Did you expect me to offer for you? Was that your plan? It would never work, you know.'

He regretted the words the instant he had spoken them but by then it was too late. High colour washed over Harriet's cheekbones and her eyes flashed.

'You flatter yourself, sir.' She spoke the words through gritted teeth, her voice low as it vibrated with fury. 'It meant nothing, and I harbour no inclinations in *that* direction, I promise you. Why did you follow me today if you have such a low opinion of me? It was clearly not from concern as to my well-being. If it was your intention to humiliate me with your insinuations and accusations, you may rest assured you have succeeded admirably.'

She snatched her hand from his arm but revealed no further hint of agitation as she walked away. She settled onto a blanket, next to a few other ladies who had already begun to eat their picnic luncheon, exchanging a few words with those nearest to her. Was it his imagination, or did that woman dressed in green—he racked his brain... Lady Fenton, that was it—twist her shoulders to casually exclude Harriet from her conversation? Were those rumours about Harriet and Stanton—true or not—the cause?

Benedict crossed to the other side of the group and sat down next to Matthew and Eleanor, where he could keep a surreptitious eye on Harriet.

'Harriet looks very charming today, does she not, Benedict?' Eleanor said as soon as the maids serving their food had moved out of earshot.

'Indeed she does,' he said. Harriet always looked charming to him, but he wasn't fool enough to say that to Eleanor.

'You have known one another a long time,' Eleanor continued. 'Were you *close* friends when you were young?'

'Ellie...' Matthew's voice held a wealth of warning.

Benedict switched his attention to his friend's wife—and narrowed his eyes as he took in her wide-eyed, innocent expression.

'We played together when we were children,' he said, as repressively as he could.

Eleanor smiled, a knowing sort of smile that set Benedict's teeth on edge. He picked up a portion of pie from his plate and bit viciously into it, pretending he could not hear Matthew chiding Eleanor for being inquisitive.

He was careful not to watch Harriet overtly but, as he ate and drank, he pondered her final diatribe. Why *had* he followed her down to the brook? He had known nothing good could come of any private exchange; his anger, his pain at being so cynically used and his sheer need were all too raw. The conclusions he had come to did nothing to vindicate him. She was right. He *had* wanted to provoke a reaction from her. When she had walked away from the picnic group on her own, he had seen his chance and he had taken it.

He had succeeded in humiliating her and he was ashamed, vowing to avoid being alone with her in future. Nothing good could come of it and—if those rumours about Stanton were beginning to grow claws—he would be wise to keep his distance if he was serious about finding a suitable wife.

Chapter Seventeen

The following Wednesday, Harriet walked along Pall Mall with Fanny and Kitty, heading for Harding, Howell and Company, the linen draper. It was the day before Kitty's come-out ball and Harriet's step-granddaughter bubbled with anticipation. Harriet tried her best to share in the excitement, but found it hard to garner much enthusiasm for anything. Her worst fears had come to pass—since the day of the picnic, her name was being linked more and more with the Earl of Stanton's and, increasingly, she intercepted sidelong glances and walked in on whispered conversations that were suddenly cut short. Edward was still out of town on business and so had not yet heard the rumours, and Fanny had said nothing, although could she really fail to be aware of them? Edward was due to return home this evening and Harriet was by now convinced it was only a matter of time before he carried out his threat. Her nerves were in shreds as a result.

'Oh, I cannot wait until tomorrow,' Kitty said, oblivious to her mother's attempts to shush her. 'Papa said someone of *particular consequence* is to lead me out in my very first dance. Do *you* know who he might be, Grandmama? Mama knows, but she will not tell me. It is to be a surprise.'

'Well, if it is to be a surprise, Kitty, I could hardly tell you, even if I did know,' Harriet said. 'Or it would no longer be a surprise and your papa would, quite rightly, be very cross with me.'

'Papa is *always* cross,' Kitty said, swinging her reticule.

'Katherine!' Fanny caught hold of her daughter's arm. 'Do stop throwing your arms around. You are supposed to be a young lady, not a child of seven. And do not speak of your papa in such a way. It is most unbecoming. He has much on his mind.'

Fanny's gaze flicked to Harriet's face, and Harriet felt a blush build from her neck. How much had Edward confided in Fanny about Harriet's visit to Tenterfield Court? She appeared as warm as ever when she was with Harriet but what, deep down, was she thinking?

'Your mama is right, Kitty. If you are not to sully your reputation, your behaviour must be exemplary at all times.' She felt her cheeks begin to burn, half her mind on her own behaviour and those dratted rumours. She felt a hypocrite, but she still needed to help guide young Kitty. 'There is nothing more likely to set tongues wagging than inappropriate behaviour in a young lady,' she went on, 'or, for that matter, unbecomingly forthright opinions.'

Kitty subsided but soon perked up when she spied her particular friend, Lady Olivia Beauchamp, perusing the display in the draper's window.

'May I go and speak with Olivia, Mama?'

'Of course,' Fanny said. As soon as Kitty was out of earshot, Fanny whispered, 'It is Lord Wincott. He and Edward have come to an agreement—Kitty and his lordship are to be betrothed before the end of the Season.'

Harriet's heart sank. 'Wincott? But…is he not rather *old* for Kitty?'

Fanny stiffened. 'He is but two and thirty,' she said. 'I should not call that old.'

Harriet had thought him older. 'He is a little staid, surely, for a girl as lively as Kitty. Is she happy with the match?'

'She does not know yet. We thought it best for them to get to know each other slowly. But it is a splendid match. He is a most moral, God-fearing man and you cannot argue with his consequence. He is wealthy, titled and his estates run alongside the land I brought to Edward as my dowry, so they can form part of the marriage settlement. That is where Edward is now, touring the estates with Wincott. And, politically, the alliance between the Brierleys and the Wincotts will be advantageous. Kitty will be thrilled when Wincott leads her out for her first dance. A marquess, no less! That is quite a coup for a seventeen-year-old.'

Harriet realised there was nothing she could say, no influence she could bring to bear. She would end up alienating Fanny, and that was the last risk she felt able to take. Poor Kitty—so open and loving, married to a pompous prig like Wincott. He was a man of a similar stamp as Edward—no doubt that was why both Edward and Fanny deemed it a good match. Harriet swallowed her indignation on behalf of Kitty. It was said that girls were happiest with men who reminded them of their fathers, so perhaps she was worrying over nothing. Fanny had stopped talking and was watching Harriet expectantly. What had she said? Harriet thought rapidly—something about Kitty's first dance.

'I am sure she will be proud to be led out by his lordship,' Harriet said, keen to smooth Fanny's ruffled pride, 'for not only does he have a most impressive title, but he is also a delightfully elegant dancer, I recall. In fact, I wonder if I might persuade him to stand up with me—a lady cannot help but show to advantage with such an accomplished partner and, as a grandmother, I fear I need all the help I can get.'

'Oh, Harriet, what nonsense—you always look beautiful, on or off the dance floor.'

'At the risk of a set-down, I second that,' interposed an amused voice. 'And if he, whoever he is, is fool enough to pass you over as a partner, then I shall be delighted to stand in his stead.'

Harriet spun on her heel. Benedict was right behind her. She could not quite meet his eyes as she tried to quash her surge of embarrassment triggered by their first meeting since the picnic, when they had not exchanged another word after their quarrel. His final words to her still stung—what a fool she had been to even hope he would contemplate marrying an impoverished widow when he might have his pick of well-born innocents. Since then she had tried to banish him from her thoughts but it had proved nigh on impossible.

'I think you will find, sir, that you are not invited,' she said tartly.

He grinned at her, his eyes glinting. 'And a very good afternoon to you, too, Lady Brierley. Please accept my abject apologies for eavesdropping and for having the audacity to interrupt your conversation.'

He bowed before glancing enquiringly at Fanny. Harriet gritted her teeth; of all the bad luck, bumping into Benedict when she was out with Fanny and Kitty. What if one of them mentioned it to Edward? Her nerves wound a little tighter and she glared at Benedict, trying to convey a warning with her eyes even as her heart pounded at the mere sight of him. His gaze flickered in her direction before he turned his attention back to Fanny.

Harriet sighed, recognising she had no choice. 'Sir Benedict Poole, might I introduce you to my stepdaughter-in-law, Frances, Lady Brierley.'

'Honoured, my lady.' Benedict bowed to Fanny.

'Sir Benedict! It is a pleasure to make your acquaintance. Why, we are almost neighbours. Of course you must come to Kitty's ball, sir—I have no doubt Brierley was unaware of your presence in town or he would have made sure your name was on the list.'

'Fanny, I do not think Edward—'

'I shall send you an invitation as soon as I return home, sir, for the ball is tomorrow night, and single gentlemen are always most welcome. I do so hope you are free?'

Harriet fixed Benedict with a look that she was sure contained the direst warning she could muster, but he studiously ignored her, his lips curving in a smile as he said, 'Oh, yes. I am free. Thank you, my lady.'

'Fanny...' Harriet seethed with a mix of anger and fear. Once Edward returned home and got wind of those rumours, Benedict's presence at Kitty's ball could only make matters worse. 'Perhaps you should not. Not without Edward—'

'Oh, Edward leaves all those decisions to me, my dear. There is no need to worry. We have plenty of room. Now, let us continue our shopping, for I simply must find some ribbon to trim my puce bonnet.'

They took their leave of Benedict. There was no help for it; all she could now do was try to avoid Benedict at the ball. Although whether even that would prove enough when Edward heard those rumours... Sick dread swirled her stomach. She was effectively trapped. Sooner or later, Edward's axe would fall and, in the meantime, she had no choice but to continue her life with a smile upon her face.

The time for Kitty's debut into society arrived. Elegant in her white gown, her dark hair fashioned in the Grecian style and threaded through with pearls, she was the belle of the ball as the Marquess of Wincott led her onto the ballroom floor into the top position for the first dance. Harriet's heart swelled with love and pride and Fanny, standing by Harriet's side, had tears in her eyes.

Edward's greeting had been noticeably chilly when Harriet had arrived earlier, and she was already halfway convinced that he was merely biding his time, waiting until Kitty's ball was over before confronting Harriet over the gossip.

Benedict had not yet arrived, to her relief. She prayed he would see sense and stay away—he must know Edward would not welcome him and that his presence would stir up trouble for Harriet. Or was that his intention? Did he want to punish her for the masquerade? Well, he need not think she had forgiven him for what he had said at the picnic, even though it was the truth. To accuse her so bluntly was inexcusable—definitely not the behaviour expected of a gentleman.

I'm better off without him!

Oh, but she could not help but feel a fool, knowing that Benedict was fully aware of her pathetic and sordid plan.

How he must have laughed at me!

She kept an eye on the late arrivals—constantly checking to see if Benedict appeared, her nerves all on edge—as Lord Wincott, slender and elegant in his evening clothes, bowed to Kitty and the rest of the dancers began to take their places in the set. As the dance progressed, a movement in the guests standing nearby diverted Harriet's attention from Kitty, and she turned to see Felicity and Eleanor both smiling at her.

'Harriet! Where have you been since we went to Richmond?' Felicity said. 'Have you been away?'

'No, but I have been busy helping my stepdaughter prepare for tonight.'

It was a white lie. She had not been involved at all with the preparations for Kitty's come-out ball, apart from yesterday's shopping trip with Fanny and Kitty, but had hidden away at home, feeling a fool, consumed with embarrassment that Benedict had guessed why she had seduced him at the masquerade and sick with worry over her future.

'Lady Katherine looks stunning,' Felicity said, watching as Kitty and Wincott performed their steps. 'And the room is beautifully decorated. Does it feel strange, seeing another family living here, when it used to be your home? I do not mean to pry, but I do sometimes wonder how Richard's mother must feel, to see me installed as mistress at Fernley Park whilst she lives at the Dower House.'

Harriet gazed around the ballroom—the walls

had been draped with swags of silver gauze and palest pink silk and large vases of artfully arranged pink flowers and delicate ferny foliage adorned the side tables placed at intervals along the long wall opposite the tall, imposing windows. The house had never looked so fine when Harriet had been mistress here.

'No,' she said. It was the truth. This had never been her home. And she had never, in reality, been mistress here. 'I prefer my little house in Sackville Street, if I am honest.'

'I can understand that,' Eleanor said. 'If anything happened to Matthew...why, I can imagine how painful it would be to continue living in the house where we had lived together. Even though Ashby Manor was my childhood home, I'm sure the ghosts would haunt me every day.'

As they haunt me, Harriet thought, barely controlling her shiver. At least Eleanor would have happy memories to sustain her. A hand touched her arm. It was Felicity, her amber eyes full of understanding. It had remained an unspoken agreement between Harriet and Felicity that they would never talk about the past, but she knew Stanton must have explained something of Harriet's marriage to Brierley. Felicity had managed to convey, without words, both her sympathy and her acceptance of what had gone before.

Harriet knew how fortunate she was to have Felicity for a friend and she was uncomfortably aware that, were she a true friend in return, she would be delighted that Felicity was with child, not jealous. She looked at the other two women. Felicity was positively glowing, as was Eleanor. Harriet buried her twinge of regret; she remembered all too well that bloom: the glossy hair, the clear skin, the shining eyes—even though hers had been diminished by Benedict's desertion and the nightmare of her marriage to Brierley.

'You are both looking so beautiful,' she said on impulse. 'And so radiantly happy.'

Felicity blushed. 'Thank you, Harriet, but beautiful is hardly—'

'Now then, Felicity Joy,' came a deep voice from behind Harriet. 'Do I hear you denigrating yourself again? Come, my *beautiful* wife, dance with me while we still can.'

Harriet watched Stanton whisk Felicity onto the ballroom floor, where sets were now forming for a country reel. She knew what his words meant—Felicity had already confided in her that they would leave town before her pregnancy began to show, and that must surely be soon. But… She turned anxiously to Eleanor.

'Do you think it is safe, Felicity taking part in such an energetic dance in her condition?'

Eleanor tore her attention from the couples on the floor. 'Trust her to know what she is capable of,' she said. 'It is an odd thing. Everyone seems determined to protect us and wrap us up safely and yet—and I know I speak for Felicity as well—we have never felt so alive.'

'I remember the feeling,' Harriet replied. Although no one had protected her. Her throat thickened.

'You?' Eleanor's voice rose in astonishment.

Harriet cursed her unthinking comment. No one knew, apart from her immediate family. She searched for words to divert Eleanor, but none would come.

'I do beg your pardon,' Eleanor carried on, 'but I had no idea… That is, I had not realised… Oh, heavens, here I go making things worse. I shall just say what I was going to say in the first instance. I did not know you had ever had a child, Harriet.'

Harriet felt the other woman's gaze on her and she averted her face, her eyes suddenly moist. She felt Eleanor take her hand. 'I'm sorry,' she said. 'Matthew always tells me I must think before I speak, and now I have upset you and I truly had no notion of doing so.'

Harriet shook her head. 'It is quite all right,' she said.

A glass of wine was thrust into her hand and she took a grateful sip.

'Would you care to sit somewhere quiet?' Eleanor asked. 'I am sorry—our excitement must bring it all back to you. It is odd, is it not, that something so natural and everyday as procreation should become so utterly absorbing when it is happening to you. And, of course,' she added, glancing around at the people close to them, 'a subject *never* to be mentioned in polite company.' She smiled her wide, infectious smile. 'I believe it is safe to say both Felicity and I have abjectly failed in *that* endeavour!'

Harriet dragged in a deep breath and tried to force a smile in return, grateful to Eleanor for trying to smooth over her emotional reaction. She read nothing but sympathy and contrition in the other woman's open, honest expression.

'I am fine now, thank you, Eleanor. And please do not think I am not delighted for you both, for I am. I...I lost my baby before she was born. But it was a long time ago now. You caught me at a vulnerable moment, with the excitement of

Kitty's come-out and realising my daughter would never…never…'

Eleanor slipped her arm around Harriet's waist and guided her to a chair at the side of the ball-room. 'Come,' she whispered. 'Drink your wine, and then dance the night away. Keep yourself so busy you will have no time to remember.'

Harriet pushed down her misery. This was not like her. She never dwelt on the past. She looked forward, not back.

Until Benedict came back into your life.

Angrily, she dismissed that voice. She would not disintegrate into a feeble, weeping woman, partic-ularly not in front of a strong lady like Eleanor. A strong, *kind* lady, she realised. She had reserved judgement about this new friend of Felicity's at first, but now she could see her true qualities. Many other women would have pried and poked and then rushed to spread the latest *on dit* amongst their acquaintances. Harriet recalled the whispers of scandal that had followed Eleanor when she had come to London the previous spring, and she knew she could trust the other woman not to gos-sip about her.

A figure appeared before her. Mr Stephen Damerel—Matthew's brother—begging her hand for the next dance, which was just forming. On the brink of refusing him, she hesitated. She could not spend her life skulking in a corner. Benedict had not appeared—perhaps, with luck, he would stay away.

She smiled at Eleanor. 'Thank you. You are right. I shall make sure to enjoy myself,' she said as she accepted Mr Damerel.

He whisked her into the dance, closely followed by three other partners. As the last of the three led her from the floor, Richard, Lord Stanton, was bowing before her. Harriet laughed up at him, her hand to her chest.

'I need a chance to catch my breath, Stanton.' She dare not risk fuelling the gossip by dancing with him. 'If you care to procure me a glass of wine, you may consider your duty done and return to your wife.'

'It is not duty, and you know that very well, Harry.'

'Maybe not.' She lowered her voice. 'It cannot be wise for us to be seen together like this, not with these rumours. They have me in such a fever of apprehension—who could have started them? Nobody knew about us. We were so discreet.'

Stanton snorted. 'My loose-tongued cousin, that's who. He confessed all last night.'

'Charles? But…but why would he do such a

thing? I thought he was my friend, and I know he would not wish to harm you or Felicity.'

'Oh, he didn't mean any harm, but you know Charles—he *never* means any harm, but he just cannot help himself at times. It seems he overheard someone expressing surprise at my choice of bride and—in an attempt to defend Felicity and before he knew what was happening—he managed to let slip that I'd had a close liaison with a very comely widow up until our wedding.' He sighed. 'You know what people are like, Harry. Once the rumour hatched it soon sprouted wings and now a load of nonsense is being passed around as fact. All we can do is ride it out. There'll soon be another scandal to take its place.'

'But my name is already being linked to yours.'

'Don't worry. No one can prove it. We did nothing wrong. And if anyone is ill-bred enough to ask outright…why, we shall simply deny it. If Felicity does not object, why should anyone else?'

Harriet bit her lip. She was tempted to confide in Stanton about Edward and his threats but pride forced her to keep quiet. It was her problem and she must deal with it. Although heaven knew how, now it was clear Benedict—who had finally arrived—would never offer for her. Every time she caught sight of him, he appeared to be glowering in her direction. Was it his intention to punish her for her ill-judged attempt to seduce him into making an offer? If so, he was succeeding. What a complete fool she had been.

She sipped at her wine, quietly despairing as she pondered her future.

Chapter Eighteen

She hadn't stopped dancing since he arrived, other than when she had been with Stanton, in what appeared to be yet another intimate conversation.

Benedict strolled moodily around the edge of the ballroom, trying, unsuccessfully for the most part, to keep his attention from wandering to Harriet too often. She sparkled. She was radiant. Her smile brightened the entire room. He *hated* the fortunate fellows who were the recipients of that glorious smile.

Begrudged them.

Deeply.

You're supposed to be searching for a wife.

Hmph! He'd already cast his eye over the young ladies at the ball. There wasn't one of them could hold a candle to Harriet.

She betrayed you. She didn't love you enough to

wait for you. How could you ever trust her? And don't forget Stanton.

Whenever he thought of Harriet with the earl the sharp claws of jealousy raked at his insides until he was ready to roar his rage. The gossip claiming it was Harriet who had been Stanton's mistress was more widespread than ever. Yet when *he* had been about to suggest a similar arrangement she had not even allowed him to speak. Once again, Harriet had chosen another man in preference to him, until she had seen him as the answer to her predicament. Well, he had seen through her game. He had taken what she offered, and he had walked away.

Except…except…it hadn't quite worked out as he had planned. His desire for her was stronger than ever and he feared it was likely to continue to plague him until such time as he wed. Then, surely, his focus would be on his own family and he could pack her back inside the box in his mind where she had lain undisturbed for so many years.

So what was he doing here?

He raked suddenly nervous fingers through his hair, the thought that it needed cutting randomly flitting through his mind. Why *was* he here? Was he so weak-willed that a week without seeing her or speaking to her was too much for him? He had spotted her in the street and, before he could question his motives or think through the consequences, he had inveigled an invitation to the ball tonight, despite knowing Brierley would object.

He glanced around but saw no sign of his host. He had deliberately come late, not wishing to stand in line to be greeted by the Brierleys and their daughter and thus afford Brierley an opportunity to refuse him entry. He had timed his arrival after the dancing had started, when the butler's stentorian announcement of his name had struggled to be heard above the music and the babble of conversation. Since then, he had taken care not to wander too close to his host. If Brierley tried to have him thrown out, Benedict was not sure he would be able to control his temper—which teetered on a knife-edge these days—and that would not bode well for his goal of overcoming Sir Malcolm's legacy of scandal.

'Sir Benedict, I am delighted you were able to come.'

Benedict closed his eyes briefly as he recognised the voice of his hostess. Perhaps Brierley would not...but no. One glance at Lady Brierley revealed a glowering Lord Brierley behind her. So much for his manoeuvrings to avoid the man.

Brierley barrelled forward. 'You were not invited, sir.'

Benedict held tight to the reins of his temper.

'Brierley, do not say so. *I* invited Sir Benedict.' Lady Brierley raised her anxious gaze to her husband.

Brierley's focus remained on Benedict. 'When did you do so? And where?'

'Why—' his lady faltered '—it was yesterday. When Kitty and I were out shopping.'

'Yesterday…when you were with my stepmother?'

'Why, yes, she is an old friend of—' Lady Brierley's eyes sharpened. She drew herself up to her full height and said, 'It makes no matter, sir, for the deed is now done. I did not know… If you had only confided in me…but there. It is of no use now. Come, we have our duties as hosts to attend to— will you spoil your own daughter's come-out by quarrelling with a guest?'

Benedict held his breath, hoping he was not about to witness a full-blown marital dispute, but Brierley—after a quick glance around the ballroom— said, 'Very well. I can see I have no choice.' He glared at Benedict. 'Enjoy the ball, sir. Come, my dear, we must not neglect our other guests.'

Benedict watched the man scan the dancers as they walked away. When the dance came to an end, Brierley headed straight for Harriet, took her arm and spoke quickly into her ear. Harriet gave no sign of what he said, but her gaze roamed the room until it settled briefly on Benedict. She replied to her stepson, a pink tinge colouring her cheeks, who then walked away from her. Her partner had already disappeared, and Harriet made her way across the ballroom to Benedict.

'So you came.' Her voice was low with accusation.

Benedict forced a careless shrug as he faced her. 'I was invited,' he said. 'It struck me as being the perfect place to meet suitable young ladies.'

'So it is. I wish you luck.'

'I am surprised you can risk being seen speaking to me.'

Her eyes glittered as she stared up at him. She looked so beautiful—almost edible in shimmering rose-pink silk clinging provocatively to her lush curves—that he itched to take her in his arms there and then and hang the consequences. Except that would hardly help his quest for the perfect society bride. It was funny how he kept losing sight of that fact—or it would be if he could find anything vaguely amusing these days.

'Edward already knows you are here. The damage is done. I came to beg you to leave—it is unfair on Kitty to court trouble on the biggest night of her life.'

Anger smouldered deep inside him. 'I am not interested in courting trouble,' he growled. 'I am simply eager to secure my future.'

'Then, I suggest you begin by engaging at least *one* of the young ladies present to dance,' Harriet spat. 'For it seems to me that every time I see you, you are staring at *me*. Or perhaps it is your intention to cause strife between my stepson and me?'

'You flatter yourself, madam,' he said, and bowed before stalking off.

His insides churned—in turmoil, as they always were in Harriet's presence. He needed to catch his breath and calm the battle between desire and distrust raging deep within his heart. He gritted his teeth and kept walking. He had a mission to accomplish: the search for a bride. And, however much he might desire Harriet, he would never ask her to marry him.

One betrayal was enough.

As he strolled around the perimeter of the ballroom, he caught sight of Miss Marstone standing with her mother and several other young ladies. He stifled a sigh. He must start somewhere and, as he was already acquainted with Lady Marstone, she would be bound to introduce him to the other girls. Pasting a smile on his face, he joined the group.

'Good evening, Sir Benedict, how gallant of you to join us, for I was beginning to wonder where all the young gentlemen were hiding.' Lady Marstone was positively beaming. 'Of course, you are already acquainted with my Bridget, are you not?'

Miss Marstone smiled up at him through her lashes: a far too seductive smile for an innocent young lady. Benedict wondered how innocent she actually was. He should know how easy it was to seduce such a girl—

Hell and damnation! Why does she keep invading my thoughts? Then he hesitated, thinking back over the words that had run unbidden through his mind. *He* had seduced *Harriet*. She was a year younger than he; she had barely known what was happening until it was too late—how had he never thought of what had happened from her point of view before?

Because you were too busy being bitter that she betrayed you by marrying Brierley.

And she *had* betrayed him, there was no denying it. They had pledged their love, but she had been seduced all over again—not by lovemaking but by wealth and a title, according to Malcolm. She hadn't been prepared to wait until Benedict inherited; she had wanted instant riches and the easy life they would bring her. Well… He came to with a start, finding himself the focus of several pairs of eyes watching him curiously.

'I do beg your pardon,' he said, smiling his most charming smile. 'I was overcome with the enormity of so much beauty and elegance in one place.' He cringed inwardly at those words—which elicited a trill of giggles—but it was expected that gentlemen should charm and flatter the ladies of the *ton*, and he was now part of this world. A surge of homesickness for the simplicity of his former life swept through him. He ignored it and continued, 'Good evening, Lady Marstone, Miss Marstone. Would you do me the honour of introducing me to the other young ladies?'

Lady Marstone began the introductions and Benedict soon became aware of the irritable looks Miss Marstone was shooting at the other girls. Still mindful of the importance of keeping mother and daughter happy to prevent Harriet's stay at Tenterfield becoming public knowledge, he asked Miss Marstone to dance as soon as the introductions were complete. She smiled graciously, but he did not miss her darting triumphal glance at her friends.

During the movements of the dance where they

could not converse, Benedict's thoughts turned inexorably to Harriet, and to her view of their past. They had never spoken of it. She had never told him why she had wed Brierley. Had it been a love match? The man had been old enough to be her father. More than old enough, in fact, for Edward was actually several years older than both Harriet and Benedict. What had driven her to accept his offer? It could only, surely, have been greed, as Malcolm had said.

Had he not suspected that was the very reason she had pursued him at the masquerade—because of his new position? With his wealth and status, no number of threats from Brierley could hold sway. She would have that comfortable, secure life she craved but…if that was truly the case, would she not have been friendlier from the start? And why did she appear to have given up so easily?

'I declare, sir, you have such a look of contemplation upon your face I would swear you have forgotten I am here.' It was said with a pout and a coquettish look that set his teeth on edge.

'Of course I have not forgotten you, Miss Marstone,' he replied smoothly. 'How could I? I am merely concentrating on the steps. I should hate to tread on your toes.'

'Oh, la, sir. You dance very respectably for a... for a...'

'For a novice?' he suggested.

Her eyes flashed with relief. 'Precisely. Tell me, sir, have you made plans for supper? Oh!' She giggled artlessly. 'Mama *would* be shocked at my boldness, but I already feel as though you and I are old friends and can be *quite* comfortable with one another.'

'I thought a gentleman was honour bound to escort his partner for the supper dance into supper?' He knew quite well that was the custom.

'But I do not have a partner for that dance, sir, and as we have only so far had this one dance...'

He ignored her dangling invitation with relief as the dance dictated a change in partner. Were all young girls this shameless, or had he just been unlucky in meeting this one? He made a mental note to scrawl his name on some other girls' dance cards before they all filled up. And the first dance he must secure was the supper dance.

As they swapped partners again, he said, 'I regret that I am already engaged for the supper dance. Perhaps a little later in the evening?'

'Perhaps,' she replied with a toss of her dark curls.

After barely half a minute of silence, she said, 'Do you like to walk in the park, sir?'

'On occasion.'

'I *love* to walk. I should walk every day, if only Mama was strong enough.'

'Mayhap she should take the carriage,' Benedict said.

'She does, but it is hardly the same, to sit in the carriage next to my mother whilst everyone else is enjoying fresh air and exercise.' Miss Marstone sighed. 'She will only allow me to walk with my friends if there is a gentleman present. Perhaps, if we should happen to meet in the park, you might offer me your arm?'

'Perhaps.'

Making a mental note to avoid the park at all costs, Benedict led Miss Marstone back to her mother at the end of the dance and then quickly took his leave, determined to secure partners for the dances to come.

After dancing with a few young ladies and successfully engaging to partner several more, he found himself standing next to Harriet during a brief lull in the music.

She immediately turned and began to walk away, but he wrapped his fingers around her wrist, saying, 'I want to talk to you.'

Her violet eyes met his warily. 'What about?'

'Brierley.'

'Edward? What has he done?'

'Not Edward. His father.'

Her skin blanched. 'I do not wish to discuss him.' He had to strain to hear her words.

'Harriet—'

'I must go. I am promised to Mr Damerel for this dance… Ah, here he comes now.' The relief in her voice was palpable.

Benedict watched his friend lead Harriet into the dance.

'Sir Benedict?' A timid voice spoke by his side.

'Ah…' He racked his brain. 'Lady Susan, is it not?'

Lady Susan was his partner for this dance. Fair haired, pretty and shy, she had been the only one of Bridget Marstone's friends he had been in the slightest taken with. He smiled, determined to put her at her ease. 'I was just coming to find you,' he said, holding out his hand. 'Come, let us show the rest of them how it's done.'

When the dance ended he returned Lady Susan to her chaperone, then looked around. On the far side of the room he spied a familiar tall figure with a pair of wide shoulders topped by a head of dark blond hair—Matthew, with Harriet by his side. Benedict started across the dance floor, his way hindered by couples forming sets ready for the next dance. He lost sight of Matthew and Harriet for a moment and then, the next time he saw them, Matthew was standing alone. He scanned the surrounding people and caught a glimpse of Harriet slipping out of the room.

He forced his way through the rest of the throng, only to be waylaid by Miss Marstone, a coquettish smile on her face.

'Do I detect that you lack a partner for this dance, Sir Benedict?'

Swallowing an oath, Benedict halted. 'You do, Miss Marstone,' he replied, keeping a wary eye on Matthew whilst Miss Marstone, in turn, gazed at Benedict. She raised a questioning brow. *Damn.* Only a blind man would not interpret that look. 'I find myself in need of a rest,' he said, hoping she would accept his excuse. He indicated his knee. 'An old injury is playing up.'

'An injury! How fascinating.' She linked her arm through his. 'You must tell me all about it.'

'Another time.' Benedict untangled his arm from hers. Matthew had begun to move away. If he was not quick, he would lose him in the crowd. 'My apologies, Miss Marstone, but I simply must find a quiet chair and rest this leg.'

He bowed and strode away, only remembering at the last minute to mime a limp for the lady's benefit. He caught up with Matthew and tapped him on the shoulder.

'Where has Lady Brierley disappeared to?'

Matthew cocked his head to one side, giving Benedict a quizzical look. 'You appear fascinated by Lady B,' he said. He then grinned. 'Not that I can blame you. She *is* a beauty, and a widow, too, by God.'

Benedict battened down his anger. *No one* should be looking at Harriet in that way, but in particular not a man who was already happily married and setting up his nursery.

Matthew held up both hands, palms facing Benedict, fingers spread. '*Pax*, old chap. She pleaded tiredness and has gone to find a quiet spot to rest,' he said, laughing openly now, his blue eyes gently mocking. Then his expression swiftly sobered. 'What is it, Ellie? You are looking pale.'

Eleanor had joined them. Benedict thrust aside his frustration at the interruption. She did look washed out.

'I am tired, Matthew,' she said. 'Would you mind—?'

Matthew wrapped his arm around her waist. 'We are going home. Now. No arguments.'

Eleanor included Benedict in her answering smile. 'He always imagines I am going to argue,' she said. 'I cannot think why. Yes, please, I would like to go home. Goodnight, Benedict.'

'Goodnight,' Benedict said. 'I hope you feel better in the morning.'

As Matthew and Eleanor turned to go, Matthew paused. 'I believe she mentioned the library,' he said over his shoulder. 'She used to live here, you know, so she knows her way around.'

Benedict nodded his thanks and followed them out of the ballroom into the hall. A footman carrying a tray of empty glasses hurried past. Benedict caught him by the arm and only by some nifty juggling of the precariously tilting tray did the servant avert disaster.

'Which is the library?' He bit the question out, not even apologising to the poor man.

'That door there, sir,' the footman replied, jerking his head towards a door on the opposite side of the hall. He then hurried away, heading towards the rear of the house.

The library was large and imposing, lined with floor-to-ceiling shelves of books. The wall opposite the door was punctuated by three heavily curtained windows that presumably overlooked the street outside. A cursory glance revealed an empty room. Benedict frowned. There were two high wing-backed chairs flanking the unlit fire-place, but they were unoccupied.

He moved towards the table in the centre of the room. Perhaps she had changed her mind and gone elsewhere in the house. He needed to talk to her. Now. He would find out, once and for all, why she had thrown away the love they had shared for an old man like Brierley. And he would find out what lay behind her fear. A gap in the curtains covering the middle window caught his eye.

He strode across the room and wrenched the curtains apart. There, curled up on an upholstered window seat, was Harriet.

Chapter Nineteen

The sudden movement of the curtains jolted Harriet from her musings. Her heart leaped into her throat and she shot to her feet, bringing her hard up against a muscled chest. Benedict, bringing with him the familiar spicy, musky scent that was uniquely him.

'I want answers,' he said.

Her pulse raced. She did not want to answer his questions. Her life was none of his business; it was nobody's business. She wanted no interrogations, no intrusions and she wanted no pity, particularly not Benedict's. All she wanted was to feel safe.

'You should not be here,' she said. She made to push past him. 'I must go.'

'No.'

He grabbed her wrist and hauled her hard against him, then wrapped his arms around her, trapping her. Harriet gasped, wriggling in an attempt to break free.

'Stand still,' he gritted out. 'I need to know—'

She had leaned back against his arms to look up into his face. As their eyes locked, he stilled and fell silent. Harriet's mouth dried at the intensity of his stare. She licked her lips in an attempt to moisten them, and his gaze lowered to her mouth. Her heart lurched and her breathing grew ragged with her rising awareness of his arousal as it pressed against the softness of her belly. The familiar need pulsed at her core, and she felt her body prepare for lovemaking.

She swallowed, aghast at the speed with which she responded to him. Was that really all it took to arouse her? Just the thought of his kiss? The tears that never seemed far away these days threatened to surface, and her pride rebelled against allowing him to see just how vulnerable she was to his allure. She could not break free of his encircling arms and she *would not* talk to him about Brierley. But, oh, how she craved his kiss. How she needed *something* to distract her from her fears over the future, if only for a short time. That need overrode all caution and stifled all the very good reasons why this was akin to playing with fire.

She stood stock-still as he traced her neckline

with one finger. She searched his eyes, one hand on his chest, aware of the hard, fast beat of his heart as she played with his top waistcoat button until it slipped free and moved down to the next one, and the next.

'Benedict...?'

She rose on tiptoe, craving the touch of his lips. She brushed her lips over his with a feather-light touch. With a harsh groan that sounded as though it was ripped from him, his arms tightened and he took her mouth, his lips moving over hers as his tongue plunged inside, tangling with hers. She slid her arms beneath his coat, around the curve of his ribcage and then drifted lower, stroking, until her hands cupped the firm muscle of his buttocks. Heat radiated from him in waves.

I want him. Here. Now.

I cannot. I must not.

She did not push him away, despite the voice of caution in her head. She ignored it, pressed closer and wrapped her arms around his neck, melting into their kiss as she weaved her fingers through his hair.

They heard the noise at the same time and they sprang apart as the door started to open. They exchanged a look and Harriet nearly recoiled at the accusation in Benedict's eyes. *He* had followed *her*, not the other way round, although she couldn't deny she had instigated that kiss, to distract him from his questions and her from her fate. And it had worked: his waistcoat hung open rakishly and his auburn hair was ruffled.

'Hide!' Benedict whispered, pushing her back onto the padded seat.

Willingly, she thought, still smarting over that look. He dragged the curtains closed, and she was once again secreted behind the curtains where she had imagined nobody would find her. Her lips felt bruised and swollen and an errant lock of hair feathered her neck where a hairpin had been dislodged. She fumbled around for her lost pin, but could not find it, so had to be content to tuck her curl behind another pin and hope it would stay in place until she could properly repair the damage.

She heard the sound of the library door clicking shut.

'What the devil are you doing here?' It was Benedict's voice, harsh with anger. 'You should not be here… The risk to your reputation if we are seen—'

'Don't be cross with me, Benedict.' A female voice—seductive and cajoling—interrupted him.

Benedict?

Harriet inched the curtains apart and applied

one eye to the gap. Bridget Marstone was pouting at Benedict. *The little cat.* Harriet knew exactly what she was up to.

'I am tired,' Miss Marstone said with a pout as she glided towards Benedict. 'I was looking for somewhere quiet to rest.'

She stopped directly in front of him and laid one hand on his chest. On his shirtfront, inside the waistcoat that Harriet had recently unbuttoned. Possessiveness spiralled up from the depths of Harriet's being, shocking her with its intensity.

How dare she?

Benedict stepped back, the door crashed open and all hell broke loose.

Miss Marstone launched herself at Benedict—flinging her arms around his neck and pulling at him as she strove to plant her lips on his—a split second before Lady Marstone, Fanny and Edward crowded into the room.

'I told you! Unhand her, you rogue! You villain!' Lady Marstone clasped her hands to her bosom. 'My baby! My innocent girl! You shall pay for this, sir!'

Benedict untangled Miss Marstone's arms from around his neck and put her from him.

'You have ruined my darling girl.'

As Lady Marstone crossed the room to clasp her

daughter in a maternal hug, Harriet interpreted their exchanged look of conspiracy. Heedless of the consequences, she swept from her hiding place and stalked into the centre of the room.

Everyone's attention was fixed on Lady Marstone, who was still in full flow.

'You enticed my poor, innocent Bridget in here to have your wicked— *Oh!* What is *she* doing here?' Her voice rose to a shriek as she glared at Harriet. 'Hussy!'

Miss Marstone took one look at Harriet and burst into tears whilst Edward's expression changed from irritation to utter fury.

'That is what I should like to know,' he snarled. 'What the devil are you doing in here with *him*?'

Harriet raised her brows. 'And with Miss Marstone, Edward. Do not, I beg of you, forget Miss Marstone.'

'As if we could,' Benedict muttered.

Harriet bit hard on her lip to silence her inappropriate urge to giggle.

'You may rest assured, Lady Marstone, that there was no impropriety,' she said, savouring the flash of fury in that lady's eyes. She was more convinced than ever that the entire farce had been a scheme dreamed up by Lady Marstone and her daughter to entrap Benedict. 'I was here the entire time and can vouch for that.'

'I know what I saw when I walked in,' Lady Marstone said. 'That wretch had my poor, innocent Bridget *in his arms*. As for you, sir—I expect you to make amends. And I warn you, if you refuse to act as the gentleman you purport to be, I swear you will never hold your head up in society again.'

'Do your worst,' Benedict said. 'What you saw was your *poor, innocent* daughter flinging herself at me. I tell you straight, madam, I have no interest in your daughter and I will not be making her an offer of any kind. If you wish to create a scandal, I would suggest your daughter will emerge the loser. Not I.'

'You have not heard the last of this,' Lady Marstone hissed, her glare encompassing both Harriet and Benedict. 'Out of the goodness of my heart and my respect for his lordship I have kept my mouth shut about your disgraceful behaviour in staying unchaperoned at Tenterfield Court, but no more, *my lady*. And, from what I hear, that is not the only proof of your immorality. My heart weeps for poor Lady Stanton—only recently wed and yet cruelly deceived by her husband and her supposed friend. Utterly disgraceful!'

She ushered her weeping daughter from the room.

There was a beat of silence after they left, then Edward strutted across the room to face Harriet. 'You have not explained what you were doing in here with Poole.'

'I was doing nothing,' Harriet said, her insides knotting as she realised the risk she had taken in protecting Benedict. She could not regret it, though. She couldn't bear to think of him trapped into a marriage with that devious cat. 'Edward, Fanny…please, you must believe me. I came here alone. I—'

'You hoped Poole would follow you,' Edward snarled. 'I saw you with my own eyes, whispering together. You *planned* this liaison. In my house, on Kitty's special night.' He grabbed Harriet's shoulders, shaking her, and she felt locks of hair again brush her neck and shoulders.

'Hold hard there, Brierley!' Benedict shoved Edward away from Harriet. 'Don't you—'

'*Do not* tell me to "hold hard" in my own house,' Edward said through clenched teeth before glaring again at Harriet. 'I warned you but you went your own way, as usual. And now you must pay the penalty. You, madam, are no longer welcome here. Go.'

Harriet's heart pounded at the implacable look in Edward's eyes.

'Fanny…?' Her appeal was met with a helpless shrug.

'Brierley—' Harriet could hear the effort Benedict made to keep his voice level even as anger flashed in his eyes '—you are making a mistake. It was *I* who followed Lady Brierley into the library. She had no idea I would follow her.'

'That is almost as bad,' Edward said. 'I think we all know what the outcome of that particular meeting would have been, had Miss Marstone not appeared.'

'I resent that,' Harriet cried. 'How dare you assume—'

'It's a natural assumption, given your past and—' his eyes raked her '—given your slovenly appearance.'

Benedict growled deep in his chest and started towards Edward, his fists clenched. Harriet grabbed at his arm, tugging him back.

Edward stood his ground, saying, 'And that just proves my point. You, sir, are no gentleman. You deserve each other. I shall attend you tomorrow, madam. I suggest you make arrangements to vacate the house in Sackville Street forthwith. I have no doubt one of your lovers will come to your aid and accommodate you, as you do them.'

He marched to the door and flung it open. Harriet stole a glance at Benedict, who was rigid with fury, his hands clenched into fists.

'Do not,' she whispered. 'Please. You will make things worse.'

'So you keep telling me. Oh, very well, but only because you ask. Otherwise…' He shot a look of disgust at Edward.

Harriet swallowed, straightened her spine and walked to the door. As she moved into the hall, Edward caught up with her and gripped her elbow.

'Fetch Lady Brierley's cloak,' he said to a passing maid. 'She is leaving.'

Am I such an undesirable character I must be escorted from the premises?

Harriet contained her bitter laugh and blinked hard to hold scalding tears at bay.

'Grandmama!' Kitty, flushed and happy, emerged from the ballroom, Lord Wincott by her side. 'Papa! There you all are. I wondered where you were… Where are you… Surely you are not leaving already, Grandmama? It is early yet.'

Harriet bit the inside of her cheek, sucked in a deep breath and said shakily, 'I am so sorry, sweetie. I am not feeling well, so I must go home.

But I have had a wonderful time and you…and you…are so very beautiful…'

Her voice failed her. She felt a hand squeeze hers briefly. Fanny. Her heart lifted a little. Perhaps all was not yet lost. Kitty threw her arms around Harriet and hugged her hard. 'I hope you will feel better soon, and I shall tell you all about what you have missed.'

'Thank you, darling. I'd like that. Never forget I love you,' she ended in a whisper.

Her cloak was placed around her shoulders. Harriet hesitated. She had travelled here with the Stantons in their carriage, as she did not have one of her own.

'Allow me to escort you home.' It was Benedict. 'My carriage, please,' he ordered.

Her instinct was to fling his offer in his face.

Why did he have to follow me? It has made everything a thousand times worse.

She had made everything a thousand times worse as well, by distracting him. She could not sidestep her share of blame. She read the righteous expression on Edward's face at Benedict's words but she was beyond caring now what he thought. She must get home somehow. She had much to think about; she had her life to organise. Edward was throwing her out of her home, and he would stop her allowance. She had nothing. She glanced at Benedict's set profile as they waited in silence. Did he imagine, now she had reached such a pass, she would fall into his arms? Allow him to support her as his mistress until he tired of her again?

Yes, she shared the blame for what had happened tonight, but most of the rest was of Benedict's doing, even her *affaire* with Stanton. His rejection of her and their baby had triggered a chain of events until she'd arrived at this point.

Childless. Homeless. Penniless.

Scorned by her family.

Her hard-won reputation in tatters.

The carriage arrived and Harriet allowed herself to be handed into it. Benedict climbed in behind her and sat by her side.

'Why did you have to follow me?' She could not hide her bitterness. 'See now what has happened.'

'If you had talked to me earlier, I would not have had to try to get you alone. I should not worry about it. It will soon blow over.'

She stared at him, incredulous. '*Blow over?* If you truly believe that, you know nothing of the machinations of the *ton*. Do not think Lady Marstone will tell the exact truth, either about tonight or about my stay at Tenterfield Court. She will embellish as much as she can, blackening both our names in the process.'

He did not speak again until they drew up in Sackville Street.

'Why did you marry Brierley?'

Fury sizzled through her. *Why?* His face was dimly visible, his expression noncommittal.

'You *know* why.'

The black-hearted *wretch*. How could he ask such a thing? Her hand itched to slap him, but at the same time she shrank from the idea of even touching him. She climbed hurriedly from the carriage, thankful that Stevens was already waiting to help her out.

'Harriet!'

She ignored him. 'No one is to be admitted to the house tonight, Stevens. Is that clear?' she said as she heard the unmistakable sound of Benedict descending from the carriage behind her. She half ran to her open front door—*not yours for much longer*—Stevens puffing behind.

'I need answers, and I will not rest until I get them,' Benedict shouted. 'Why did—?' His words were cut short as Stevens shut the door behind them.

Now what?

Harriet's mind spun, but she could find no solution. Should she wait until Edward turned up tomorrow, in the hope he might have mellowed? Or should she retain what dignity she still possessed and leave of her own accord? She did not have the luxury of that option, she realised. Her only resort would be to move into the house in Cheapside, or to go to her mother and aunt in Whitstable. Neither option appealed, and both were only short-term answers to a dilemma that needed a long-term solution.

Marriage. Her stomach knotted. There was no one she could trust enough to put her life in their hands.

'Milady? Are you quite well?'

Stevens's question shook her from her thoughts. She was standing in her hall, her cloak still around her shoulders.

'I'm sorry, Stevens,' she said. 'I am quite all right.'

And the servants. What would happen to them? They would all lose their jobs… Sick despair rolled through her from her head to her toes. Accompanied by a wave of guilt. She'd thought she could handle Edward. She'd been wrong, and she had jeopardised her entire household's future.

'I shall retire now, and I suggest you do the same.'

There had been no thunderous knocking at the

door, such as she had feared. Benedict had clearly washed his hands of her, too. As she climbed into bed, misery engulfed her and she turned onto her side, curled into a ball and wept.

Chapter Twenty

Edward slammed out of Harriet's salon as the clock struck noon the following day. She stared at the door in a daze. Far from softening his attitude to her, he had grown more implacable overnight. He had been unmoving. Kitty's future was in the balance and Edward was determined the match with Lord Wincott should go ahead for political, financial and social reasons. Wincott had already expressed his disquiet about Harriet's charity, believing such charitable work was tantamount to encouraging immoral behaviour in the serving classes. Now, unless Edward dealt once and for all with the connection between his family and Harriet—before the sordid story of her behaviour became common knowledge—he feared Wincott would never come up to scratch.

'And does Kitty have a say in who she weds?' Harriet had asked. That had been a mistake. Edward had exploded in righteous indignation that she should have the temerity to question a system of arranged marriages that had proved advantageous for the aristocracy for centuries.

'My marriage was arranged,' Edward said, his face darkening, 'as was yours, madam. What would have become of you without my father rescuing you as he did?'

Harriet had been beyond caution—her temper had been teased to breaking point, and all her pleading and cajoling had got her nowhere. '*Rescuing* me? You simply do not see what you do not wish to see, do you, Edward? Your father was a tyrant. You ask what I would be without him rescuing me. I would be a *mother*. I would have a daughter, and no amount of money in this world can ever make up for her loss.'

'That is hardly my father's fault.'

Harriet had paced the room in her agitation. 'Oh, yes, it is!' She'd struggled to speak, her throat had been so tight. 'He pushed me down the stairs. He *laughed* when I lost my baby. He gloated it would save him money and that my "swollen belly" would no longer interfere with his pleasures.'

'There is no talking to you if you are set on inventing stories to blacken my father's name,' Edward had said, but some of his bluster had abated.

He'd marched to the door. 'One week to pack up and to leave. One week, madam.' And he had gone.

What was she to do? Where could she go? She would not allow Edward to banish her to the isolated cottage on the Brierley estate that he had offered. With no horse or carriage, she would effectively be cut off from the outside world, completely dependent on Edward and Fanny.

The door opened and Stevens came in. 'Will you see Lady Stanton, my lady? She arrived just after his lordship. She has been waiting in the drawing room.'

Harriet scrubbed her hands over her face. 'I don't know,' she said. 'I can't...I can't even *think* straight. I—'

What was she saying? She should not speak like this in front of Stevens. Before she could refuse to see Felicity, however, Stevens said, 'Her ladyship was most insistent, my lady. She—'

'She will not be denied.' Felicity's voice sounded from the doorway. 'Do not blame Stevens, for he did his best to put me off, but I simply must speak to you, Harriet.' She crossed the room to sit next to Harriet and take her hand. 'Thank you, Stevens, that will be all.'

Harriet held her emotions in check until Stevens closed the door behind him, and then a huge wave of exhaustion, misery and hopelessness swept over her.

Later, after she had wept out her despair in Felicity's arms, she sat up.

'I must look frightful,' she said. 'I am so sorry. I do not know what came over me, but I am better now. I was just tired and… Why did you come?'

'After you left last night, there was talk. I was worried about you.'

'Talk?' *Dear God, already?* Her stomach twisted. There truly was no going back; her reputation was in tatters. It was only a matter of time before the tattle mongers remembered her humble beginnings and shook their heads in their superior conviction that blood was everything.

'Yes, about you and Sir Benedict,' Felicity said. 'That awful Marstone woman was spreading all kinds of malicious gossip. We tried to stop her, but not even your stepson could silence her. Oh, Harriet, I am so very sorry.'

'You have nothing to be sorry for, Felicity.'

'Oh, but I do. You went to Tenterfield Court for *me*. If you had not—'

'If I had not, then all this would have blown up in some other way,' Harriet said miserably.

'Do you want to tell me about it?'

Harriet unburdened her heart, telling Felicity all

about her youthful love for Benedict, her fall from grace and Benedict's rejection of her. And she told her something of her marriage to Brierley—glossing over the worst of his violence and his part in the loss of her baby daughter—triggering a fresh paroxysm of grief as Felicity squeezed her hands, her own eyes glinting with tears.

'No wonder you made such an effort to help me find out who was responsible for Emma's plight,' Felicity said. 'And as for *Sir Benedict Poole*—his treatment of you was appalling. Now I wish I *had* allowed Richard to call him out!'

Her friend sounded so fierce, a laugh gurgled from Harriet's swollen throat. 'That would solve nothing.'

'No, but it would make *me* feel better,' Felicity declared, her small hands clenched into fists.

'What am I to do?' Harriet asked in despair. 'Edward has all but disowned me. I am to l-l-leave this place. He has stopped my allowance—'

'Can he do that?' Felicity said.

'Yes. I talked to the solicitor and he c-confirmed it. I have nothing. And now I do not even have my reputation.'

'Well, as to the first, you are always welcome to stay with us,' Felicity said.

'I could not possibly.'

Felicity fixed Harriet with a stern gaze. 'If you are feeling awkward because of what happened between you and Richard, then please do not.'

The knot in Harriet's stomach tightened further. Although she was aware Felicity knew of their *affaire*, it had never been mentioned between them. 'How...how can you speak of it so calmly? You should be spitting fire at me, and yet you have remained my friend, and you are here when I need you.' She could not imagine she would be so magnanimous in the same circumstances.

A rueful smile lit Felicity's face. 'I lived through my father's and my stepfather's infidelities,' she said. 'Had your liaison with Richard taken place after our marriage, I could never forgive either of you for that, although I know many wives do accept their husband's *affaires*. But to take against you for something that happened before I was even betrothed to Richard...? No, that would be unfair, although I confess I found it hard at first to forgive you both for not telling me the truth as soon as you and I became friends.'

'I'm sorry.' Harriet hung her head.

'Oh, it was not your fault, I am aware of that. My penitent husband admitted you had advised him to tell me the truth, but that he thought it best to say nothing and hope I would never find out. And even that I cannot be angry about, for it finally forced Richard and me to be honest with one another, and our marriage is happier and stronger as a result. So, I repeat, I will not see you on the streets. You are welcome to stay with us if the worse comes to the worst.

'We *can* do something about your reputation, however. You have done nothing wrong, and you are not to skulk in here as though you have.' She stood up. 'Get some rest, and I shall collect you at four thirty. Put on your best carriage dress, for you and I are going to dazzle them all in the park.'

Harriet's heart sank. 'Felicity, no. I cannot. I—'

'You can and you must,' Felicity said gently before stooping to kiss Harriet's cheek. 'You will not go down without a fight. I shall not let you.'

It was worse than Harriet feared.

Felicity had driven to Sackville Street in her phaeton and pair, her groom perched behind. Harriet had dressed in her best blue carriage dress and matching bonnet and sat by Felicity as she expertly drove to the park and steered the vehicle onto the carriageway.

As usual at that time of day, the park was thronged with walkers, riders and people taking the air in their open-topped carriages. They were people Harriet had come to know over the past eleven years since her marriage to Brierley. Most had been friendly enough towards her, even though Harriet had mostly kept herself to herself after Brierley's death, finding it hard to fully trust others—the legacy of her marriage, she supposed. Others, however, had merely tolerated the vicar's daughter who had become a countess by marriage. And some—since she had begun her crusade to protect vulnerable maidservants—had given her the cold shoulder. They were no loss—she had no desire to socialise with such people in any case. But now...today...her ears were burning, as was her face, as one after the other turned from her.

Snatches of conversation as they passed reverberated as loudly as a town crier's announcements to Harriet in her sensitive state.

'Her own granddaughter's ball...'

'Shameless...'

'Low breeding, my dear...'

'Tenterfield Court...'

'On his deathbed...'

'No shame...'

'No gentleman...'

'Miss Marstone...'

'Lucky escape...'

'Felicity,' she said, as they bowled along the drive, 'please take me home. I cannot bear this.'

Felicity, however, slowed her ponies to a walk and pointed with her whip to three gentlemen trotting towards them on horseback. Harriet's heart quailed, but then rallied as she recognised Stanton as one of the three. He, at least—surely—would not cut her.

'You are not running away,' Felicity said fiercely. 'You have done nothing wrong.' She turned her attention to her ponies, who tossed their heads, sending their identical flaxen manes rippling on their necks, as the three huge horses were reined in alongside the phaeton. 'Whoa, Spice. Steady, Nutmeg.'

Harriet saw, with a nervous lurch of her stomach, that the other two men were the Duke of Cheriton—one of the most powerful noblemen in the *ton* and, she knew, Felicity's former guardian—and his younger brother, Lord Vernon Beauchamp.

'Good afternoon, Cousin Leo, Cousin Vernon,' Felicity said. 'You are both acquainted with Lady Brierley, I think.'

All three men doffed their hats. Stanton smiled at Harriet, his chocolate-brown eyes warm.

'Don't look so petrified, Harry,' he said. 'You do know that, whatever happens, Felicity and I will always stand by you. And, in the meantime, His Grace has expressed a wish to promenade. So—' Stanton swung elegantly from the back of his huge dapple-grey gelding and strode to the side of the phaeton, holding out his hand to Felicity '—if you ladies would care to join us, I can think of no more pleasurable way to spend the next half an hour.'

He then addressed the groom perched on the phaeton. 'Dalton, please hold Gambit—' he proffered his horse's reins '—and her ladyship's ponies, whilst we take a short stroll.'

In the meantime the duke, suave and elegant as always, had also dismounted. He tossed his black's reins to his brother, who tipped his hat, smiled and said, 'I'd better keep these two on the move or war is likely to break out. See you back here shortly,' and nudged his horse into a walk.

Harriet absorbed all this manoeuvring with an inner *Hmph*. That the whole encounter had been planned by Felicity she did not doubt, but she was grateful for the effort. Whether it would do any good or not was anybody's guess, although— she looked into the duke's silver-grey eyes as he handed her from the phaeton—if anyone could sway public opinion, it was the Duke of Cheriton.

Hope filtered into her heart. No one would dare

to snub her whilst the duke and the Earl of Stanton championed her.

They began to stroll.

'So when are you going to tell me what happened after I left last night, you dog?' Matthew said as he relaxed back in a chair in the coffee lounge at White's late that afternoon. 'There's a new bet in the Book, that Sir B— P—will make a significant announcement before the week is out. Don't tell me you've found yourself a bride already? That's quick work, even for you.'

'Why must it be about a woman? It could refer to the imminent murder of my business partner.'

'Hah! You wouldn't last five minutes without me to prop you up. Seriously, though, I should warn you—you're unfamiliar with the ways of the *ton*. If you are raising expectations enough to be noticed, you will be expected to make an offer. If you don't, then the parents of decent young ladies will warn them against you and your reputation will suffer. I presume you're still serious about restoring the Poole name?'

'Oh, I'm serious, all right. And no, I have not raised any expectations.'

'So what does the wager mean? Come on, old

boy, if there's some inside information you can give me, I might have a flutter myself.'

He really didn't want to discuss it but he'd barely slept, wondering what damage had been done to Harriet's wider reputation. Brierley's black opinion of his stepmother was already, he feared, a lost cause.

'What about a widow's reputation?' he asked.

Matthew tilted his head, a knowing smile lurking in his eyes. 'The Lady Brierley again? What *have* you been up to, old chap? And what is the story between you two? Eleanor has been badgering me to find out ever since you met at our house the other week, and *particularly* after your reluctance to discuss the subject at the picnic. She is convinced you two have *history.*'

Benedict ignored Matthew's questions. The past was no one's business but his. But he needed to know what might now happen. 'A widow's reputation is not as vital as an unmarried girl's, is it?'

'Vital in what context?'

Benedict told Matthew what had happened after Matthew and Eleanor had left Kitty's ball.

Matthew whistled through his teeth. 'And Lady Marstone came in with both the Brierleys, you say? She was setting you up, old chap.'

'I know.' Benedict clenched his jaw as he realised his friend was trying not to laugh. 'It is not funny.'

'It wouldn't have been had you ended up shackled to Bridget Marstone,' Matthew said. 'Seriously…I would have had to reconsider our partnership. And to think of having Lady M as a mother-in-law! Thank God for Harriet, eh? So what is the problem? There were enough witnesses to confirm you were never alone with Miss Marstone.'

'Yes,' Benedict said, 'but none to swear how long I was alone with *Harriet.* When Lady Marstone realised I was not about to make an offer for her daughter, she made threats. I'm not concerned about me, but for Harriet.'

He had no choice, he realised, but to confide in Matthew about Harriet's visit to Tenterfield Court.

Matthew straightened in his chair, frowning and suddenly serious, and Benedict found himself thinking that he preferred his friend's mocking banter, irritating as it was at times.

'What did Brierley do last night?'

'He made Harriet leave. I took her home in my carriage.'

'Bloody fool. Brierley, I mean,' he added. 'He missed a perfect opportunity to smooth things over by putting on a united front with Harriet.'

Benedict sighed. 'I think he's moved way be-

yond wanting to smooth things over. He's set on
throwing Harriet out of her home and stopping
her allowance. I need to know how her reputation
will suffer, Matt. Brierley is more concerned with
securing an offer from Wincott for his daughter
than with the damage his actions will do to his
stepmother.'

'Self-righteous fool! When you consider what
his father was like—'

'His father?'

'He's the reason Harriet set up her charity,' Matthew said. 'Eleanor was full of it after she heard
about it. Brierley got two of his servants with child
and then dismissed them. Harriet helps other girls
in a similar situation—it's sickening to realise how
many *gentlemen* feel perfectly justified in washing
their hands of those girls and their children. Harriet works hard to persuade the men responsible
to pay up and support their by-blows, making her
somewhat unpopular in some quarters.'

Benedict felt sick. Harriet might have betrayed
him, but she was a decent, caring woman, and his
thoughtless action was hurting her. 'And they will
no doubt happily spread scurrilous rumours about
her if they hear about last night.'

'Oh, yes,' Matthew said. 'They will be in their
element. From what I've heard, there have been a

few who have tried to discredit her in the past, but she has always taken care to guard her reputation.'

'And I suppose, there I have my answer,' Benedict said slowly. 'Her reputation will suffer because, until now, it's always been spotless.'

Matthew smiled in sympathy. 'It looks that way.'

What would Harriet's answer be? Despite her manoeuvrings at the masquerade, she still might throw his offer back in his face, but at least he would have tried to make things right. He must accept responsibility. What was happening to her was his fault—if he had not followed her, she would not be in this predicament.

Chapter Twenty-One

Benedict rapped on Harriet's front door. Stevens answered it almost immediately.

'Is her ladyship in?'

Benedict went to step over the threshold. Stevens moved to block his way. Benedict scowled at the man.

'Has her ladyship told you to bar my entry?' He was in no mood to be denied; his decision was made and the sooner he asked the question and she accepted, the sooner the damage he had caused could be repaired.

'Her ladyship is not at home, sir,' Stevens said.

Benedict eyed the man, trying to decide if he was telling the truth or if he was merely obeying instructions. If the potential scandal was as bad as he now feared, where would she go? It was far more likely she was hiding away at home.

There was a clatter of hooves in the street behind him. A phaeton and pair, driven by Felicity, Lady Stanton, had turned into Sackville Street, and there she was.

Head high, facing the world. His Harriet.

Your Harriet? Since when? She's never been yours.

She will be now. The reply instantly soothed his agitation and he knew, suddenly, he had made the right decision. He wanted Harriet and if this was the only way he could have her, then so be it.

He barely noticed the three gentlemen riding behind the phaeton until they reined to a halt outside the house. Stanton and two of his cronies—although whether it was quite the thing to call a duke and his brother cronies was another matter. He had never formally met either man, although he knew them by sight, and he now found himself the target of hard looks from the three men. Stanton spoke to the duke's brother and swung from the saddle. He strode over to where Benedict waited on the doorstep.

'What the devil are you about, coming here?'

Benedict locked eyes with him. 'I'll go where I please.'

'You've done more than enough—'

'This has nothing to do with you,' Benedict snarled. 'It is between—'

There was a flurry of skirts and Harriet and Felicity joined them, Felicity linking arms with her husband.

'Thank you, Stanton, for all you've done,' Harriet said. She raised her voice and called to the duke and his brother, 'And thank you both, too. I'm very grateful.' She turned cool violet eyes on Benedict. 'Did you have something to say to me?'

'Yes. But not here. Inside.'

She stared. 'Have you learned nothing of the ways of this world? If I allow you inside my house now, do you not realise that all our efforts to repair the damage of last night will have been for nothing?'

Benedict was aware that Stanton had shrugged free of Felicity's restraint and had ushered her away from the door before coming back to stand next to Harriet. He still did not know for certain if those rumours about the earl and Harriet were true or false. If they were, would Felicity and Harriet be such friends? It was yet another question for Harriet to answer.

In the meantime, the duke had dismounted and stood beside Felicity, one hand around her upper arm.

Keeping her out of harm's way. Benedict felt his eyes narrow and his blood began to pound through his veins. He had faced many situations like this in his life—men bristling with menace, protecting their own, whether it was their women, their possessions or merely a jug of ale. A brawl, or even heated words, would do nothing to help his cause but, God help him, he would not back down from these dandies. Although—looking again at their stances and their expressions—*dandies* was no more accurate a description than *cronies*.

He concentrated on Harriet. 'I have come to repair the damage,' he said. 'To make things right. I wish to speak to you. In *private*.'

Sudden understanding flashed in her eyes and a myriad of expressions crossed her face, so fleeting he hardly had time to interpret them, and then she blinked and was again unreadable. She locked eyes with him, probing, and he tried to convey his deepest feelings by expression alone. He must have succeeded, for she released a tiny sigh, turned to the others and said, 'Thank you so much for all you have done for me today. It will be all right now, I assure you.'

'We can come in and wait in the hall,' Felicity said, clearly reluctant to trust Benedict. 'At least, that way, the proprieties will be observed if Sir Benedict is… If he does not…um…' Her voice tailed away as her cheeks flamed.

Benedict pushed past Stanton and crossed the pavement to stand in front of Felicity. 'You have my word,' he said softly. 'I will make things right. Thank you for caring.'

Amber eyes searched his. 'Very well,' she said eventually. She glanced up at the duke. 'Would you help me into my phaeton please, Cousin Leo?'

Cousin? That explained a lot. Harriet did move in exalted circles these days. He felt a tremor of unease. What if she would not accept him? He was but a lowly trader compared to these men.

You are a baronet, now, don't forget, and rich, too.

Oh, yes! Wealthy and a title. How could she refuse? She married for the same before, don't forget.

He dismissed his sudden uncertainties as he walked back to stand by Harriet, ignoring the large form of Stanton, still hovering protectively by her side.

'Well?' He'd stated his case. He would not beg.

She nodded and said, 'Come inside.'

About to follow her across the threshold, Benedict turned to Stanton and thrust out his hand. They would have to learn to get along, with Harriet and Felicity such fast friends.

'Thank you for looking after her,' he said. 'It's

good to know she has friends to rely on when her own family are so quick to believe the worst.'

Stanton gave him a hard stare as he gripped his hand.

'You make sure *you* look after her,' he said. 'Or you will be hearing from me. I will not have my wife upset. Do we understand one another?'

'We do.' Benedict followed Harriet inside the house.

'Thank you, Stevens,' Harriet said as she handed him her bonnet. 'Please come this way, Sir Benedict.'

She led him into the salon where he had taken her after she had fainted in the street. It seemed like a lifetime ago, not just two weeks. How had his life taken such an unexpected turn? From being set on marrying a virtuous girl of impeccable breeding, here he was on the verge of offering for a…for a… His thought process stalled. And then he realised.

It simply did not matter what Harriet was or was not. He loved *her*. He had always loved her. And now, more than ever, having seen her vulnerability, he knew it was his destiny to be the man to protect her. The sight of Stanton taking that role— the role that destiny dictated was Benedict's—had made his blood boil.

She had crossed the room to stand by the window, waiting for him to speak. Cool, calm, composed. Hands clasped loosely before her. The perfect lady.

Except now he knew the passion that ran deep below that unruffled exterior. Despite his intention of keeping his distance from her after the night of the masquerade, he had been unable to. And his need had triggered last night's disaster—his need to see her, to speak with her, to learn everything about her, had driven him into following her into the library.

He still did not entirely trust her. He still suspected there was something she was hiding but those questions could wait. He had a lifetime to learn the truth. The way she had responded to his kisses and caresses last night reassured him that, whatever else she felt for him, she felt the same desire he did. He could not wait to make her his wife.

He crossed the room to stand in front of her. She tilted her head to look deep into his eyes.

'Will you marry me?' He should speak of his love but, somehow, the words would not form. This felt vulnerable enough—he could not expose himself further by admitting his love for her. His heart beat faster as she held his gaze, her huge eyes solemn. His entire body was rigid with urgency, his skin stretched so tight it felt it might split if he made a sudden move. He realised he was holding his breath.

'Thank you. Yes.'

No outburst of joy. Barely a glimmer of a smile.

What do you expect, when you have told her nothing of what you feel?

What is he thinking? He looks so stern. Has he only asked me because of last night, or does he have some feeling for me other than lust?

What does it matter? Your problems are solved, and you know you will always be safe in a marriage to Benedict.

She ignored the uneasy thought that she was being unfair in accepting his proposal. She had—eventually—got the result she had planned for on the night of the masquerade. Security. Safety. Maybe even a child, if God saw willing to grant her that blessing. Her heart skipped a beat at the thought. A baby! How she yearned for a baby of her own. Resolutely, she cast aside her guilt.

Benedict *owed* her.

And she loved him. Even though that love was layered under years of anger and resentment, it had survived. Would she ever dare to open her heart to Benedict and admit her love? She shrank from that thought. What if he rejected it? He could still do so, even within a marriage. She could not imagine risking such heartache ever again.

An awkward silence ensued, though their gazes remained fused. He reached out and took a pin from her hair, dropping it to the floor. His eyes never wavered from hers as he felt for another pin and removed it. And another, until her hair was falling loose around her shoulders. She did not move. Waiting, her heart racing as anticipation spiralled up through her entire body.

He lifted her heavy tresses, weighing them in the palms of his hands, much as he had weighed her breasts on the night of the masquerade. Then he threaded the fingers of one hand through her hair to cup her head.

'Harry...'

The groan came from deep within him. Tormented. Heartfelt.

At last. Her bones were melting. Her blood on fire.

He pulled her to him, against his chest, and his lips crushed down on hers. She moulded her body to his hard, lean frame, winding her arms around his neck, clinging to him, returning his passion.

At least we have this.

* * *

'We will wed as soon as possible,' Benedict said some time later. 'I shall consult my solicitor tomorrow and have the settlement drawn up. You will never again be beholden to Brierley.'

A wave of such relief swept through Harriet at Benedict's words she felt she might cry. She blinked several times and swallowed hard before she dared to answer him. 'Thank you. That means more to me than you know.'

He had been standing by the fireplace, but now he came to her and sat by her side, placing his hand over hers where it lay in her lap. 'Tell me,' he urged.

She turned her hand palm up and laced her fingers through his. She forced a light laugh. 'Oh, it was merely a figure of speech. I have to say I am looking forward to telling Edward our news. And to seeing Lady Marstone's face—she made sure everyone believed you would never stoop to taking on a humbly born, penniless widow.'

His fingers tightened around hers. 'She was wrong,' he said gruffly. 'You are more of a lady than she will ever be.'

'May we go and see Edward now? Together?'

'Of course,' he said, but he made no effort to

move. His head bent, he watched the interplay of their entwined fingers. 'Do you miss him?'

'Edward?'

'No. Brierley.'

Harriet pulled her hand from Benedict's and stood up. 'No,' she said. 'Come, let us go now before it gets too late.'

They took a hackney to Upper Brook Street. Harriet sneaked a look at Benedict as he stared out of the window, his jaw set. He did not have the look of a man joyously anticipating his forthcoming nuptials. Was he thinking about the coming interview with Edward, or was it their betrothal and all that it meant that was on his mind? She tried to ignore those ever-present pangs of conscience.

Edward received them in his study, standing squarely in front of the hearth. He did not offer them a seat.

'Well?'

'We have come, as a courtesy, to tell you that we are betrothed,' Benedict said. 'The wedding will take place as soon as the banns have been read.'

'I am pleased you are finally making an honest woman of her, Poole,' Edward said.

Harriet felt Benedict stiffen by her side. Well, he deserved that gibe—if he had taken responsibility for his actions years ago, a great deal of heartache might have been avoided. But she had no wish for the two men to be constantly at odds with each other. Edward and his family would still be a part of her life. She slipped her hand into Benedict's and squeezed.

'I trust you will do the decent thing and allow Harriet to remain in her home until our marriage,' Benedict said. 'After all, a continued crusade against your own stepmother can only reflect badly on you.'

Edward scowled. 'There was never a crusade,' he said. 'I had my duty as head of this family not to allow my stepmother to scandalise society with her behaviour. Thankfully, that responsibility will lie with you henceforth. I dare say you will be more equal to the task than I.'

Harriet bit back her retort and lightly tugged at Benedict's hand in a silent attempt to prevent him reacting as she feared he might.

'You may as well come to the drawing room and tell Fanny and Katherine,' Edward added grudgingly. 'Wincott is there, too. I make no doubt *he* will be relieved that scandal has been averted.'

'Lord Wincott? Has he made his offer for Kitty?'

'No.' Edward led the way from his study to the drawing room. 'We have agreed to give her time to enjoy some of her first Season before he offers, although he very nearly backed out after the deplorable goings-on last night.' He halted and faced them both. 'He was utterly horrified by your behaviour.'

'I am sure Lord Wincott is as mindful of the advantages of the match as you are, Edward.' Harriet chose her words carefully. Wincott was, in her opinion, a pompous ass—a bit like Edward himself—and that was no doubt why Edward thought he would make a good husband for Kitty, but Harriet worried about her lively granddaughter being tied to such a dull spouse. 'Lord Wincott should count himself fortunate to win a bride with so many fine qualities. And the political alliance will benefit him as well as you, so do not be too quick in thinking all the benefits flow in your direction. He will gain, as well.'

For the first time since their arrival, Edward's face softened. 'I had forgotten quite how perceptive you can be at times,' he said. He heaved a sigh, then held his hand out to Benedict. 'I suppose I must welcome you to the family.'

'Edward is not a bad man,' Harriet said some time later, as Benedict's carriage conveyed them back to Sackville Street. 'He is merely inflexible in his views.'

A sarcastic laugh escaped Benedict. 'Inflexible? How I didn't plant my fist in his smug face, I do not know. Or in Wincott's. Patronising poltroon. God help the country, with men like that at the helm.'

'I am pleased you did not,' Harriet said. She had seen the effort Benedict had made to remain polite and agreeable. 'At least you must allow that both Fanny and Kitty are delightful.'

A rumble of acquiescence sounded deep in Benedict's throat. 'Although how in hell they have remained so with that stepson of yours as husband and father, God only knows,' he said. 'Poor Kitty has my sympathy. She'll be going from the control of one pompous windbag straight to another.'

Harriet shivered at the reminder of the control a husband exercised over his wife.

'What is it? Are you cold?'

'No, indeed.'

How could she feel the chill when he sat so close by her side, his heat warming her even through their clothes? He put his arm around her shoulder anyway and she snuggled closer. Maybe, in time, she would learn to forgive him for the past but, in the meantime, she felt safe and she felt secure, and if she could not have her independence that, surely, was the next best thing.

'We have not discussed tonight yet,' Benedict said.

Heady, sensual anticipation swirled at Harriet's core. 'Tonight?'

'Yes. I thought we should show our faces somewhere, even if it is only the theatre.' He nuzzled her ear, whispering, 'We need not stay until the end as long as we allow ourselves to be seen.'

The swell of passion deep inside her burst to the surface, heating her skin. *Heavens!* Was she really that shallow? It seemed he was not the only one consumed with lust. Then reality—plans already made—intruded into her thoughts.

'But it is Matthew and Eleanor's musical evening tonight, and we have both promised to attend.' She shifted on the seat and stared at him. 'You surely had not forgotten?'

Benedict coughed, and then cleared his throat. 'I may have done.' He glanced down at Harriet with a twinkle in his eye—the first sign of humour since he had proposed. 'Be warned, however, that I shall never admit to it if you let on to Eleanor. She is one lady I don't want to get on the wrong side of.'

'She is forthright in her views, certainly, but she has a kind heart,' Harriet said, recalling Eleanor's compassion at Kitty's ball. 'And she has had her share of troubles.'

She recalled the whispers when Eleanor had spent the Season in London the year before—her first visit in several years. They hadn't been acquainted then, but Harriet remembered the rumours about Eleanor's mother having caused a scandal when Eleanor was young, and then—although Harriet had never learned the full story—someone had tried to kill Eleanor.

'Yes. Matthew has told me what happened last year,' Benedict said. 'They are fortunate to have found each other.'

'Indeed.' Harriet conjured up a mental picture of Matthew and Eleanor: a couple very much in love. Could she and Benedict ever be half so happy and content? 'I might not have known Eleanor long, but I like her very much and should not like to offend her by not attending tonight.'

'Then I shall sacrifice my personal preference for spending most of the evening in bed with you, my dear, and I shall escort you to the musical evening. I warn you, though. I am not a lover of music, unless it is a sea shanty or an impromptu tune played in an alehouse somewhere. I did not think Matthew was, either. Strange how marriage can change a man.'

His voice had grown thoughtful. Harriet stole a look at him. All trace of good humour had once again vanished. 'Are you regretting—?'

'Not at all.' His response was blunt and immediate, and Harriet chose to believe him.

Chapter Twenty-Two

The Poole family solicitor was standing at the window of Benedict's study when he entered it the following morning.

'Mr Swain, thank you for coming. Please, take a seat.'

Benedict indicated the visitor's chair and settled into his own chair on the opposite side of his desk. Mr Swain approached the chair, bent slightly to examine the seat and then, very gingerly, he swept his coat-tails aside and perched on the edge. Benedict bit his lip. He had only met Swain once before, and this action only confirmed the opinion he had formed on that occasion.

'Laurence informs me that you are the man I need to speak to with regard to drawing up a marriage settlement.'

Swain straightened, placing long-fingered hands

on the rim of the desk. 'Laurence,' he said. 'I have not seen him for a while. How is he?'

Benedict stifled his sigh. This promised to be a lengthy meeting. He was used to commercial transactions: an offer, a counter-offer, brisk negotiation, a handshake.

'Laurence is very well and is kept inordinately busy answering all my inane questions about the estates and Sir Malcolm's investments,' he said of the young man who had been Malcolm's secretary and whom he had inherited, along with the rest of Malcolm's retainers and advisers—including old-fashioned, fastidious solicitors, he thought, eyeing his visitor.

'Good, good,' said Swain. He shifted back a little in the chair and regarded Benedict through his spectacles. 'Marriage settlement, you say. Well, well. And who is the lucky lady, might one enquire?'

'Harriet, Lady Brierley. She is the widow of the Earl of Brierley. The third earl, that is.'

Swain was back on the edge of his seat. 'The widow Brierley?' There was a pause. 'Good heavens.'

Benedict felt his brows draw together in a frown as Swain removed his spectacles, took a handkerchief from his pocket and began to polish vigorously. He then replaced his spectacles and looked up. Benedict curbed his desire to urge the man to get on with it.

'Now, this will take some planning but…yes, yes, it can be done with very little additional expense to you, sir.' A smile of satisfaction revealed long teeth. 'Yes, very little additional—'

'What do you mean by "additional expense"?'

'Well, of course, the *current* settlement will cease and the capital will revert to you, but that is all to the good, for it would not serve our purpose at all. Indeed no. Not with the dividends being paid through his lordship—'

'Whoa! Hold on. You've lost me, Swain. What current settlement? Which dividends and, for that matter, which "his lordship"?'

'Why, the present Lord Brierley, of course. You are joint trustees.' Swain regarded Benedict with an avuncular smile. 'It is quite all right, sir. No need to worry your head about it—no one expects you to be *au fait* with the entirety of Sir Malcolm's business. Not yet. Shall we discuss figures? Would you think the same amount sufficient? Or would you wish to increase it? It is not over generous for a man with your wealth, but then the lady will have you to settle her major expenses once you are wed, so it will only be in the nature of pin money.

And there must, of course, be provision made for any children.'

Benedict stared at Swain, his mind whirling as he tried to piece together the fragments of information the solicitor had scattered through the conversation.

'Let me understand this,' he said slowly. 'Are you telling me that there exists an investment, made—presumably—by my cousin, and that the income from that investment is paid to Lady Brierley?'

Caution crept through Swain's expression. 'That is the gist of it, yes.'

'Why?'

'I beg your pardon, sir. Why what?'

'How did it come about? Why would Sir Malcolm invest *any* money on behalf of someone he barely knew?'

'Well, I… As I recall…the money was settled on her at the time of her marriage. Her father was the minister at the local church, you know, and your cousin—second cousin, I should say—agreed to provide a dowry as her own father could not.'

It made no sense. Malcolm had not had an altruistic bone in his body. Why would he provide a dowry for Harriet?

'The settlement was subject to certain conditions set by Lord Brierley, as I recall,' Swain continued, 'and, although I cannot bring them all to mind, I do remember that the dividends were not to be paid direct to Lady Brierley but to go to her through her husband and now, of course, through the present Lord Brierley. Unusual condition, but his late lordship insisted upon it, and Sir Malcolm did not seem disposed to argue against it. And the Reverend… Yes, I forget his name now… Lady Brierley's father just seemed grateful someone was providing a dowry at all.'

That made even less sense. Malcolm had provided the dowry and yet *Brierley* had dictated the terms? Benedict was loath to question Swain further until he had thought through the implications of this news.

'You said the current investment will revert to me? Presumably that will be because her ladyship is remarrying?'

Swain beamed. 'Yes, yes, that is a standard condition in these deeds, of course, if there is no issue from the union. The capital will revert to you, as Sir Malcolm's successor, and you will be able to reinvest that sum—ten thousand pounds, if my memory serves me correctly, *most* generous of Sir Malcolm—for her ladyship when you marry. Quite a neat solution, all told. Was there anything else,

Sir Benedict, or should you like me to proceed with drafting the new deed of settlement?'

Benedict thought quickly. He had intended to settle a large enough sum on Harriet in order that if anything should happen to him she would have financial security. He must also make suitable provision for any daughters or younger sons. Now he hesitated. Had this information changed anything? His thoughts were too random to come to a sensible conclusion. Why had Harriet not told him? But…Brierley had stopped her allowance, and had threatened to do so more than once. If she had known there was money settled on her, would she not have used that to argue her case?

Then he realised. Other than the need to satisfy his own curiosity, it did not matter for, whatever the truth, it would not change the fact that he and Harriet were to marry.

He stood up. 'Thank you for attending me, Mr Swain, and yes, please do get on with drawing up a new deed. I shall instruct you later as to the amounts as I intend also to include a house for her ladyship's use if she should survive me. I will summon you again if I have any further questions.'

He actually had a thousand more questions swarming through his brain, but he doubted the solicitor could answer the question that was uppermost in his mind: the burning question of *why* Malcolm had provided a dowry for the local vicar's daughter.

'Very good, sir.' Swain stood up and brushed both hands over the seat of his trousers.

Swain left and Benedict sat back, hands laced behind his head. The myriad doubts that had hovered beneath the surface of his conscious mind now untangled themselves, fighting their way free of the restraint of his longing to simply trust her.

Why had Malcolm paid Harriet's dowry? Many reasons came to him, and most were dismissed. The few possibilities remaining were the ones he liked least. And the thought that floated to the surface time after time churned his gut with anger, jealousy and despair. He knew Malcolm had a taste for young girls. Had Harriet succumbed to him? Had she, once he had returned to Cambridge after that last glorious summer they had spent together, become embroiled in his cousin's sordid sex games? She was a passionate woman. That was undeniable. Had that passion, once he had awakened it, driven her to seek excitement?

He was loath to believe it. It did not tally with her reputation as a virtuous widow, but who knew what really went on in another's life? And her behaviour at the masquerade... If he had not been there, would she have targeted some other man to flirt with? Or more?

Growling an oath, he shoved his chair back and stood. It was time to ask Harriet.

During the journey to Sackville Street his thoughts turned to the future and what this marriage between himself and Harriet would be like. Last night, at the musical evening, he had watched Matthew and Eleanor—besotted with one another, gloriously happy—and the same envy he had felt before had infused him. Could he and Harriet ever be that happy? Or would their shared past always be a barrier between them? He could only hope not.

Stevens showed Benedict into Harriet's salon, and she came to him, hands outstretched, smiling.

'This is a pleasant surprise. I did not expect you to call this morning.' Then she hesitated, her hands falling to her sides. 'What is it? What is wrong?'

'I have a question, and I want to know the truth.'

She stilled. Not a single muscle in her face so much as twitched but, somehow, her expression blanked. Her guard was raised.

'What is your question?'

'It is about your allowance—the one that Brierley pays you.'

Her fair brows drew together into a puzzled frown. 'What about it?'

'Why did you not tell me my cousin settled a sum of money on you when you married Brierley?'

'I…I do not know what you mean.' She sank onto the sofa behind her, staring up at him, her eyes huge in her pale face. 'Your cousin? Do you mean Sir Malcolm? What sum of money? Who told you that?' She sounded genuinely perplexed.

'My solicitor, when I consulted him today about drawing up our marriage settlement. He told me that when you married Brierley, Sir Malcolm provided your dowry.

'I want to know why.'

Harriet tried desperately to take in what Benedict was telling her. What did it mean? Sir *Malcolm* had provided a dowry? For her? But…

'No. I had no dowry. My father was poor. He could not pay a dowry.'

She was uncomfortably aware that Benedict was watching her closely. Too closely, his green eyes narrow. He was suspicious, but of what? What had *he* to be suspicious of? *He* was the one who had abandoned *her*. She remembered as if it were yesterday the agonising pain when her father had told her of his interview with Sir Malcolm and Benedict, and of Benedict's refusal to take responsibility for her and their baby. Yet he appeared to have wiped that from his mind.

How delightful it must be to have no conscience.

She loved him, she no longer denied it, but she still could not forgive him and that memory festered. She longed to shout at him, to scream out her anger and frustration over what he had done to her, and yet she could not process her thoughts swiftly enough to work out what reaction that might provoke. What if it caused him to break off their betrothal? What would she do then, and how...*how...* could she survive if he rejected her again?

One day—when she was brave enough, and strong enough, to broach the subject—she would have to tell him the truth of how she felt. But once that truth was spoken, would there be any future for them? Could they work together to rebuild her trust in him, or would their troubled past destroy any hope of a happy life together?

At the masquerade, she had been certain marriage to Benedict would solve all her problems. And so it would—her practical problems. But what of her feelings, and what of his? Her emotions pushed and pulled at her heart until she could no longer be sure what was for the best and what it was she really wanted.

She could not decide what to say for the best, and so she said nothing.

She waited.

Benedict paced the room before he returned to tower over her. She tensed against the instinct to shrink away from him.

'Why did Malcolm settle such a large sum on you?'

'I do not know. I did not know that the money came from your cousin.'

Uncertainty churned her insides. *Why is he angry?* Shadows from the past rose up to haunt her. *Is it my fault?*

Benedict paced the room again as he continued to fire questions at her.

'So you *did* know there was a settlement.'

'No. Yes.' She remembered the dreadful meeting with Mr Drake. 'But I only found out recently— that day you came to my aid outside the solicitor's office. I assumed the money was settled on me by my husband.'

'Did you never think to ask?'

'I… No. I—'

'Why were the dividends paid to Brierley?'

Her head was spinning. She gripped her hands so tightly together in her lap her knuckles turned white. 'I don't know.'

What had Mr Drake told her? There was a condition attached to the settlement, that Brierley would pass the dividends onto Harriet as long as she did nothing bring the Brierley name into disrepute. Except, of course, her late husband had never seen fit to pay her those dividends.

Nausea churned her stomach and forced its way higher to burn her throat as she felt the full weight of her worthlessness bear down upon her. She tore her hands apart and pressed her fingers to her lips to prevent a sob from escaping. Benedict had not wanted her—still did not want her, not truly—and Brierley, that lecherous, brutish old goat, would not even take her without a handsome bribe.

'You must ask Edward,' she said finally, for want of something better to say. 'I know nothing more than I have already told you.'

She rubbed her hand across her forehead and rose to her feet, her legs shaking. 'I am sorry,' she said. 'I am unwell. I must go and lie down.'

Benedict was by her side in an instant. He scooped up her hands and clasped them to his chest. 'No, do not say sorry. It is I who must apologise,' he said. 'I have done nothing but fire questions at you since my arrival. I will do as you suggest, and talk to Brierley.'

Chapter Twenty-Three

'What did Edward say?' Harriet asked later, as she and Benedict travelled in his carriage to dinner at Stanton House in Cavendish Square.

'He was at the Lords,' Benedict said, 'taking part in a debate that's expected to continue into the small hours. I left him a message that I will call on him tomorrow morning.'

Harriet had spent all afternoon sifting through the past in the light of the information that Sir Malcolm had paid Brierley to marry her. She should be accustomed to humiliation. No wonder Brierley's favourite taunt had been that Harriet belonged to him, body and soul. But, if she considered the transaction from Brierley's position, it made sense. He would be faced with the expense of raising another man's child except, in the end, it had cost him nothing. But it had cost her everything.

She cast a glance at Benedict. He was frowning. Again. It appeared to be his constant expression since Kitty's ball, she realised with a start. He was not happy about their betrothal, that was clear, but what she could not fathom was why he was so incredulous that Sir Malcolm had paid money to provide for her. He knew she had been with child. What had he expected? Did he think when he rejected her that there would be no further consequences, and that his guardian would cast her adrift with no means of support, like so many gentlemen did to their maidservants in the same circumstances?

The incredulity that had smouldered ever since Benedict had told her about the dowry finally sparked into rage, exploding through her. This was Benedict, not Brierley. She must not fear punishment for speaking her mind. If he objected to her words enough to break off their betrothal, then so be it. Better to live a pauper than to constantly fear to voice her opinion.

'*Why* do you persist with this fantasy? Is it really so unbelievable that your guardian paid Brierley to marry me?'

Benedict stiffened before twisting to face her. '*Fantasy?* What is that supposed to mean?'

'I mean that you are making this into a drama when you know *damned* well why he did it. You might not have been told that he had provided financial support for me, but you must be able to work it out.

'Not speaking of a thing does not mean it did not happen, Benedict, or have you managed to completely wipe the past from your memory?'

Benedict hauled in a deep breath, battening down the urge to grab Harriet by the shoulders and shake her meaning from her. A glance out of the window revealed the carriage was even now approaching Cavendish Square. He rapped the ceiling of the carriage with his cane and it drew to a halt. He opened the door and leaned out to speak to the coachman. The carriage lurched on its way, and Benedict sat down.

'I've told Atkins to take a turn around the park,' he said, 'whilst you explain to me exactly what you are talking about.'

He crossed his arms across his chest and waited. Harriet's ragged breathing was loud in the carriage, but he battled his instinct to take her in his arms and soothe her distress. Or was it anger? Whichever it was, she had spoken from the heart and she must continue to do so if he was ever to learn the truth of the past.

'The money was for the baby.'

The air whooshed from his lungs. *Baby?* He could not speak. His heart jolted and lurched in his chest as her words reverberated right through him. *No. It could not be.* But… He dragged in a tortured breath, his chest swelling and burning with the effort. He looked back over the years… They had been inseparable, confident in the throes of first love and the unassailable belief of youth that nothing could spoil their vision for the future. They had made love. The first time, for each of them…

'What baby?' His voice was strained as it emerged from his thick throat.

'*Our* baby.' She glared at him. 'Do not pretend you did not know. Papa *told* me.'

His thoughts charged onward, skimming over what had taken place that summer and the following autumn: the best, followed by the worst, time of his life. He had blocked what had happened from his mind for the most part; he had not examined those events but buried them securely in a compartment in the depths of his mind. Now he must bring them into the light and look again. What was the truth?

He had returned from Cambridge that Christmas to find her gone. Had he ever questioned Malcolm's glib announcement that she had married

Brierley for his title and for the riches he could provide?

'What did your father tell you?'

'He told me what you said to him.' Tears sparkled in her eyes and glistened on her lashes. 'I w-was a bit of f-fun. You were sowing your *wild oats*.' The disgust in her voice affected him even more than even those words did. 'Y-you wanted n-nothing to do with m-me or…or our b-baby.'

Fury blacker than he had ever known thundered through Benedict. He clenched his fist and slammed it into the carriage door, which shivered in its frame. The carriage once more lurched to a halt. *Damn and blast it!* He stuck his head from the door again. 'Keep driving until I *tell* you to stop!'

He turned to Harriet, who sat shaking, her arms wrapped around her torso, head bowed.

'It's not true.'

She lifted her head and glared at him. 'Papa wouldn't lie. Not about something like that.'

He sat down again, prised her arms away from her body and enfolded her in his arms. 'I am not lying to you, Harry. I knew nothing about the baby. What… But where is the baby?'

Tremors racked her body and a sob escaped her.

'Harriet?'

'She—she died. Before she was even born.'

Benedict freed one of his hands to scrub it over his face. He couldn't take it in. He'd only just learned he'd fathered a baby, and now it was as if she had been snatched from his arms. Grief engulfed him for a tiny life he had not even known existed until a few minutes ago.

'Why didn't you tell me?' His words sounded harsher than he intended. He cupped Harriet under the chin and forced her head up to meet his gaze. 'Why?'

'You *knew*!'

'Harriet…no. I didn't know. I swear.'

Before his eyes, she withdrew, retreating behind a mask that foiled the eye of the observer quite as effectively as the mask she had worn for the masquerade.

'Talk to me, Harriet, please. I—'

'We will be late,' she said. 'Richard and Felicity are expecting us.'

Richard! The same jealousy spiked through him and burst from him before he could consider his words. 'Stanton! Heaven forbid we upset *Stanton*. Are the rumours true? Is he your lover?'

She jerked away from his touch. 'We are not lovers.'

'But you were?'

'That is neither here nor there.' Her voice wobbled.

He worked hard to tamp down his anger and moderate his tone. 'We should go home and talk about this.'

'I am not ready to talk about it. Not yet.'

'How much time do you need? You've had eleven years to think about it…to talk about—'

'I've had eleven years of *not* talking about it. To anyone. Do you understand?' A bitter laugh escaped her. 'No, of course you do not. You have had eleven years of living a life of blissful ignorance. Now, please, may we continue to Cavendish Square? I do not want to be late.'

To look at her, nobody would now suspect anything was wrong. She hadn't been that way when he'd first known her—he had often joked she was like an open book—but since they had met again, there had only been an occasional glimpse of the spirited Harriet he used to know. Such as just now, when she had lost her temper. Why did she retreat behind a mask whenever there was a danger of confrontation or whenever her emotions ran high? It was as though she was scared of letting go…of saying what she really thought. She had erected a barrier as effective as a brick wall, and he could not find a way to breach it.

Or could he? He could take her in his arms and kiss her, encourage her to talk about her deepest feelings…but would it be a mistake to push her now, at a time when both of their feelings were raw and time was limited? He was afraid of widening the gap between them rather than breaching it. Maybe it would be better to tackle it tomorrow, when they'd both had time to calm down.

As he instructed the coachman to drive back to Cavendish Square he promised himself that tomorrow morning—early—they would sit down and they would talk this thing through.

And then he would take her in his arms and kiss her and tell her—for the first time in eleven years—how much he loved her.

What was she to do?

Harriet sat in her boudoir, gazing unseeingly from the window, until the rosy light of dawn fingered the rooftops opposite. She was numb, her brain frozen with indecision. She had picked over her memories until the bones of the past were stripped bare. Either Papa had lied or Benedict now lied. She wanted neither of those two to be true. And that was impossible.

How she had survived the evening before without screaming out her pain and frustration she did not know. But she had. And her heart had twisted a little tighter each time she'd observed Matthew and Eleanor or Richard and Felicity together, and recognised the love that bound them, shining out for all to see. She had watched Benedict, too. Read the signs of strain in his features; traced with her eyes the furrows on his brow; recognised his discontent in the downward turn of his mouth.

He escorted her home from the Stantons' house in near silence, depositing her at her home and then leaving in his carriage. And Harriet had climbed the stairs and dismissed Janet and had sat and thought.

It was not just their argument about the baby and about Stanton that had caused Benedict's low mood. He had been frowning and unhappy before that—she had noticed it more than once since Kitty's ball. And the thought crept unbidden into her mind that she was the cause. She viewed the decisions she had made and the actions she had taken since Benedict's return to London and she reached the conclusion she was no better than Bridget Marstone.

Oh, she could fool herself that she had not deliberately trapped him into a proposal at Kitty's ball. She had convinced herself at the time that the whole farce was his fault because he'd followed her into Edward's library. And yet…she could not deny she'd deliberately set out to seduce Benedict on the night of the masquerade with every intention of prising a proposal from him—because she'd felt aggrieved, because she'd blamed him for everything that had gone wrong in her life and because she'd thought he deserved to suffer as she had.

Her plan had not worked. He had seen right through her and he had *chosen* not to propose to her. He did not want to marry her but now he was trapped and… What if he was telling the truth? What if he had *not* known she was with child? Did she want him to suffer in a marriage he did not want? Could she live with herself, knowing what she did about her motives and knowing that there would be no betrothal had it been Benedict's free decision? And would he ever forgive her when he found out the truth about her and Stanton?

He was due to call on her at ten.

She loved him. She did not want him bound to her from a sense of obligation or duty.

Benedict no longer had a choice, but she did. Suddenly, she knew what she must do.

Chapter Twenty-Four

Don't worry?

Benedict ripped the letter in half and in half again, and dashed the pieces to the floor of Harriet's salon. She'd done it again—led him on and then betrayed him! Broken off their betrothal and gone. He rammed his fingers through his hair and paced up and down, fury boiling in his gut. Then his steps slowed as common sense began to penetrate his anger. Her wording—she had *released* him… Had she gone for his sake? He must believe she had. He must not allow the lies of the past to cloud his judgement.

Where would she go?

To Brierley? Hardly.

The Stantons? Possibly.

That charity house of hers? Where was it again? Cheapside? Again, possible.

What had she said again? He retrieved the ripped

letter, strode to a table by the window and laid the pieces out, fitting them back together.

Dear Benedict,

I have been unfair, both in not believing you last night and in accepting your proposal. I therefore release you from our betrothal: I have come to realise that to be forced into an unwanted union can never provide a solid foundation for a happy marriage such as our friends demonstrate.

I have gone to find the truth of what happened eleven years ago.

Do not worry, I beg of you. I am no longer your concern and I shall be perfectly safe. I have written to Edward to inform him that our betrothal is at an end and that I shall accept his offer of a cottage at Brierley Place, so you will no longer need to worry about me. If what the solicitor told you is true as to the source of the monies, I imagine Edward will not be so churlish as to withhold my allowance for very long! And I dare to hope that, after Kitty is settled, he will again countenance my presence in London.

I wish you good fortune in your search for

a bride, and I hope that your union will be blessed with children and you will lead a happy and contented life together.

Do not worry about me. I will see you upon my return and tell you what I have discovered.

Your good friend,
Harriet

Three times she had told him not to worry. What did the foolish woman think he would do other than worry? Why the *hell* hadn't he made her talk to him last night? Why had he decided it would be better this morning after they'd both had a chance to calm down and think things through?

Because you were scared of what you must admit, and of what you might hear, if you both spoke from the heart.

Now she had gone and the ache in his heart rippled through his body until he could feel it in his toes and the tips of his fingers and in his jaw, which was clenched tight against his tears.

Where would she go?

Thoughts flitted in and out of his mind, never settling for long enough to allow him to examine them.

Calm down, slow down, think!

He sat on a nearby chair, head bowed, his hand resting on the torn letter as if he could absorb her thoughts through his fingertips.

Think logically.

I have gone to find the truth of what happened...

Who would know? Malcolm, Brierley and her father were all dead. The present Lord Brierley? He shook his head, frustration mounting. Who else was involved? Harriet herself. The solicitors!

He surged to his feet and was halfway across the room before he realised the three men who had planned this would have had no need to confide the whole truth to their solicitors.

Planning—what had they planned? If it was true about the baby, and he could not, having witnessed Harriet's distress, disbelieve it then the men—her father, his guardian and her future husband—had conspired to keep Benedict in the dark about Harriet's pregnancy, and Harriet in the dark about Benedict not knowing. They'd told Harriet that Benedict had rejected her and they married her off to Brierley. The whole thing stank of Malcolm. He had made no secret of his disapproval of Benedict spending time with the village children and of his plan to find a suitably well-bred bride for his heir. But Harriet's father was complicit in the deception.

And *that* must be where Harriet had gone—to

see her mother—the only person who might still know the truth of what had actually happened.

He dredged up a memory… Harriet, talking about her mother and her aunt… The sea air… Whitstable. That was it.

Benedict headed for the door.

'What time did her ladyship leave?' he asked Stevens, who was hovering outside the salon door, an anxious expression on his face. 'Did she say where she was going?'

'She took a hackney at seven this morning, sir, carrying a portmanteau. Janet says her bed wasn't slept in and that she packed her bag herself. I heard her direct the hackney to Lad Lane so I can only assume she is going to Brierley Place, but she did not say so.'

Or Whitstable. The Swan with Two Necks was in Lad Lane, and the stagecoach that ran from there to Canterbury would pass through Faversham, a scant five miles or so from Whitstable.

Benedict whipped up his horses and arrived back in Grosvenor Street in record time.

'Order the carriage round,' he said to Reeves as he strode into his house. 'I am going into Kent. Fletcher!' He had kept Malcolm's valet on as well, after his kinsman's death, despite having little use for one. Fletcher appeared at the top of the stairs as

Benedict took them two at a time. 'Pack a bag—enough for a couple of nights away, please.'

'Am I to accompany you, sir?'

'No. No need.' He did a quick calculation in his head. With any luck, and frequent team changes, he should be in Whitstable by six.

'She is not here, as you can see.' Mrs Rowlands showed Benedict into the empty sitting room of the small house she shared with her widowed sister. On the opposite side of the hallway he had glimpsed a dining room through an open door. It, too, had been unoccupied. Involuntarily, he glanced at the ceiling.

'My sister is resting in her bedchamber.'

Benedict gazed at Harriet's mother in frustration. Small likenesses to Harriet, glimpsed in isolation, smote at his heart—her elegant posture, the shape of her brow, the set of her chin. They stood facing one another. Mrs Rowlands had not taken a seat—the implication being that Benedict was not welcome to stay—and neither had she offered him refreshments.

'Have you heard from her?'

'I received a letter about a week ago.'

'Well—have you any idea where she might have gone?' he asked in desperation.

The woman was as uncommunicative as it was possible to be, without out-and-out rudeness.

'I am afraid I cannot help you,' Mrs Rowlands said. 'I suggest you return to London and wait for Harriet to contact you, if she chooses to do so.'

The woman was a poor liar, but he could not fault her for trying to protect her daughter. Harriet was here. He felt it in his gut but, short of forcibly searching the house, there was little he could do. Did Harriet know he was here and was hiding from him? Or had Mrs Rowlands taken it upon herself to shield her daughter from him?

'She told me about the baby.'

Mrs Rowlands flinched. 'We do not speak of that.'

So it *was* true. 'Why was I never told?'

'What could *you* have offered my daughter? You were just a youth, with nothing in the way of prospects until Sir Malcolm died, and *he* held all the power. You ruined our daughter's life and broke our hearts. We lost her when she married that man.'

'Lost her? How?'

Mrs Rowlands walked to the door. 'It can do no good raking over the past. Leave it where it belongs. If Harriet wishes you to know, I am sure she will tell you when she is ready to. I am sorry for your wasted journey.'

'It is of no consequence. If you *do* happen to see Harriet, tell her I was here. Tell her that I am gone to Tenterfield Court, when she is ready to talk to me.'

He had no choice now but to leave. He trod down the short path to his carriage and then looked back at Harriet's mother. 'And tell her that, in my eyes, our betrothal still stands.'

'Betrothal?' Mrs Rowlands' voice rose in sharp enquiry. 'What betrothal?'

He ignored her and opened the carriage door.

'Where to now, sir?' Atkins called from the box as Benedict mounted the carriage steps.

'Tenterfield Court.'

He settled against the squabs as the carriage rocked into motion.

...to be forced into an unwanted union can never provide a solid foundation for a happy marriage...

Those words had haunted him the whole journey from London. An unwanted union. Did she mean unwanted by her? If so, he must accept he was chasing a lost dream. Or did she—as he hoped and prayed she did—mean unwanted by him? He must trust Mrs Rowlands to give Harriet his message and he must trust Harriet to understand why he had given her this opportunity to come to him freely. It was time they were open about the past, and about their present feelings, if they were to have any chance of happiness.

He would give her until the day after tomorrow. If she did not come, he would return to Whitstable and, this time, he would find her. But he hoped against hope that she would come of her own accord.

When Harriet awoke, sunlight was flooding through the open curtains in an unfamiliar bedchamber. She squinted and rubbed at her temples, which throbbed. A loud gurgling accompanied a churn of her stomach and the events of the day before came tumbling out of her memory and into her conscious thoughts. She was at Mama's, in Whitstable. As if in confirmation, the haunting cry of a seagull echoed outside the window.

Her stomach rumbled again, reminding her she had not eaten since yesterday, when she had managed to grab a quick slice of bread and cheese at one of the inns when the stagecoach had pulled in for a change of horses. She frowned. That would explain the headache, but why had she not eaten when she arrived here in the middle of the afternoon? Those memories—her actual arrival—remained hazy. But she recalled with absolute clarity the reason for her impromptu journey to the Kent coast.

Benedict. Their betrothal. The burning question she hoped her mother could answer.

She got up and crossed to the washstand in the corner of the neat, impersonal guest bedchamber. There was clean water standing in the jug and she poured it into the basin. It was cool, but it would help to wake her up. She washed quickly and pulled on the same dress she had travelled in yesterday. Someone, she noted, had brushed the dusty evidence of six hours of travel from the blue fabric. She brushed her hair and roughly plaited it before going downstairs.

The clock on the mantelshelf in the sitting room read quarter to eleven.

'Good morning, Mama.' Harriet crossed the room to the window, where her mother sat—embroidery in hand—and bent to kiss her cheek.

Her mother smiled. 'You are looking better, my dear. That tincture of laudanum worked—you have slept for almost seventeen hours. You had better have something to eat. Go and ask Joan to prepare toast and tea, will you, please?'

'Mama, I need to ask—'

'Yes, yes, my dear, but first you must have something to eat.'

She put her embroidery on the arm of her chair and rose to her feet. She framed Harriet's face with her hands and shook her head, smiling. 'Listen to your mama, stubborn girl.'

Tears welled up to thicken Harriet's throat and she turned away before Mama saw. 'Yes, Mama,' she said.

Oh, how she wished she could return to her childhood, to a time when life was uncomplicated and full of promise. How she wished she could forget everything—Benedict included—and stay here in peace with her mother and her aunt. She silently berated herself for her ingratitude, and vowed to cease this self-pitying nonsense. Look at all the women and girls who had fared so much worse than she had. The workhouses were full of them, single mothers who had no option but to rely upon the parish to survive.

When she returned from speaking to Joan, Harriet said, 'I cannot remember what I said—or did, for that matter—when I arrived yesterday. How is Aunt Jane?'

Mrs Rowlands filled her in on her sister's various ailments until Joan brought in tea for two and buttered toast for Harriet. Once she had left the room, Harriet opened her mouth to question her mother, but she was beaten to it.

'He came looking for you.'

Harriet gaped at her mother. 'Who? Benedict?' She started to her feet. 'Where is he?'

Mrs Rowlands grabbed at Harriet's sleeve. 'Sit down. He is not here. He came yesterday in the early evening.'

'What did he say? How did he seem?' She studied her mother's expression. 'You did tell him I was here?' There was a beat of silence, during which Harriet drew her own conclusion. 'Oh, Mama! How could you? Where did he go?'

'I did not tell him you were here because I had no way of knowing whether or not you would wish to see him,' Mrs Rowlands said, her exasperation clear. 'What was I supposed to think? You arrived here without warning, exhausted, distraught and nigh on incoherent. The words you did say made no sense. The only information I could glean was that, once again, Benedict Poole appeared to be the cause of your distress. Of *course* I told him you weren't here.'

'I'm sorry, Mama.' She recalled the nightmare of a journey on the stagecoach. She hadn't expected to feel so vulnerable, or so unworldly, when she'd made that spur of the moment decision to come to

Whitstable. A sleepless night…over seven hours crammed into an airless coach…no food to speak of…no wonder she could barely recall her arrival. 'I can see you were trying to protect me.'

She squirmed under Mrs Rowlands' penetrating gaze.

'You still carry a torch for him, don't you, Harriet?'

'I cannot help it, even though I know…at least, I thought I knew…how badly he treated me before. Now I am confused, and I want—'

'Now you want the truth?'

'Yes. Did Papa lie to me?' She waited for the answer to the question, not knowing what she wanted to hear, not knowing which option would be the most painful to endure.

'Yes, but Sir Malcolm left him no choice.' She took Harriet's hands in hers, holding her gaze. 'We both lived to regret our decision, but by then it was too late to change anything. Once you had married that…that…' A deep sigh, seemingly torn from the depths of her mother's soul, accompanied a shake of her head. 'Sir Malcolm was adamant he would never permit you and Benedict to wed. We were frantic. You were disgraced, and your baby would be…'

Her mother fell silent and Harriet felt her chest

swell with pain at the memory of her tiny, tiny daughter, held once in her arms before being taken from her.

'It was unthinkable to your papa...to *us*...that your child, our grandchild, should grow up with the stigma of being born out of wedlock. Sir Malcolm offered a solution. The *only* solution, as far as we could see, but only on condition we backed his story that Benedict had rejected marrying you. He even offered to settle money on you—we had nothing to offer as a dowry—and he threatened... he threatened...' Mama's voice cracked and her eyes filled. Harriet squeezed her hands. 'You must believe me, darling... If we had *known*, no threat to take Papa's living from him would have made us agree. But...but...'

She hauled in a shaky breath.

'I thank God you have another chance. Go to him, Harriet. Go to Benedict and try to put right that dreadful decision Papa and I made all those years ago.'

Harriet gazed from the window of the chaise and four, eager for her first sighting of Tenterfield Court. She hoped and prayed Benedict would still be there, for what if he had tired of waiting and was even now on his way to London? She picked at her soft kid gloves, impatient to be doing and not just sitting and yet dreading the conversation to come. If she—if *they*—were to sort out this mess and ever find happiness, she knew she must find the courage to tell Benedict the whole truth.

Her mother's words rang in her head. *He said to tell you that, in his eyes, your betrothal still stands.*

That message gave Harriet hope—and yet she didn't dare to hope too much—that Benedict might still harbour some tender feelings for her, apart from his obvious lust. But if that was so, why had he not offered for her after the masquerade ball? It made no sense and yet, during that journey, she gradually realised she still did not know the whole story. She now knew why Papa had lied to her, but she still had no idea what Benedict had been told to explain her marriage to Brierley. Was that the key?

The chaise jolted to a halt in front of Tenterfield Court. Harriet gazed up at the imposing red-brick mansion and her heart flipped before climbing into her throat. Her entire future would be decided in the next few minutes. A footman opened the carriage door for her and handed her down.

'Thank you, Cooper,' she said with a smile.

'It is a pleasure to see you again, my lady.'

Crabtree was at the door, waiting. He bowed as she approached.

'Good afternoon, Crabtree. Is Sir Benedict at home?'

Her stomach knotted as she waited for his reply. *Please let him still be here.*

'No, milady.'

Harriet's heart plummeted. She was too late. He had tired of waiting for her and returned to London. The butler's measured tones penetrated her inner panic.

'I beg your pardon, Crabtree. I missed that.'

'I said, before he went out, the master left instructions that if anyone should ask for him, I should say he is at the folly.'

Harriet bit at her lip, excitement stirring deep within her. He was waiting for her. 'I will go to him there,' she called over her shoulder as she dashed out of the front door and down the steps.

The slope up to the folly seemed steeper than ever to Harriet as she dragged air into her lungs and her calves ached with fatigue. *Or you are not used to such strenuous exercise.* She paused, her hand to her heaving chest, the thud of her heart tangible beneath her fingers. The folly towered above her, silent and grim, silhouetted against the grey sky. Doubt assailed her. It looked deserted. Was she a fool to read such hope in his message?

Her breathing eased, but her heart still raced—from nerves now rather than exertion. There was no choice. She had come this far. If they could not reconcile the happenings of the past now, they would never do so. She walked to the door, her steps leaden with trepidation.

The door was unlatched. Harriet pushed it open.

Chapter Twenty-Five

The interior of the folly had changed beyond rec-ognition. Candles flickered, banishing the gloom of the day and illuminating the red Chinese-style carpet that had been spread on the floor, and the cushions of all colours that had been arranged into two facing heaps. In the centre of the rug, be-tween the piles of cushions, was a wicker basket, the neck of a bottle protruding. A flicker of move-ment caught Harriet's eye. Benedict, eyes glitter-ing in the light from the candles as he sat on the old tub chair pushed back against the wall on the far side of the tower from the door. He watched her. Waiting.

She stretched her trembling lips into a smile. 'I owe you an explanation,' she said.

'You do.' In one lithe movement he was on his feet but he did not approach her. Instead, he ges-tured to the cushions. 'It is comfortable enough,' he said, 'although the resilience and enthusiasm of youth made it seem more comfortable back then than we might find it today.'

Harriet folded her legs and sank down onto the cushions. Benedict did likewise, the basket between them. So near and yet so far. Would he understand?

'Have you eaten?'

She shook her head. He unpacked the basket and spread bread, cheese and fruit before her and then uncorked the wine and poured each of them a glass. He appeared totally at ease, lounging on the cushions, propped up one elbow, wine glass in hand.

'Why could you not talk to me the other night?'

Brutal honesty was required, however hard it was for her and however shameful. She knew instinctively that he would struggle to ever fully trust her if she could not now summon enough confidence to tell him everything.

'I was afraid.' She bent her legs and hugged her knees close to her chest.

His brows snapped together. 'Of me?'

'You were so angry when I told you about the baby. I panicked and I couldn't work out what to say in case it made you angrier.' She gulped a mouthful of wine.

'What about the truth? All I wanted was the truth. What did it matter even if it did make me angrier?' He straightened, leaning towards her, staring at her, probing. 'What has made you fear a man's anger, Harriet? Brierley?'

Even his name made her want to curl into a tiny ball and disappear from view. She nodded.

'But you must know I would never hurt you,' he whispered achingly.

There was pain in his eyes, and the urge to comfort him overrode her dread of finally talking of her ordeal.

'Oh, I do.' She reached out impulsively and he met her gesture halfway, taking her hand and rubbing his thumb across her knuckles. She stared down at their joined hands. 'Sometimes...' She paused, trying out the words inside her head. 'Sometimes...something happens that brings the past back and it is as though I cannot separate the now and the then.' She looked up, anxious that he would understand. 'When we met again. At Tenterfield. That night you ran up the stairs behind me and I...I...'

Her throat squeezed shut, leaving a torrent of words dammed up inside, as they had been for years. She dragged her hand from his and pressed her palms to her face, pushing her fingers to her closed lids.

'Harry? My love?' There was a rustle and Benedict was beside her, nestling her into the crook of his arm, stroking her hair.

'Tell me, sweetheart.'

'He th-threw me down the stairs.' She clutched at Benedict, her words muffled against his chest. 'I was s-seven m-months' pregnant. I l-lost our b-baby.' Huge sobs racked her as he held her and soothed her, rocking gently. 'I didn't think I c-could b-bear to carry on living—I didn't w-want to survive. I had lost you, but knowing that I carried your baby s-somehow made it b-better. I s-still had a part of you and then…I had n-nothing. Nothing b-but p-pain and misery and fear and disgust.'

She wept on his shoulder, his deep murmurs soothing her until eventually her sobs subsided and she pulled back to look up into his beloved face. His jaw was taut, his features etched with pain. A tear sparkled on his lashes. Wonderingly, she reached up and wiped it away. He feathered a kiss to her forehead.

'Oh, Harry, my darling, I can't bear to think of you going through all that alone.' His words vibrated with anguish. 'Our poor, defenceless baby, robbed of the chance of life. You don't need to mourn her alone anymore, my love. I mourn with you. I am here for you. I will be with you forever.'

Hope blossomed with his words, and yet there was something she must say…something Benedict must know before he committed himself and felt honour-bound to stand by his word.

'Ben…what if…what if I can no longer carry a child?' Her worst fear, out in the open. 'You n-need an heir. And in seven years with…*him*…I never got with child. What if I am b-barren?'

'Then, we will adopt children and we will love them as our own. Oh, *God*, Harriet! All that wasted time!'

A muscle in his jaw bunched and his chest expanded as he dragged in a breath.

'*Why* did I trust Malcolm?' he gritted out. 'Why was I so ready to believe you would betray me by marrying for wealth and a title? I should have known better. I should have known *you* better.'

She placed her palm to the side of his face. 'You were young. We both were. Is that what they told you? That I married Brierley for status and money?' She read the shame that dulled his eyes. 'You were young,' she said again. 'I would rather learn now that you made such a mistake than still believe you heartlessly abandoned me.'

'Which is the thought you have lived with all

these years.' He hugged her close, resting his cheek on her hair. 'All those wasted years over one lie… All that wasted energy, resenting one another for something that did not happen.'

He pulled away and tilted her chin, looking deep into her eyes. 'I can understand why Malcolm lied. He made no secret of his ambition for a great match for me, perhaps to atone for his own failure to wed and produce an heir. I doubt he would have spent a single second feeling guilty, but…your father—I cannot understand why he didn't tell you the truth. Why would such a pious, honest man lie about something so fundamental to his only daughter's happiness? Did your mother explain *why* he went along with Malcolm's lie? For I swear to you I never said those ugly things to him.'

She stretched up to press her lips to his. 'I know you did not,' she whispered. 'I knew, in my heart, that you were telling the truth the other night, but I was torn. I hated that my memory of my father would be tainted by these lies…but now…I realise I did not go to my mother for proof you were telling the truth but to understand *why* my father had lied.'

She moved away from him, shrugging his arm from her shoulders, then shifted her position so she fully faced him. He watched her intently, his green eyes sombre, as she took his hands in hers.

'My mother guessed my condition before I even knew it myself. I had missed my courses, and then I began to be sick in the mornings. She confronted me...' Harriet paused, recalling the horror of that conversation, and her shame when her father had discovered the truth. Poor Papa. He had been devastated.

'When Papa went to your cousin to tell him I was with child and to demand you marry me, Sir Malcolm was adamant he would never allow us to wed. As you said, he had much higher ambitions for you and, as your guardian, you would need his permission to marry. My father was equally determined that his first grandchild should not be born out of wedlock—that would have offended every precept in which he believed. So my parents' only option was to find someone who would marry me before the child was born.

'As you might imagine, Sir Malcolm was only too keen to help them out with finding someone, and he suggested Brierley. My father was so grateful for his help and to have his daughter married to an earl, and his grandchild brought up in such splendour... That was far more than he, or my mother, could ever have imagined for me.

'I was utterly horrified when they told me I was to marry Brierley. I refused. I cried. I told them we loved each other and that I knew you would marry me—that we would elope if Malcolm wouldn't give us permission.'

She smiled, shaking her head at the memory. 'I had a very hazy notion of what elopement might entail,' she said. 'All my knowledge had come from reading novels, much to my mother's despair. Anyway, that is when they decided a white lie was in my best interests, according to Mama. If I thought you wanted nothing to do with me or our baby, then I would stop hankering after you. I would find my peace and settle into my new life more easily.'

He squeezed her hands, then lifted them to press his lips to her skin. 'Poor Harry. I wish you had written to tell me what was happening.'

'I wish that, too, but it all happened so very fast after Mama realised I was with child that by the time I caught my breath, the arrangements had been made with Brierley and I had been told—and I believed—you did not want me. If I had written, it would have been to tell you how I hated you.'

A rumble rose from deep within his chest as he pulled her back into his arms. 'I would have come back straight away to shake some sense into you. Tell me about Brierley.'

'I can hardly bear to even think of that man,' Harriet said, shuddering. She must be brave, though. No more secrets. 'He hid his true character well, although the fact that he was a friend of Sir Malcolm's should perhaps have been warning enough. But my parents were not worldly people and I do not think it occurred to them Brierley might be so very cruel. Not even Edward fully realises his father's depravity—from what I have gathered over the years, Edward's mother was a most upright, moral woman and his father worshipped her.'

She swallowed, the memories looming large, threatening to overshadow her new-found joy. 'Perhaps it was I who caused such vile behaviour—I could never match the perfection of his first wife. He constantly compared my appearance and my behaviour to hers, accusing me of not being fit to take her place.'

She hesitated, dredging her past for the truths she must now reveal if she and Benedict were to have a chance of happiness together.

'He would punish me,' she whispered into his chest. It was easier to admit to such sordid details when she could not read the disgust in his eyes. 'It started with the occasional blow if I displeased him, but eventually I could *never* please him, no matter how hard I tried. And he seemed to…seemed to…'

She stopped, unable to control the wobble in her voice, tears flowing again. Benedict rocked her. 'Shh,' he murmured into her hair. 'You don't have to tell me. Leave it in the past where it belongs. You're safe now.'

Harriet rubbed her eyes and forced another swallow past the lump in her throat. 'No,' she said. 'I need to tell you. I need you to know about Stanton.'

He stiffened. She could *feel* the anger radiating from him. Her courage almost failed her, but she had come this far; she did need to tell him all. She could not allow suspicions to fester between them.

'Are the rumours true?'

She forced away her instinct to appease him by saying what he might want to hear, to deflect his anger by lying.

It's Benedict. Even if he is furious, he will never hurt you. Not physically.

'Yes,' she said, her heart quailing as she accepted that, although he might not hurt her physically, he had the power to crucify her emotionally, once he knew the truth of her *affaire* with Stanton.

The silence seemed to stretch forever, his chest rising and falling beneath her cheek.

'Tell me,' he said eventually.

She dragged in a torturous breath. 'Brierley… When he…he couldn't…' She could not say the words. She hoped Benedict would understand. 'He *liked* to hurt me. When he…when he…'

'When you were intimate?'

'Yes.' Harriet felt her cheeks burn. Confessing such things, even to the man she loved—or perhaps *especially* to the man she loved—was as hard as she had imagined. 'He made me…*do* things and, if I did not please him, he would punish me again. He would…restrain me, sometimes for hours. Usually naked. To await his pleasure, he would say. Because it was all I was good for. And he would force me to accept his advances, at all times of the day or night. I know a wife is expected to accommodate her husband's needs, but I grew to hate and fear any sort of intimacy and I hated *him*.'

She sighed. 'I have never admitted this, but I was *glad* when he died, God forgive me. He cut me off from everyone. I was only permitted to go out if he was with me. I was not allowed to visit my parents, and he read their letters to me and would only frank my letters to them after he had read them. I was entirely dependent on him and his servants.'

'And Stanton?'

Ah. Stanton. Will he understand?

She must be brave. Harriet levered herself upright so she could look into Benedict's eyes.

'I have always wanted a family and I was heartbroken when I lost our baby—'

Benedict put his fingers to her lips. 'You did not lose our daughter. Place the blame where it belongs. Brierley killed her. You and she were both innocent victims.'

The burden of guilt in her heart eased a little. How many times had she wondered if—had she said or done something differently—Brierley would not have lost his temper with her and pushed her on the stairs? How many times had she blamed herself, as Brierley had?

'Thank you for understanding.' She sucked in a deep breath, praying for the strength to continue; to admit her calculated decision to use another man to help her forget. 'Although I longed for a baby, I never wanted a child with Brierley and I thank God I did not have one. But then, after he died, I thought I might…' She paused, chewing on her lip. 'I thought of remarrying, but I found I was too afraid to trust *any* man. I could not even contemplate allowing any man such control over me, so I put my desire for a family to the back of my mind and I focused my energies on the charity I founded.

'And then I was invited to a house party. Lord Stanton was there, and I heard some of the other ladies discussing his prowess.'

Benedict glowered at those words and, despite knowing what else she must admit to, Harriet had to bite back a smile at his expression.

'He was well known as a ladies' man before he married Felicity,' she continued, 'but nobody expected him to marry when he did—he was known as the Elusive Earl for his ability to avoid the snares put out for him. And I began to wonder if someone like him—if *he*—might help me to overcome my distaste for...for the marital act.'

Her cheeks burned. 'This sounds so sordid and... and calculating,' she said. 'I'm sorry.'

'For what?'

For what indeed? She forced a laugh. 'If I am honest, I suppose am sorry for myself. I am sorry that I must admit out loud that I would even contemplate asking a man to help me with such a thing, let alone actually do so. So I made a point of getting to know Stanton. We became friends and, when I felt I could trust him, I asked him to help me.'

'You told a man you barely knew about things you have been unable to tell me?'

'It's odd, is it not, that I found it easier to approach Stanton than to tell you? Mayhap it was because my feelings were not involved. And I did not tell him much. I…I told him my husband had found me unsatisfactory, but after a few times I think Stanton guessed there was more to it than that.'

'I don't think I care to hear any more,' Benedict growled, leaping to his feet to take a hasty turn around the room.

Harriet watched him anxiously. Would he be able to accept the past, and what she had done? She was well aware that men set great store on their brides being chaste and pure. Not only was she a widow, but she had just confessed to having a lover—one that she had pursued, and one with whom she still enjoyed a close friendship. She could not guess what was going through his mind now, but she had confessed thus far and she would finish her tale.

'We agreed no one should ever know, and we only met at my house. I will not lie to you, Benedict. Stanton and I did become close, but there was never any question of love on either side. When Stanton became betrothed to Felicity—quite unexpectedly—he ended our arrangement.' She huffed a laugh. 'He was mortified when Felicity and I became friends.'

Benedict stood staring out of the window, silent

except for the harsh sound of his breaths. Harriet rose from the cushions to go to him. She did not touch him; she did not quite dare, he was so stiff and unyielding.

'Can you forgive me?'

He spun round to face her. 'Forgive *you*?' He placed his hands on her shoulders. 'Harry, how can you ask such a thing—there is nothing to forgive you for. It is I who should beg *your* forgiveness.'

He kissed her fiercely, his lips and tongue possessing her mouth as he cradled her face.

'I cannot forgive myself for all you have gone through. I am astounded you can even bear the sight of me, let alone... You are an amazing, beautiful, generous woman.'

His words demolished the last remaining barrier around her heart, allowing a flood of hope and joy to cascade through her, filling her with wonder and love.

'Now—' he stepped back and looked at her, a teasing glow in his green eyes as his hands slid from her face, across her shoulders and down her arms to clasp her hands '—what is this nonsense about releasing me from our betrothal?'

'It is not nonsense. It is another thing which I am not proud of, although I honestly did not plan to entrap you at Kitty's ball... You were right...I

did plan…I did intend… Well, it did not work—'
she caught at her breath, which was coming out in
frantic-sounding gasps '—and you did not fall for
my scheming at the m-masquerade…but I am still
g-guilty and I cannot bear for you to be t-trapped
into a marriage you do not want.'

A light lit his eyes. 'That masquerade,' he said
slowly. He tasted her lips again with a low, satisfied hum. 'How could I ever forget?'

'You do not want to marry me,' Harriet said desperately. 'You would have asked me then.'

Benedict threw his head back and laughed.
'Sweetheart, you do not understand me very well if
you think I would *ever* allow myself to be trapped
into making a proposal against my own wishes.'

'B-but…you *were* forced into proposing after
Kitty's ball. You cannot deny it, and *I* cannot
l-live with that knowledge.'

'That is true,' he said slowly, frowning. 'And if
you truly cannot live with the guilt that you have
entrapped me, I must thank you for releasing me
from any obligation to marry you. I accept.

'Our betrothal, as of this moment, is over.'

Harriet's heart cleaved in two and tears blurred
her vision. He might have forgiven her, but he did
not love her.

'Harriet. Look at me, please.' She raised her eyes to his, feeling a tear slide down her cheek.

Benedict lifted her hands to his lips. 'My darling Harriet, will you please do me the honour of becoming my wife?'

'But...'

'You goose! Did you really believe I proposed to you against my will? I was *relieved* to be forced into it—I could then excuse myself from being a fool for trusting you again and pretend I was merely acting the gentleman.' He hesitated then, his face suddenly serious. 'You do *want* to marry me?'

She gasped. 'Of *course* I do. There is nothing I want more. I love you, Benedict Poole, with all my heart.'

'Then, that is that,' he said with a huge smile as he took her into his arms. 'For I love you, too, with all my heart.'

She tilted her face to his and silence reigned for several satisfying minutes.

'Do you think you can learn to accept my friendship with the Stantons?' Harriet asked when they eventually came up for air.

He gave her a little shake. 'Will you please stop fretting? Yes. If Felicity can live with what happened before she and Stanton wed, then I'm damned sure I can. I cannot blame either of you for what happened before we met again…and I thank God that we did meet again,' he added, smiling down at her.

'And I, too. And,' she added, feeling decidedly naughty now her worries had been put to rest, 'it turns out Brierley did me one favour.'

She laughed as Benedict lifted a brow. A weight had been lifted from her and her life now stretched before her, full of hope and pleasure and love.

'I have certain skills.' She lowered her voice to a purr, half closing her eyes as she traced a path down Benedict's chest to his groin and closed her fingers around his manhood. 'Skills to please gentlemen.' With her other hand, she pulled his head lower to flick her tongue in his ear.

A strangled noise sounded deep in Benedict's chest and he hauled her to him, capturing her lips in another passionate kiss.

'Skills to please *this* gentleman alone,' he growled. 'You are *my* woman from now on. Mine alone. You are the breath in my lungs and the song in my heart.

'I love you, Harriet. I've always loved you. It's only ever been you.'

Epilogue

October 1813

'Four…five…six.'

Benedict slammed to a halt mere inches from the drawing room door, which stayed stubbornly closed, even in the face of his most ferocious glare. He spun on his heel and paced back across the room. Six lousy paces. He swore viciously under his breath. He had become accustomed to the screams. But there had been nothing but silence for ages. That was even worse.

A hand landed on his shoulder.

'You'll wear a hole in the carpet if you don't stop this,' Matthew said. 'Come and sit down. Ellie will come and tell you as soon as there's any news.'

'I *can't* sit and do nothing. I've a mind to go up there and…'

'Whoa! You'll scandalise the whole neighbourhood if you go near Harry while she's…while she's…well…you know. It's not men's business. Why don't we go to the club and have a drink? Take your mind off things.'

Benedict turned and stared at his friend. 'Take my *mind* off… Did *you* go off drinking whilst Ellie was going through this torture?'

'Well. No. Now you come to mention it, I do believe I wore a track in our drawing room carpet, too,' Matthew said, his blue eyes twinkling. 'But it's worth it. You'll see. You'll have a littl'un like our Thomas and life will be ten…no, a *hundred* times better than you ever thought possible.'

'I hope so,' Benedict muttered. Never in his life had he felt so utterly helpless. 'Why's it taking so long?'

Matthew shrugged. 'It always does. It's nature's way.'

'As long as Harry is all right.' Benedict's throat squeezed tight at the thought of all the things that could go wrong. He gripped Matthew's arm with sudden urgency. 'I don't know what I'd do if—'

He broke off at a sound from the hallway. Running feet. Then the door flew open and Eleanor burst into the room, her cheeks flushed, her eyes bright, a huge smile on her face.

'Come on, Papa Poole. It's all over, barring the introductions.'

Benedict was past her in a trice, across the hall and up the stairs two at a time. The bedchamber door was closed and, as he reached it, he hesitated, suddenly uncertain. The unmistakable mewl of a baby sounded from inside the room, shaking him from his momentary attack of nerves. His son. Or daughter. He opened the door. Walked in. There were others in the room but he had eyes only for Harriet.

His Harriet. His beautiful wife—tired and flushed, but beaming.

Her arms were full. He couldn't... *What?* Benedict stared, his brain trying to make sense of the sight of his gorgeous, beloved wife and the babies in her arms. He looked again, resisting the urge to rub at his eyes.

'Twins?' he whispered.

Harriet's smile widened. 'Twins,' she said. 'One of each. A boy and a girl.'

Benedict crossed to the bed as if in a dream. He reached to stroke Harriet's cheek. Harriet, who had made his life complete and who had banished all the hurt and loneliness of his past, and now... He reached out tentatively with one finger and touched the rounded cheek of the baby nearest to him. How soft. How delicate. How *perfect*. He watched as the pink lips pursed and a tiny frown flickered across the babe's forehead and his heart swelled, so full of love it felt as though it might explode. Wispy strawberry blonde curls peeped out from the edge of the white shawl it was wrapped in.

'Your daughter,' Harriet said. 'Is she not perfect?'

Benedict tore his eyes from his daughter to search Harriet's face. Always sensitive to her moods, he caught the faintest whisper of pain in her voice. Pain for what might have been. He bent and pressed his lips to her forehead. 'We will never forget our first girl, my love. Never. But we will give these two the most joyous, secure childhood they could wish for.'

'We will,' Harriet said as Benedict brushed a kiss on first his daughter's head and then his son's, his chest near bursting with pride and with love.

'It is fortunate we selected names for both a boy and a girl, is it not?' Harriet said with a weary smile. 'William and Rebecca—they sound very well together, do they not?'

'They do indeed.'

Benedict reached for William, taking the tiny bundle of his son into his arms and cradling him to his chest as he perched on the side of the bed, unable to tear his gaze from his tiny hand as it waved in the air, fingers splayed. He tickled his palm with the tip of his little finger, amazed at how huge it looked, then gasped with delight as William closed his tiny fingers around his.

His vision blurred and he blinked hard. A gentle hand touched his and he looked up into the glorious violet eyes of his wife, watching him with tenderness and love.

'I love you, Ben,' she whispered, and her eyes were now heavy with sleep. 'So very much.'

He leaned over and kissed her gently. 'I love you, too, my Harriet. Sleep now. You need your rest.'

'Will you stay with me…with us…awhile?'

'For as long as you want, sweetheart. You have made me the happiest man on earth, and there is nowhere else I would rather be.'

* * * * *

MILLS & BOON®

Why shop at millsandboon.co.uk?

Each year, thousands of romance readers find their perfect read at millsandboon.co.uk. That's because we're passionate about bringing you the very best romantic fiction. Here are some of the advantages of shopping at www.millsandboon.co.uk:

* **Get new books first**—you'll be able to buy your favourite books one month before they hit the shops

* **Get exclusive discounts**—you'll also be able to buy our specially created monthly collections, with up to 50% off the RRP

* **Find your favourite authors**—latest news, interviews and new releases for all your favourite authors and series on our website, plus ideas for what to try next

* **Join in**—once you've bought your favourite books, don't forget to register with us to rate, review and join in the discussions

Visit **www.millsandboon.co.uk**
for all this and more today!